PRAISE FOR
JASON PARENT

"*Down In The Deep, Dark Places* by Jason Parent hooks you in with the first story. It's a collection of horrible fates, some more disturbing than others. The book will leave you breathless by the end. A few of my favorites include: Eleanor, Agon, Scan For Life, and a Boy and His Dog. Such a great horror collection!"

—Author Jonathan Tripp

"This collection of chilling short stories shows that horror lurks everywhere: at sea and in the desert; in broad daylight and in dark caverns; in the form of gods and monsters, vampires and zombies, and all-too-human beings. Read them with the lights on."

—Kim H., Proofreader, Red Adept Editing

"Immersive and eye-opening. Parent's unique prose and cutting dialogue are both just as rotten as they are refreshing."

—Author Aron Beauregard

"Horror at sea. Death in a rainforest. Subterranean vampires in Afghanistan. There is something for everyone in *Down in the Deep, Dark Places*. Jason Parent's writing is hypnotic, pulling you into each unique tale right up to the twisted end. A masterful writer. You're in for a dark treat with this collection of terrifying short stories."

—Jeremy Bates, author of Suicide Forest

"Jason Parents new collection of stories *Down in the Deep Dark Places*, touched on all of my core fears and loves in horror. It was as if the author wrote the stories with me in mind. I am usually not a short story fan. I feel like in many collections the stories are very similar to each other, maybe a common theme. This is not the case with Jason's collections. Each of the stories is unique and different. This has always been a selling point for me with Jason Parent. He writes in so many styles and genre, whether it is subterranean, ocean, ghost or monsters, he writes in a way that sucks me in. While I loved all of the stories in the book, a few really stuck out to me. Glimmer is just an amazing ghost story that really pushes the limits of how far would you go for your child. The struggles that poor Ed experienced with his corgi in Violet hit very close to home on many levels and the imagery and detail Jason's uses describing the ocean in Agon is some of the best writing Jason has ever done. I highly recommend this book to anyone who loves good writing and great story telling."

—Frank Spinney

"One of the most versatile and engaging writers today, Parent demonstrates his willingness to unnerve his readers with his newest collection *Down in the Deep, Dark Places*. This one doesn't let up one bit! "

—Steve Stred, 2X Splatterpunk-Nominated author of
Mastodon, Father of Lies, and Churn the Soil.

DOWN
IN THE
DEEP
DARK
PLACES

[signature]
8/5/03

DOWN IN THE DEEP DARK PLACES

JASON PARENT

GALLOWS WHISPER

ISBN: 978-1-957121-47-5

Text © 2023 by Jason Parent

Editor, Curtis M. Lawson

Cover art © 2023 Nick Greenwood

Publisher, Joe Morey

Interior and cover design by Cyrusfiction Productions

Gallows Whisper
An imprint of Weird House Press
Central Point, OR 97502
www.weirdhousepress.com

TABLE OF CONTENTS

FOREWORD

Modern horror fiction is an ever-growing and increasingly diverse ecosystem. Contemporary writers of the macabre draw from a rich history and take the genre into dark new places. Online retailers are overflowing with books in countless subgenres and styles of horror. King-inspired coming of age stories. Gritty, ultra-violent splatterpunk novels. Modern takes on Gothic tropes.

There is cosmic, folk, sci-fi, and comedy horror. Some authors tell tales of classic monsters, such as werewolves or vampires. Others create fresh nightmares drawing from modern sensibilities and 21st century anxieties.

One can drill further down, into micro genres, if one chooses. Thursian cosmic horror. Anti-natalist weird fiction. Erotic body horror.

The rabbit hole never ends.

My point in all this is that many authors find a comfortable niche and hunker down in a small biome they feel comfortable with. They settle into tropes or styles, if not for their whole careers, at least for significant periods. The best among such writers may redefine a sub-genre. The rest tend to get stuck in a quagmire of derivativity and nostalgia.

Jason Parent is not one of these writers. His legacy will not be as the king of a tiny fiefdom within the field, nor as a desperate imitator of what came before. Jason's writing can't be confined to a small region of the horror ecosystem. He is an explorer, overwhelmed with literary wanderlust, and his work is a safari through the entirety of the genre.

Jason has proven himself skilled at writing tense horror in historical settings with stories such as *Where Wolves Run* and *Wrathbone*. In his book *Eight Cylinders*, he merged *Mad Max* style action with Lovecraftian Horror to great effect. *What Hides Within* and *White Trash and Dirty Dingoes* both exhibit Parent's strong comedic gifts, merging humor with horror and crime fiction, respectively.

In this collection, you will see Jason's incredible diversity on display. These are stories from the mind of a well-read author with a rich assortment of influences. A knowledge and love of horror fiction emanates from every page.

As the art on the cover suggests, the book you hold in your hands is filled with horrors lurking just beyond the light. *Agon* is wonderfully strange piece of weird fiction, which merges aspects of the classic man against nature story with glimpses of the supernatural. In *Glimmer*, we find a poignant exploration of grief and desperation set within the walls of a haunted hotel. *Akin* reminds us that the gruesome can be fun and offers a laugh amidst some of the more serious tales.

While there is a diversity to the tales within this book, and while Jason's tone and style change from one piece to another, there is also a consistency to the work you are about to read. While he writes across the breadth of dark fiction, the core of Jason's voice shines through in each story. There is an underlying sense of wit and whimsy, even in the darkest and most dread of these tales. Perhaps whimsy isn't the right word, so rather let me say that you can tell that Jason is having fun with each piece. While he approaches his craft with passion and dedication, his fiction is never pretentious, nor does it take itself too seriously.

With all that said, I invite you to turn the page and embrace the myriad horrors ahead. Walk across cursed deserts where shadows stalk living prey. Prowl the streets of Providence, where Eldritch Gods creep into our world. The time has come, dear reader, to follow Jason Parent down into the deep dark places.

—Curtis M. Lawson
Providence, Rhode Island
April, 2023

AGON

When she pushed me off the cruise ship, I was at first fairly calm about the whole thing. Beyond the initial shock—not all that shocking, really, given the turn our marriage had taken these past few years—I didn't then have a true sense of the danger. An appreciation for the vast expanse of insolubility, the endless miles and unfathomable depths of poison water that surround the continents, eating at their edges to eventually consume all, sure, I had *that*. But I guess I figured someone on a vessel as large as a continent itself would have seen me fall, heard my shouts for help, thrown me a literal circle of life so that I might not become part of the figurative one.

As if I could escape it.

That was hours ago, back when the sun was high in the sky, now barely more than a pink lipstick stain on the horizon. I've gone through panic and rage, hysteria and denial, then through them again many times over. My tears and my tantrums, my curses and promises of revenge have expunged much-needed energy as I struggle vainly—nay, hopelessly—to cling to life.

Without accounting for its toil upon my mind and soul, living is not so hard as one might think. I am an expert swimmer. The same chemical makeup that would leave me dehydrated despite an endless supply of drink also keeps me buoyant. My sneakers and jeans, and with them my wallet and sole means of identification should something happen to my fingers and teeth, have long since been discarded in favor of floatability. They lie somewhere far below, on an ocean floor unlikely to be otherwise touched by man—certainly not in my short lifetime. Perhaps they will be discovered by far-future explorers, from this world or beyond.

Or below.

My effects might end up in the belly of an ocean behemoth, clang against the great dome of Atlantis or some other lost civilization, or disturb the eons-old resting place of a sleeping god. I'll never know. I'll not likely wake with the dawn.

All I must do is close my eyes, lie back, relax, and let the waves carry me where they will. If only I could slow the rise and fall of my chest to match the ocean's swell. My mind is my first and foremost enemy; allowing it to fall into despair and madness is certain doom. I struggled against it for hours but have come to a fragile peace, insanity nevertheless lingering at the back of my skull, its tendrils searching for cracks through which to seep.

If I survive panic, then any number of deaths await me: drowning, dehydration, exhaustion, exposure... What is the word for being eaten alive? If given the choice, I'd rather be eaten dead. But it is thoughts like these that threaten to melt the glue keeping me whole.

For now, I float easily and undisturbed as I stare up at the emerging stars, clinging to the smallest fraction of hope. I must be stranded in the path of another cruise ship or maybe in a shipping lane, though I have little knowledge of such things to be certain.

At least, I suspect I was. God only knows where the currents have taken me. And if I must die, then I hope these currents take me directly to Him.

If He'll have me.

Other beings have taken interest. Occasionally, an amphibious creature brushes against me or a curious fin idles by, amorphous shapes in the dark. At most, their attention is fleeting, toying even. I've heard somewhere that sharks feed at night. Perhaps I need a little more marinating before I'm done.

If they are going to take me, I'd rather it be sooner than later. End this waiting. Kill the hope, for the hope is killing me. I am easy pickings, a dying fish floundering on the surface.

I picture my wife, sipping wine on our room's balcony, the same one she heaved me from, pleased with her crime and confident no fingers will point toward her. No body, no murder—at least that's what all those cop shows say. No one will ever find mine out here.

It's funny how much the night sky looks like an ocean. Puffy clouds roll over it like whitecaps. Stars twinkle like moonlight on dark water. As above, so below.

My ears underwater, I listen to whale songs and the deeper tones of lower things as my body rocks with the gentle ebb and flow of the tides. I watch as the moon, full and bright and far bigger than I've ever seen it before, climbs into view as if rising out of the water itself, so close I can almost reach it. It looks like a giant eye, studying me as I study it, wondering what this strange growth might be on its ocean mistress. Its full orb fills the sky, open and aware. Are its phases just how long it takes for a god to blink?

I tread water and take in its unusual grandeur. Its many craters and canyons, with their own unknowable depths and darkness not unlike those below my feet, make strange striations in its surface. They do not appear random, instead more like runes or ancient symbols carved by hands beyond my mind's ability to conjure. The sheer scale of such a creature would erase all semblance of sanity, striking me dumb as a baby turning in the womb, terrified of what comes with light and enlightenment.

In an attempt to drive out these morbid thoughts—understandable given my rather morbid predicament—I view the moon in light of its eerie, almost mystical beauty. It may be the last thing of beauty I witness in this world and the last thing to see me.

I am neither a good man nor a bad one. I am just a man. Perhaps I could have been a better husband. I tried, but maybe not hard enough. My heart cannot contrive forgiveness; not yet and perhaps not in life. Maybe someday she will have enough forgiveness for the both of us.

The moon's refracted light shines like a corridor that cuts across the water directly in front of me. The celestial sphere hangs in the sky just over the horizon, which, in that otherworldly radiance, doesn't seem so far away. If I swim hard enough and fast enough, I feel as though I truly could reach it. A part of me recognizes the absurdity of the notion, but other forces work upon me. The waves, for one, push me toward the moon as if urging me to try. Something unseen, something stronger than the inertia of the ocean itself, compels me toward that great eye in the sky. I am caught in its gravitational pull and see no cause to resist.

And so I swim, the glowing corridor my swim lane, the water growing ever stiller like the soft rush and fizzle of dying waves reaching the end of their roll. Still pushing on my back, but gently now, caressing. The soothing hand of a mother drawing circles on my skin to coax me to sleep.

Not only is the moonlight brighter now, but the water, too, seems alight. Neuron blasts illuminate the sea like lightning through a dark sky, the stars above matching their strobe-like effect as if the two surfaces are communicating in Morse code. I know my efforts will deplete my remaining reserves, but I must continue. The pull is too strong, the promise of the moon too enticing. Its song beckons me, and whether menace or madness, I must heed its call.

And as I race forward, kicking and slapping water with violence and haste, I touch something. My heart thuds in my chest as only it can when one realizes he is not alone in the darkness. But I do not stop, cannot stop. My hand makes contact again, swiping first through water then through a soft, semisolid muck as it circles down and back.

Land? It can't be. Somewhere, perhaps a mile back, I must have died, or else I'm dreaming. I stop, make to tread water, but my toes collide with thick mud, sinking in before I can plant them and pitching me forward onto my knees. And there I stay for a moment, head and shoulders above water, a penitent man offering a prayer. *Please, God. Let this be real.*

On shaking legs, I rise. For the love of God, I'm standing!

But on what?

The ocean has gone quiet around me, unnaturally still and black as subterranean night. But it is still ocean, in all directions, as far as the eye can see. I must have found a sandbar, must be close to land, only it's too dark to see it. If I could just stay here, hold fast and survive the night, I may actually have a chance at life. Morning's light will reveal all.

I yank off my T-shirt and wring it out. Particles of light sparkle in the falling droplets. Others tingle on my skin. The moon seems so close now I feel as though I could lean forward and kiss it. I dare not for fear of its mistress's wrath. And something else causes my breath to hitch, an atmosphere growing cloudier and steamier, as if someone has poured water over the coals in a sauna. Or hot breath. The air is cloying, or maybe it is the tiny particles of luminescence on my body, droves of them swarming closer, filling the water with brilliance that acts like a lantern through the fog. They pile against my boxers, creating tiny sandlike drifts wherever they collect.

Two black obelisks protrude from the water, one almost directly in front of me, the other fifteen meters or so to its right. How I had not noticed them before causes only a moment's alarm, for surely they are more evidence of the land I seek. They can only be rocks, and yet they are oddly symmetrical: conical on their inner sides and arching like train tunnels on the outer sides, slightly curved toward me, rising out of murky depths like sacrificial alters to a lunar deity.

And they continue to rise. *I*, too, am rising.

I look down to see the water only inches high but lapping against my knees, the rest of my legs sunken in quagmire. The light critters form a circle around me. They slide with the muck upward over my thighs and belly, climbing. I gasp and swipe them away, managing to dislodge swaths of them while others, seemingly sensing my attack, disappear as if burrowing under my skin. And still they keep coming like an army of ants whose mound I have disturbed but with no biting, no pain, but creating that impulse to be free of them, that sensation of wrongness that comes from skittering things on skin. Bigger things slither like eels across my legs and over my feet, and I am thankful I cannot see them under the mud.

All the movement stirs the ocean bed. Bubbles pop on the surface, releasing noxious gases that reek of dead fish, rotten meat, and the odor of catacombs breached after having been sealed for ages. The bones of unidentifiable creatures rise to the surface, fossils of beings that had been much larger than me but whose fate I now seem to share.

The ground continues to rise, and I continue to sink. The mud is at my thighs, the water gone, the light creatures creeping higher still like strangling vines. With every frantic swipe, more swaths emerge and others disappear, and although I do not feel them, I am certain they are inside me.

I cannot fathom what this place is, know only that I am where no man should ever be. I cannot move, my legs entrenched in slimy, abhorrent mire. Earth that I have disturbed and should have left alone. Earth that had never before been corrupted or maybe always had been.

The sparkling parasites continue their upward climb, worming their way up and into me. Comprising me. *Becoming* me.

A milky film forms on the outer side of the obelisk in front of me, now as tall as a house. My mind reels as I think of my grandmother's cataracts. A vertical slit in that film shifts forward. In it, I see the doorway to Hell. I laugh as tears squirm from the corners of my eyes. My broken mind again wonders how long it takes for a god to blink.

And yet I continue to look. God help me, I look. I see it, and it sees me. We share light and enlightenment, and my mind shatters with all that is exchanged. And as I open my mouth to scream, sparkling creatures pour down my throat.

§

I awake, floating in the water. How I survived falling asleep in the ocean is beyond me, for the monstrosity to which I bore witness surely could only have been the stuff of nightmares.

But no, I am… changed.

I hear a horn. A ship is approaching. Not just any ship—*my* cruise ship, its name emblazoned on the side. Someone must have seen me fall, after all. I am saved!

Or do I have something else to thank for my life? As I tread water, waiting for the lifeboat to approach, I sense I am not alone. And it is not the marine life in the water that causes me concern. A nagging in the back of my mind tells me I should dive down, the human part that yet remains, a mousy voice amid the screeching of the others.

In a matter of minutes, hands are pulling me from the water. A blanket drapes over my shoulders, smiling faces and mouths exclaiming miracles, disbelief that someone could possibly have survived a week in the water. I am offered food, told to drink. I want none of it, but I suppose I must keep up appearances.

For now.

My wife and her betrayal seem of no consequence now. The moon will be out in full again tonight, and I have the light of the stars to share.

REVENGE IS A DISH

"**W**hy'd I ever take that fucking job? Why'd I ever take that fucking job? Why'd I ever take... that fucking... *job*?"

Maurice shouted the words up at his captive audience, the blinding ball of fire scorching his already sunburned skin. He howled as he slammed his fists into the water, and it spat back, salt stinging his eyes. Helios and his fucking chariot couldn't race across the sky quick enough for his liking. His boiling, blistering skin and cracked, dry, and bleeding lips cried for sunscreen.

He took a long, slow breath, trying to calm down and conserve his strength. But as the calming dispelled his anger, he gave way to despair and began to sob. "I don't even like boats. I hate the freaking water, I hate the constant rocking, and I fucking *hate* rich people."

But he sure as hell didn't mind screwing them, at least not that gold-digging slut, Olivia. Even she had turned on him, though, left him for fish food.

Just two months ago, Maurice had been a rising star in the culinary world. He had a reputation for making exquisite new creations from standard ingredients or using exotic and sometimes unheard-of fare in more common dishes. After a rather public dispute with the owner of *Mes Amis*, who made unfounded (or at least unproven) allegations that Maurice had embezzled from the restaurant where he'd served as head chef, he took a break from the Manhattan elite cuisine scene. A week later, he received a call from Dr. Nigel Flickenhoffer at the behest of his wife, Olivia, a regular at the restaurant during his head chefdom.

Dr. Flickenhoffer was a retired curmudgeon of inexhaustible means, despite his trophy wife's exorbitant attempts to exhaust them. At one-third her newly wedded husband's age, Olivia—the name she'd given the old fool, though Maurice suspected she'd gone by Trixie or Lexus in a former life while employed at some truck-stop strip club or its nearby parking lot—had a seemingly inexhaustible sexual appetite, the kind a limp dick like Flickenhoffer couldn't satiate, not with all his hoity-toityness and fancy things or all the Viagra in the world. Her vocabulary was as small as her waist, but her fake tits were the best and biggest money could buy, no doubt a gift from Doc Asshole, as Maurice preferred to call him. It didn't take long for Maurice to realize he hadn't been selected for his cooking skills but for his pretty-boy looks, piercing blue eyes, strong arms, and chiseled abs, the kind only years of exercising and eating right could provide. Olivia took him for a test drive during his *tête à tête* interview and seemed pleased with the results. Four times pleased, by his count.

The job seemed simple. The couple intended to sail their yacht, a ninety-foot Princess, around the world. To do so, they required a chef to provide the daily meals for them and their small crew. Freshly returned to the job market, Maurice needed a paycheck, and Olivia needed a fuck buddy to fill the void, *her* void, while her dickhead husband fulfilled his egomaniacal, global-explorative fantasy.

"Come with us," the doctor had said, "and see exotic locales and forgotten cultures, worlds you never knew existed." Maurice was all too willing to say yes, enjoying the pay and the perks Olivia's proposal offered. He signed on the dotted line two minutes after he'd spilled his seed on her back and was out to sea only a few days later.

In the six weeks he'd spent in that smoking-jacket-and-boating-shoe-wearing, George Hamilton wannabe's employ, Maurice had kept everyone well fed and Olivia well satisfied. Everything was perfect.

Until he got caught with his dick in Doc Asshole's most prized possession.

Even on a boat as big as the *Wakemaster*, it was easy to run out of places to hide. Their secrecy was not aided by the facts that Olivia was a screamer and a lust-crazed whore. Her aggressive and insatiable grinding had chafed Maurice raw. Her indiscretion had gotten him fired. He'd barely had enough time to pull up his shorts before the old bastard and his captain threw him overboard.

He floated on a lifesaver that one of the deckhands, a teenager named Samuel, had been kind enough to let slip from the back of the boat as it drifted away. Maurice clung to the hard white doughnut as if it were the only thing in the world that mattered. Out there, surrounded by deep, dark ocean as far as his eyes could see, it *was* all that mattered.

That, and revenge.

If I somehow make it out of this cesspool alive, I might only take a finger or two from good ol' Samuel. The rest of them will rot in hell, but not before they suffer. They're in for a whole fucking galaxy full of hurt.

He gritted his teeth. *Especially that twat, Doc Asshole.* "I'm gonna kill you for this, you motherfucker!" he screamed at the sky.

Maurice slumped over the lifesaver. The thoughts of revenge, the anger, the wild schemes and planned torture his imagination concocted, those were the fuel that kept him floating. But with every passing hour—twenty-seven or so by his best estimate—the voice of doubt and hopelessness grew louder in his mind, a voice that told of a future far more likely, a future without his pipe-dream revenge.

A voice that told him he was going to die.

He sobbed quietly, unable to hold it back. Last he knew, the *Wakemaster* was drifting lazily somewhere north of the Solomon Islands. He had no idea which way the currents had taken him, could barely tell direction at all, his only indicator being the downward arch of the cruel afternoon sun.

As much as he despised that burning globe and the damage it was doing to his smooth, boyish face, he feared its setting. Maurice knew so little about the ocean. He knew nothing about sailing or nautical miles or currents or buoyancy or surviving alone at sea. He barely even knew how to swim. Yet somewhere in the far recesses of his mind dwelled a tidbit of information he believed to be true whether it was or not: sharks feed at night.

The opening scene of *Jaws* flashed behind his eyes. He gripped the life preserver a little tighter.

The irony of a chef becoming food for another creature was not lost on him. He laughed that nervous sort of laugh one has while walking through a haunted house, pretending to be brave. The fear of what hid beneath him in that infinite expanse of deadly water seeped through his body like the icy touch of a howling blizzard.

He would not survive the night.

He would not have his revenge.

Maurice had made it through the first night thanks to the sheer power of denial, defiance, and rage. Reality had since kicked him in the ass with a steel-toed boot. Dread sent a hollow pain through his chest, and he winced as another sob caught in his throat.

Something touched his leg.

The slightest brushing, probably just a swish of water, tickled the hair on his calf. He'd felt it a hundred times since he'd entered the water, and each time, his heartbeat fluttered. Each time, it had turned out to be nothing.

Because it was *nothing. Just my imagination.*

The water temperature rose, and he wondered if he'd been so petrified that he'd pissed himself. But the water didn't cool. Heat seemed to pulsate through it as if it were tangible and alive.

"Fuck!" Something slid, slippery and eel-like, across his shin. *It's just my imagination just my imagination just my imagin—*

"Ah!" He swiped his hand across his calf. "What the fuck?" Something had bit him, *really* bit him this time. He lifted his leg, relieved to find it whole. His fingers prodded the skin around a small bump. It wasn't a bite. It burned as though it had been pressed against a hot oven.

He had little time to consider it before electric pain jolted through his other leg. He hollered in agony. Instinctively, he jumped atop the lifesaver, his body commanding as much of itself as possible out of the water before his mind could piece together the cause of his duress. He balanced precariously on a tiny island, his buttocks sinking through the hole.

His legs remained submerged up to his knees. He growled, half in anger and half in pain, as needle-like stabs poked junkie tracks across his skin. Something curled around his ankle, where flesh was thin and nerve endings shallow. Maurice squealed. Tears ran from his eyes. He ripped his foot free of the water, tottering backward and nearly plunking himself into the drink.

Long, thin strands of what looked like vermicelli slid limply from his ankle and fell to rest atop the waves. More strands streaked across the surface, dozens of them, some dormant while others writhed like inchworms.

Nearest to Maurice, the strands were spaced as wide apart as a foot. He traced their length twenty yards away, the distance between them narrowing like that of guitar strings up the frets until they began to overlap. A patchwork quilt formed close to a bulbous, off-white membrane that bobbed in the water like an upside-down buoy.

The membrane was getting closer.

"Shit." Maurice turned onto his stomach. His legs sank deep into the water. The stinging was immediate and tormenting. Still, he kicked, the pain making him kick faster. When one adventurous tentacle caressed his thigh, he bit into his lip so hard that he drew blood. Maurice welcomed its copper taste, a reminder he yet lived. It took everything he had to fight the panicked urge to reach down and swipe the tentacles away.

After a minute, new stings stopped coming, but the old stings ignited every nerve cell in his legs. The water simmered. His flesh was on fire. He kicked until his legs couldn't kick anymore then collapsed into the lifesaver. His teeth chattered, a deep cold icing his insides and causing him to shiver violently while his legs and forehead scalded. Where salt water didn't soak him, sweat did.

Tears in his eyes, he cursed Doc Asshole and the occupants of the *Wakemaster*, wondering how he could replicate and inflict all his pain and anguish upon them. A thousand wasps, stirred into a frenzy and set loose on those sons of bitches, seemed like a decent appetizer but hardly par for the main course.

If he'd only get the chance.

He looked up at the sun, low in the sky, and sank into the preserver. He rested his ear against its curved surface and closed his eyes.

\#

When Maurice woke, he gazed up at a sky full of stars. In his initial daze, he found it beautiful. Then he vomited out the sour-tasting contents of a stomach he'd thought empty.

His head spun. A splitting headache pounded a heavy metal drumbeat through his skull. His skin radiated heat, while his insides were colder than a grave. Every muscle ached as if he had just completed back-to-back decathlons. His legs coasted weakly, the skin numb, the water strangely soothing.

Content to float, thirst scratching at his throat, hunger gnawing at his belly, Maurice let fate do with him as it would. He had been foolish to think he'd had any choice in the matter. He cupped his hand in the water to wash the retch from his chin. His fingers tangled in a mass of stems and leaves, their color indistinguishable under the moonlight.

Seaweed. He'd used it in a few dishes, but he had never cared enough to research what it looked like in its natural, nondried state beyond the nasty shit that gathered on the shores of Staten Island. He lifted it out of the water, wondering if it was edible. As salted and saturated with seawater as it was, Maurice guessed that eating it would only make him thirstier, if not violently ill.

Maybe it will speed along my death. The thought wasn't entirely unwelcome.

Another thought came to him, and he sprang up in excitement. An idea, a flash of information the truth of which he was certain—*like sharks feeding… Oh, God, it's night*—blossomed like a flower at the forefront of his mind. He shook off his fear. A faint light of hope, a dying ember at best, needed fostering.

Land! Kelp like this grows closest to land!

Despite having no idea where he'd heard this *fact*, Maurice was so sure of its veracity that he paddled frantically forward into a mass of lush flora. It tangled his arms and legs, slowing his momentum. His efforts were at first like trying to sled down a snowless hill, then like trying to sled with no hill at all. Soon, he was swallowed by a living, underwater jungle.

Immobile.

He squinted to see through the thick black of night. If land was out there, which direction it lay was not a guess he was willing to make. The water and sky both shimmered with moonlight, but everything in between hid behind darkness. Shore, his salvation, could have been less than a half mile away for all the good it would do him. He couldn't see a fraction of that distance.

He frowned. *Does kelp even grow in tropical waters? Is this even kelp? I wouldn't know kelp from seaweed or any other fucking kind of ocean plant or algae or whatever the fuck it is.* The growth around him was alive. That much seemed certain—that, and that there was a lot of it. His chin dropped. *I am going to die out here.* His heart thumped in his chest. He thought he might cry again, but before he could, he took several cleansing breaths and pulled himself together. *Relax. Save your strength. You'll see what's what in the morning.*

Somehow, Maurice did begin to relax. He turned to his back and let his head dip into the water. The night was clear and beautiful. His mind began to drift, and he was back in his home, enjoying a cold beer and a fat, red burger, its juicy blood running down his chin. He licked his lips and closed his eyes. For one blessed moment, he allowed himself to forget his dire circumstances and simply exist in silence and in peace.

Water splashed nearby, a light disturbance in the surface beyond the gentle sway of the ocean's ebb and flow. Maurice froze. His eyes shot open, and he held his breath. A splash came again, and he caught sight of its maker. A small fish wiggled as it bit into the thick growth. A similar splash came from behind him then another off to his right.

Maurice let out his breath. The splashes came sporadically, but the fish that made them paid him no mind. He stared at the water as it rippled across the leafy tips of the underwater vegetation. *It's nothing. Just some little fish having a snack. These plants must be the feeding grounds for tons of them.* He imagined all sorts of bright-colored fish, beautiful, harmless creatures like those he had hand fed in Cancun.

His reasoning seemed logical, but an uneasiness lingered at the back of his mind. He remembered the graduation card his parents had given him when he earned his Culinary Arts degree. *Be a Big Fish in a Big Pond*, it read. A picture of the food chain was drawn on its cover, that oft-used image of a tiny fish about to be eaten by a slightly larger fish, which in turn is about to be eaten by an even larger fish, and so on and so on. Except this card added a new component to the image. The pool in which all the fish swam was actually the inside of an Earth-sized fish's mouth that took up most of the card's cover. The mouth curled into a sinister grin.

A shark's grin, full of pointed teeth.

"Why in fuck's sake would you want to think of that?" Maurice asked himself aloud. Surely, he was being paranoid. He had enough to worry about without adding his irrational fears to the pile. He hadn't seen a shark the first night, though he might have been too out of his mind to notice one tap dancing on the water directly in front of him, and he hadn't seen one yet that night.

Yet.

Stop it.

As soon as it was light enough to see, he would swim for shore. *If there even is a shore. If there—*

"Ow!" Something bit him. He yelped again as another bite came.

Whatever had bit him wasn't in the water. It was on his chest. He slapped his skin. Something squished.

He raised his hand in front of his eyes. A sort of jelly with hard, greenish chunks in it spread across his palm. Tiny sticks jutted from one of the larger chunks. He brought his hand closer for a more critical inspection just as an inch-long bug skittered around his knuckle. It resembled a centipede, having too many legs to be an insect or spider, its smooth shell segmented like that of an armadillo.

Its sharp pincers speared Maurice's skin.

He gasped and emitted a terrified squeal that might have called his manhood into question had anyone been around to witness it. He thrust his hand into the water and swished it as if it were on fire, trying to free himself of the dead bug and its very-much-alive friend.

A chill ran down his spine as he glanced down at himself. His skin crawled. So did the swarm of isopods on it.

He trembled. They were in his hair, under his clothes. He had to get them off. He needed them off that instant.

In his panicked swatting, he tumbled into the water. Sinking beneath the surface, he tore off his shorts, clawed at his hair, and patted every inch of his body. When he calmed enough to take in his surroundings, as blind in those depths as he would have been lanternless and several hundred feet below ground, he used his hands to see. They led him through a maze of shoots, which he grabbed to pull himself forward, his legs frog-kicking to assist.

The plants grew everywhere, and though they parted easily enough for him to pass, Maurice feared them all the same. He imagined them belonging to something conscious and evil, like the tentacles of the jellyfish he'd already endured, except these were trying to drag him down to a watery grave: cold, empty depths where the souls of millions of others lost at sea waited with open arms and hollowed-out eyes.

Instead of swimming up, he tried to swim out. His breath grew short. Air bubbles escaped his lips. His lungs ran on empty. When they could operate without oxygen no longer, he swam for the surface.

Only then did he realize how far he had sunk.

He scissored his legs with all his might. His lungs burned, begged for air, but air seemed a mile away. Maurice couldn't tell where water ended and night began. Something nudged him. Something solid and sleek. He screamed. Salt water seeped into his mouth, leaked down his throat. He tried to swallow it all, but liquid squeezed its way into his lungs. He coughed behind lips he couldn't keep closed. His arms turned in maddening circles. He choked, gagged, panicked as life seemed forfeited.

His grasping fingers found air.

He wheezed as his mouth breached the surface then fell into a coughing fit that depleted the oxygen he'd just inhaled and sprayed seawater spittle from his mouth. Even as he coughed for another minute, his eyes looked left then right then left again, scanning the surface for that horrid monster that had touched him, praying it would not touch him again. He saw nothing, heard nothing beyond the wind and the waves. Still, his heart pumped in rapid-fire staccato.

A splash came from directly in front of him. He couldn't see what had made it, just the white froth where the creature had once been. The ripples in the water, the sound the animal had made as it cut across the surface, led Maurice to believe it had been no minnow or goldfish. No, the creature was big, big and monstrous, probably with lots of teeth.

He stared straight ahead. The danger revealed itself. A black fin, like the tail of an airplane, sliced through the water a mere thirty yards away.

Twenty-five.

Maybe it's a dolphin. He wished to God that it was, but when it was only twenty yards away, he saw the second fin zigzagging gracefully about six feet behind. *A dolphin's tail fin is horizontal. Sharks' are—*

Maurice didn't need to finish his thought. He didn't have to see the rest of the animal to know it. A shark headed his way, and if the distance between dorsal fin and tail fin was a trusted indicator, this particular shark was enormous.

He pictured a giant mouth with pointed teeth curled into a sinister grin, the cover of the graduation card his parents had given him. His heart pounded so hard, he thought it might explode, hoped it might. His head spun. The world blurred.

The shark closed in.

§

The sun was cooking the sky from purple to pink when Maurice woke, sputtering and floating on his back in water shallow enough to stand in. He saw a beach and beyond it, a thick forest and the promise of an end to his nightmare. At first, he thought he was dreaming, or perhaps he'd found the afterlife. He slapped his cheeks and felt the sting.

Is this real? I'm alive? How?

A clicking sound, like that of an egg timer cranked slowly, emitted from the beak of a charcoal-skinned dolphin with smiling eyes. Another beside it bobbed its nose in and out of the water, splashing Maurice.

Not two fins from the same *animal. Two fins from* different *animals. Two dolphins!* Had they saved him? He'd heard stories about shipwrecked sailors being rescued by dolphins, but he'd never believed them to be true. The playful creature splashed him again, and he splashed it back, laughing, slowly letting himself accept that the worst was over. Tears of joy ran rivers down his cheeks.

"I wish I had something to offer you, you beautiful bastard." He smiled at his saviors, their bright faces innocent like children. He'd never loved any person or thing as much as he loved them then. "Thank you. Thank you from the bottom of my heart."

Naked and humiliated, his penis shrunken and wrinkled like a California raisin, Maurice waded to shore, part of him thankful it appeared deserted. When he reached it, he collapsed on the sand, embracing the beach and making promises to God to live a better life.

After he had his revenge.

Once his joy had tempered, he stood to gauge his surroundings. He had escaped the perils of the sea, but he had no idea where he was or how he was going to get back home. It wasn't long before he spotted his answer.

A large, white craft lazed in the water off in the distance. Maurice threw a hand over his eyes to shield them from the sun. "No fucking way!" He must have died. Either that or the jellyfish stings were making him hallucinate. He knew that vessel.

The *Wakemaster*.

It can't be. I must be losing it. Maurice rubbed his eyes, blinked the blur away. The ship was no illusion. He squealed with glee like a toddler. He knew that she-bitch, Olivia, forced the captain to stop at every good sunbathing beach and that her husband forced the boat to stop whenever the notion to explore fancied him. But right there? Right then?

Maurice rubbed his hands together. His luck had done a complete one-eighty. Or perhaps it was that other she-bitch, Karma, come to bite those motherfuckers in the ass. The dolphins hadn't just saved Maurice's life. They had towed him to other people.

And a chance for revenge.

How he wanted to kiss those slippery sons of bitches. He didn't know why the boat was docked there and didn't care. Maurice had one mission: get to the ship before it left him stranded a second time.

A mosquito bit his forearm, and he smacked it. The small splatter of blood its flattened form left behind caused him to chuckle. *Anything else want to take a bite out of me?*

Maurice thought back to those nasty kelp critters and examined the welts on his skin. He thought back to that moment of sheer horror when he thought a shark would make him into sushi. He wanted those on the *Wakemaster* to know that feeling, the fear of being eaten alive by something sinister and predatory. He wondered if that sort of terror was something he could cook up.

The pipe dream spurred him into motion. At first, his legs protested—they had forgotten the feel of solid earth—but soon, they were sturdy beneath him as he sprinted the winding beach, keeping out of sight close to the tree line.

The scalding sun had risen high by the time he approached the yacht. Sweat glistened on his red-brown shoulders, dripped from his hair. All that separated him from the boat was half a football field of wide-open beach, followed by a five-minute swim. Despite nearly two full days in the ocean, Maurice coveted that swim, his body already like dry brush ready to ignite.

He steadied his mind, forced himself to examine the boat, watch for signs of life. But the ship sat silent. *Is everyone sleeping?* He smiled then tiptoed across the beach. To his right, he spotted what he first mistook for felled trees until he saw that they had been hollowed out.

Some sort of canoe? He crouched and rolled forward, which probably would have drawn more attention to him if someone had been watching. Feeling exposed, he wondered if the beach was as deserted as he'd thought. Keeping low, he held his breath and waded quietly into the water.

He swam much of the distance underwater, only coming up for air when he absolutely needed it. The ladder started a foot above the water. He pulled himself up and made his way to the top, where he peeked over the lip. No one stirred. Maurice climbed aboard.

Where the hell is everybody? He scanned the deck, half expecting a trap. But no one jumped out at him. Master and crew had simply... *vanished?*

He made his way from bow to stern, his wet feet slapping the deck, announcing his presence with every step. He loitered at the stairwell down to the living quarters, listening for chatter, snoring, anything, but heard nothing.

As he slunk below deck, every creaky stair made him cringe and stop to listen. He searched room after room. Still, he found no one. When he reached the kitchen, he ran to the refrigerator and yanked it open. He cracked open a bottle of water and let it spill down his throat and seep from the corners of his mouth. The cold water felt like heaven. When the bottle was empty, he placed it on the counter and wiped his mouth with the back of his hand. Then, he grabbed another bottle and a plump, red apple.

The loud crunch as he bit into the apple made him freeze. He chewed slowly and put the apple down, then grabbed a large butcher knife from the chopping block and a bottle of vinegar from the cabinet. After finishing his sweep of the cabin, satisfied he was alone, he rummaged through his bedroom, happy to find his stuff had not been thrown overboard. He grabbed a clean shirt and shorts and headed for the shower.

Cool water cascaded over his damaged skin and rehydrated his pruned lips. He scrubbed clumps of seaweed from crevices and wiped dead things from his skin. Red and purple welts tracked across his legs like bubble wrap filled with blood. Some of the bubbles had burst, leaving open sores that looked like rare roast beef. He laughed. He'd heard once that certain jellyfish could kill a man in less than five minutes. Apparently, he'd been exposed to the pussy kind, even though his legs throbbed worse than anything he'd ever experienced.

All mirth left him as he poured vinegar over the wounds. His eyes squeezed shut. His teeth clenched tighter than a virgin's legs. His free hand gripped the handicap railing so hard that his knuckles bleached white.

But he was alive. He was clean. The copious amounts of aloe he applied to his face and body were already resurrecting his skin.

He had only his mind left to attend to.

It demanded revenge.

Maybe I'll just take the boat, leave them here to rot. That's much better than how they left me. Better than they deserve.

Maurice didn't even know where *here* was. He certainly didn't know how to pilot a yacht or navigate the high seas. The others could have been partying at some rich island estate owned by Doc Asshole or one of his asshole friends. Maybe they were only minutes away from a city or civilization. His idea might leave him worse off than they were.

He finished washing, dressing, and tending to his wounds then searched the boat for weapons. In addition to his butcher knife, with which he had carved the best damn sashimi that side of Tokyo—*the way southern side*, he assumed—he grabbed a flare gun from the emergency kit and a gaff hook that looked like it could haul in Moby Dick.

He stared over the rail at the bow, scanning the shore and the lush palms beyond as he gobbled the rest of his apple. The fruit was a light snack to test the agreeability of his stomach. He wondered if he should pack some food but decided against it. If his plan was a success, he'd have plenty of time to come back and eat his fill. And if it was not successful, he figured he would have no need of food then.

He spotted one of the yacht's lifeboats, its back end lolling in the shallows, just waiting for the undertow to drag it away. He wondered how long it had been there, why it had been left forgotten. The more pressing questions concerned what its owners were up to and how Maurice could exact his revenge.

Planning had never been his forte. He knew he wanted to see Doc Asshole, Olivia, and the entire crew—*except maybe Samuel*—dead at his hands but hadn't the faintest idea on how to bring that about. The knife in his grip seemed a good start, but how was he going to stab one without the rest noticing? He could ambush them on the boat, but that would give him little room to maneuver unseen. He'd get one, maybe two, before the rest overcame him.

On land, he could sneak up behind them, take them out one by one, ninja-style. A ninja he was not, but the idea had a certain appeal to it. Regardless, his best odds of success seemed to be on solid ground.

He counted his fingers: one, two, three, four, five. *Five!* There was the captain, the two deckhands, Logan and Samuel, Doc Asshole, and his blushing bride. The doctor was the least threatening. Maurice grinned. He'd save him for last. Olivia was a hellcat, though. She scared him the most, even more so than the brawny captain.

You can do this, he told himself, trying to summon confidence. *Why should they get to live when they left you to die?*

His legs throbbed their agreement. His back and shoulders ached their hurrahs. His fever still hadn't broken, but he knew the heat in his face had more to do with his festering anger than what ailed him.

He lowered the remaining lifeboat and tossed the gaff hook and knife inside it. He tucked the flare gun into his belt, climbed into the boat, and rowed to shore. The physical exertion punished already exhausted muscles. His body yearned for his cozy bed.

I'll sleep when this is over.

Maurice had never been a violent man. He'd never been overly moral, either. Still, nothing about his intentions seemed wrong. He bit into his lower lip, thinking black, delicious thoughts. His plan may not have been right, but it sure as hell felt righteous.

On the shore, he found tracks leading from the other lifeboat into the jungle. They were set in groups of three, side by side, too many to belong to just the crew. *Unless they came and went more than once.* It could be the same group; the outer footprints in each threesome were made by bare feet and those in the center made by shoes scuffing the sand.

After pulling both lifeboats farther up the beach, he followed the tracks toward the trees. Just before sand yielded to thick underbrush, two sets of footprints veered off to the right in long strides. Maurice followed them twenty feet, where they stopped abruptly. Spots of what looked like raspberry jam dotted the white sand. Tracks then veered into the jungle. Two narrow grooves were dug in the sand as if something, or *someone*, had been dragged.

He followed the tracks as far into the jungle as he could before he lost them. He was no tracker and tread carefully, guessing that the dangers of the jungle likely matched those of the sea. At least on land, feet firmly planted, he stood a fighting chance against anything thrown his way.

He scratched his head. What would possess Doc Asshole and his crew to leave the safety and comfort of the yacht for the wilds of an untamed land? Maurice would have to watch his step, but he was determined to pursue his revenge before the island could take it for him.

The smell suddenly made him forget all that. Like the blissful aroma of a Brazilian rotisserie, the scent of sizzling meat wafted toward him on a warm breeze. It revitalized his stomach's longings. The apple had been nowhere near enough to abate his hunger. He swallowed the saliva pooling in his mouth. *God, what I wouldn't do for a taste of that.*

Led by his nose, Maurice pressed farther into the jungle. The gaff hook hung loosely over his shoulder, its point jammed into a wine cork. His butcher knife, firmly in his grasp, pierced the air as he held it in front of him. Every now and then, he used it to bat away a fern or branch that blocked his path.

He knew he should be cautious, but his stomach would have none of it. If he died of snake venom or malaria or some other bullshit, at least he'd die after a satisfying meal.

A low moan, carried on thin wisps of smoke, made its way toward Maurice. It quickly crescendoed, becoming the mad howls of human suffering. Maurice stopped dead. The hairs rose on his neck. He held his breath. The screaming turned his blood to ice. He was sure a man was being tortured. Or skinned alive.

Or roasted.

His stomach gurgled and turned at the thought. The pool in his mouth went stagnant. Yet the smell of the meat remained savory and inviting.

At the sound of a dull thud, the screaming stopped. *Run, moron!* He knew he should, but his feet crept forward. The knife quivered in his hand. Smoke writhed in thick tendrils like a giant squid searching for Captain Nemo. It billowed over leaves, covered Maurice in haze, and burned his eyes. He nearly stepped into the clearing before he saw it, throwing his back against a tree at the edge of the open space before, he hoped, anyone could have seen him. He clutched the butcher knife to his chest.

He chanced a glance into the clearing but saw nothing in the split second he allowed himself. He crouched low and looked again, spotting a crackling fire and two long, dark, cylindrical animals skewered over it. They were thick like boa constrictors but not quite so evenly shaped.

Deer legs? No, not deer. Maurice covered his mouth. He looked away. *Human.*

The rest of Samuel lay beside the pit. His legs had been removed a few inches above his knees, the stumps blackened, cauterized to stop the bleeding. Flies flew circles around the wounds and the spitted meat. Samuel's eyes were closed. He wasn't moving except for the faint rise and fall of his chest.

Christ, he's still alive! Maurice bit his knuckle to hold back a scream. His first instinct was to help Samuel, and he acted on it before logic could hold him in check. The young deckhand had at least tossed Maurice a lifesaver, while the others just turned their backs like the cowards they were.

"The others," he whispered as he crawled hastily to Samuel's side. The boy was unconscious, his arms tied behind his back. His hair was matted against his skull. He appeared to have been clubbed. His legs crackled and charred above them. Rivulets of blood boiled and bubbled and ran fiery trenches through ashen fields of flesh.

But where were the others? *Did they do this to him for helping me? Have they all gone mad?* Maurice sawed through Samuel's bonds, unable to

22

take his eyes off his task for fear of stabbing the boy and taking off more parts than the poor kid had already lost. He hadn't seen the others, hadn't spotted who had done this to Samuel, not until he grabbed the deckhand under his arms and straightened to drag him away from his savory-smelling other half.

And saw the pointed tips of spears aimed at his face.

He dropped Samuel and slashed at the air, but the knife did nothing to slow his attackers' approach. He ripped the flare gun from his belt, and the five dark-skinned islanders jumped back. One dropped his spear and ran. The others stood their ground, but their weapons trembled in their hands.

"So you recognize guns?" Maurice had acted without thinking, had no time to be afraid, but the flare gun had bought him some time to think. The island's natives seemed terrified of it. Yet there were four spears to one flare gun and one knife. Maurice did not like his odds. Still, the fact that he didn't yet feel sharp points stabbing into his back made him think there might not be many natives other than those who stood before him. White men with guns might have had something to do with that.

The two men and two women stood mostly naked except for the women's grass skirts and the men's banana hammocks, which were held up with twigs. Necklaces circled their throats like chokers, with bones and teeth—human, dog, and others Maurice couldn't identify—dangling from them. Each held a six-foot spear with a wooden shaft and a stone blade. They were hunters; Maurice could tell by the deft way in which they handled their weapons, but they were not successful ones if their emaciated frames told a story.

Or perhaps they had just run low on their preferred game.

Others stood behind them, well out of harm's way. Two small children hung by their mother's side as a babe nursed from her tit. An old man with a malformed arm glowered like a wild dog whose meal had been stolen from its snapping jaws. Seeing their teeth filed into points and Samuel's legs roasting over the fire, Maurice didn't have to guess whose company he kept: cannibals, and by the looks of them, the worst kind—hungry.

If he didn't see them with his own eyes, Maurice might not have believed cannibals still existed in the civilized world. But he was far away from what he considered civilization and had recently drawn the conclusion that what he mistook for civilized society wasn't truly civilized at all.

"Is that Maury?" a woman's voice called from an animal pen at the other side of the clearing. "Help us, Maury! They're cannibals!"

"No shit."

Olivia stood behind a row of tall, wooden spikes thatched together to form a crude picket fence. Her clothes were tattered and revealing, and Maurice couldn't help the movement in his pants when he thought of her glorious fake tits. *Hardly the time for it*, he chided himself, but he was just a man.

Behind Olivia, the remaining crew of the *Wakemaster* rose along with the good doctor. They appeared to have been roughed up a bit.

Tenderized.

Maurice considered his options. The right thing to do, he supposed, would be to try and save them. The smart thing to do would be to walk away, take the yacht and retreat far from the island, leaving the rest of them to their well-deserved fates. The idea curled up the corners of his mouth, even if revenge would not come at his hands. With four sharp spears between him and their freedom, Maurice figured walking away was the only chance any of them had of surviving.

One surviving was better than none.

As he stood deadlocked with four starving cannibals, his arm began to tire. But one of the hunters lowered his weapon first. He pointed a finger at Samuel, who lay at Maurice's feet. Then he slowly brought his hand to his mouth and opened wide to stuff it full of air. He repeated the gesture, only this time he pointed at Maurice after he raised his hand to his lips.

Is he offering to share? Maurice's gaze fell upon the fenced-in prisoners. Doc Asshole glared back at him, not pleading for forgiveness, not begging for help, but instead wearing that same smug asshole face that only pretentious, know-it-all smug assholes wear, beady eyes peering down a narrow asshole's nose, mouth pressed asshole flat, and arms asshole-crossed as if his patience was dwindling and his entitlement to rescue had never been in question. Seeing that face, Maurice's rage rose so quickly that it spawned a third option.

That motherfucker. Maurice seethed. He hadn't survived two days at sea, having every hell visited upon him the ocean could muster, only to be ridiculed by a man certain to die unless *he* did something. *Oh, I'll do something all right, you piece of shit. I'll fucking do something. Who says revenge is a dish that has to be served cold?*

He lowered the flare gun, hands steady and deliberate as a surgeon's, though his eyes twitched with just a hint of madness. He tucked the gun into his belt. The islanders raised their brows and cast quizzical looks at one another. Maurice made no sudden movements. He crouched beside Samuel.

"I'm sorry," he whispered, though the words rang hollow. "It's too late for you." With a grimace of effort and concentration, he slid his knife into the boy's muscular thigh and began to shear meat from bone. Samuel's eyes burst open. His mouth contorted as if he were yawning. His fingers clawed deep grooves into the earth at his sides. A silent scream froze on his face as his eyelids fluttered, and he passed back out.

Maurice severed an eight-inch slab of human. He slid the gaff hook off his shoulder and speared the meat with it as if he were going fishing for leviathans. The curled point looked like a giant teriyaki beef skewer. He held it over the fire but not too close, patiently letting the meat cook evenly while the islanders watched with savage curiosity. Any fear seemed to have dissipated along with their murderous intent, as if the cooking muscle had a hypnotic power over them, lulling them into quiet hunger.

Minutes passed, with Maurice passing the hook between hands as one tired. "A fine cut," he muttered. "Hardly any fat." He let the blood rise to the surface before rotating it, browning the meat and searing the outermost edges to add a smoky flavor, leaving the center red and juicy. He licked his lips, unable to deny his own hunger and the fact that properly cooked human at least *smelled* delicious.

When Samuel's thigh muscle had cooked to a fine medium rare, Maurice waved the gaff hook in the air to cool it. He handed the spear to the native closest to him, a woman with thick, coarse hair and devilishly black eyes set deep above pockmarked cheeks. "Careful. It's hot."

The woman didn't take the gaff hook right away. She stepped back and shouted what sounded like *laleo*, then looked to her companions for guidance. The others grunted. She stepped forward like a wild animal, wanting the proffered treat but fearing the hand that held it out to her. She touched the hook, then recoiled, only to snatch the tool from Maurice's grasp a moment later. As if immune to the heat, she grabbed the meat and tore it off. After sniffing it and turning it around in her hands, she bit off an enormous chunk.

The others watched in silence as she chewed. She grinned widely, then laughed with her mouth full. Chunks of meat hung like bats from a ceiling in the gaps between her teeth.

The other three islanders lowered their spears. Each took an impressive mouthful of Samuel's thigh muscle in turn. When the last of the four had bit off more than he could chew, he passed the fist-sized leftovers to Maurice.

"I'm good." Maurice didn't take it. The islanders frowned. They gripped their spears a little tighter.

"Okay, okay." Maurice took the meat, shocked by how quickly he'd folded. Did part of him actually *want* to try it? He let out a breath. *I can do this.* Before he could overthink it, he shoved the morsel into his mouth.

And smiled.

Warm blood ran down his throat, so naturally flavorful, no seasoning or marinating required. "It's… it's amazing!" he said with so much fervor that the islanders flinched. They all laughed after he did.

He kept chewing. By God, he wanted more!

The two children ran over to him, apparently given the okay from their breastfeeding mother. He handed the rest of the meat to them. They tugged at it as if it were a wishbone, the little girl getting the larger chunk. She beamed with pride as she gnawed it ravenously. The little boy seemed content to nibble on the lesser half.

In the pen, Logan was hurling, and Maurice remembered that the deckhands were somehow related. Maurice shrugged. He knew he should be sick, too, but that part of him that saw and understood the wrong in his actions didn't *feel* it. He had less ill will toward Samuel than he had for the rest, but the boy was as good as gone by the time he'd found him, the nearest hospital only God knew where.

The others were as good as gone too. They just didn't know it yet.

Or maybe they did. Olivia cried, loud sobs Maurice might have thought melodramatic had she less reason for drama. The captain huddled in a corner, hiding his face behind his hands. Doc Asshole remained defiant, smug asshole face firmly fixed.

Maurice chuckled. *You're next, asshole.*

The huntress with the onyx orb eyes handed back the gaff hook. She had a wildness to her that no longer frightened him. In fact, he kind of liked it. She snapped her fingers and pointed at Samuel, who looked as pale as death. His eyes were open, but they were glazed over.

Lifeless.

Maurice felt nothing. He certainly didn't feel responsible. He raised his hand to his mouth, copying the gesture one of the males had made earlier. The huntress grunted and smiled. Maurice readied his knife, a chef once again.

They ate most of Samuel that afternoon. Maurice made steak tips out of the charred legs, flaying most of the charred skin for a few mangy dogs that lingered around the campsite. He paired Samuel's ribs with roasted sago, pan-fried banana, and some kind of grub the islanders fussed over. He hesitated to eat the larvae then laughed at the irony. There were other parts of Samuel—parts that even Maurice's surprising indifference to human consumption wouldn't permit him to eat—and they did not go wasted, the tribe picking them clean. All that was left of the boy was a pile of bones.

Waste not, want not. Maurice had more than his fill, and the rich meat and gristle bloated his stomach, but not once had his stomach turned. Not once had he felt even an ounce of regret. The meat tasted too damn good. After what those bastards did to him, they were getting their just desserts.

"Desserts!" Maurice was already contemplating tomorrow's meal. He sat in the dirt, absently drawing figures in it with the little boy. Devil Eyes tapped him on the shoulder. She pointed up to what looked like a giant bird's nest approximately forty yards above the ground. It was big enough to accommodate twice as many as those comprising the tribe, a treehouse with a thick, knotted banyan tree serving as its main support, bolstered by stilts and crossbeams, and roofed with umbrella-sized palm leaves.

Devil Eyes smiled and closed her eyes, pressing praying hands to the side of her face. She grabbed Maurice's hand and tugged him to follow. But he stayed put, watching the tribe, including the children and the deformed old man, climb up a tree-trunk ladder and into their home. Maurice figured he'd head back to the ship for a good night's sleep in the master bedroom.

Having broken bread with the tribe, consumed the flesh of man, Maurice had apparently earned a place among them. The clearing was his as the tribe prepared for the night, the sun sinking into a thin black line. He marveled at the innocent, almost naïve trust they placed in him, an outsider.

He rested, let his meal digest, then walked over to the pen. He felt good, carefree. His fever had broken. The throbbing in his legs was gone. And the best part: not so much as a twinge of remorse.

"You'll burn in hell for that," Doc Asshole called out as Maurice walked by. Maurice stopped.

Olivia ran to the gate. Tears turned her made-up face into a clown mask. "Don't listen to him, Maury. He's just a limp-dick asshole, like you always said he was."

Maurice started walking away. Slowly. Smiling. The rest of the prisoners stared silently, eyes pleading for help just as his had pled for theirs. He'd give them the same answer they'd given him.

"Let me out of here, babe," Olivia begged, tears beginning anew. "We can fuck all you want. Maury? Let us out, Maury. Maury!"

Maurice had passed the enclosure. But before heading back to the yacht, he turned for one last look. Olivia had fallen to her knees. Somehow, someway, Doc Asshole still stood way up high on his pedestal, looking down.

Maurice just laughed. He pointed at the doctor. "You look a little tough. I think tomorrow, I'll teach these islanders how to tenderize meat and fix a proper steak. A good marinated steak always tastes better when you cook it slowly. We'll start small, hands and feet probably. There's always a learning curve. Who knows how many lessons these locals will need to get it right?"

The doctor looked away, but not before Maurice caught a glimpse of a face stricken with horror. Whistling, he returned to the ship, wondering what seasonings would spice up old meat.

DESERT SHADOWS

Monday, April 5, 1943

We're flying blind. Lost—somewhere over the sea.
Have to hurry. Fuel low. Two engines out.
Have to jump.

If you find this diary, tell my family I love them.

—Vernon Moore

Tuesday, April 6, 1943

Praise God! I'm alive, and I'm not alone. I may yet see my family again.

My name is Vernon Lewis Moore. I am a proud son of Rutherford and Ethel Moore and a loving brother to Norman, Evelyn, Virginia, Donald, Robert, Richard, and Betty, all of whom I miss dearly and pray are safe and well back in Ohio. I am a staff sergeant in the USAAF and the gunner and assistant radio operator of the B-24 Liberator, *Lady Be Good.* Or I was, anyway, up until yesterday.

Though our situation is bleak, we all remain hopeful. Should fortunes prove ill, Second Lieutenant Robert Toner and I have decided to journal our plight. This, we hope, is only a precaution, a record for our families in case we never see them again. We understand that death here is a possibility that can't be discounted but not necessarily a *probability*. Our *Lady* is down and yet we stand. Surely, God has more in store for us. I certainly don't plan on dying out here—not today, not tomorrow, not ever.

Still, we're lost in a strange place, so far from home. I'm not certain where we are, but I can tell you how we got here. Only two days prior to this writing, the newly assigned crew of the new long-range heavy bomber *Lady Be Good* left Soluch from the Berina airstrip for a bombing mission over Naples. In addition to myself, eight others left Libya on our *Lady*:

First Lieutenant William Hatton, pilot
Second Lieutenant Robert Toner, copilot
Second Lieutenant DP Hays, navigator
Second Lieutenant John Woravka, bombardier
Technical Sergeant Harold "Rip" Ripslinger, flight engineer
Technical Sergeant Robert LaMotte, radio operator
Staff Sergeant Guy Shelley, gunner and assistant flight engineer
Staff Sergeant Sam Adams, gunner

The nine of us were assigned to the 514th Bombardment Squadron, 376th Bombardment Group, Ninth Air Force. The intended bombing was our *Lady*'s maiden voyage, and it was doomed from the start.

A twenty-five-plane formation set out from Soluch that afternoon. At takeoff, a sandstorm whipped over the airstrip, forcing two of the other Liberators back to base. The *Lady*'s engines took in dangerous quantities of sand, but Lieutenant Hatton did not abort. Even after we made it through the storm, harsh winds blew us off course and away from the formation. When we neared Naples in cloud coverage and long after the rest of our boys had released their payloads and gone, Lieutenant Hatton turned the *Lady* around, and we dropped our weight into the Mediterranean. As we headed back to Berina, our automatic direction finder malfunctioned. We were flying blind.

No one seemed to know where we were or what we should do. We radioed the tower for help but received no response. I can't figure out why they ignored us; the equipment appeared to be operating.

Nevertheless, we put our faith in Hatton, Toner, and Hays to steer us home. We believed they would right up until two in the morning, April 5, when the last of our fuel went up in flames and we were forced to jump.

And I thought we were still over the Mediterranean! Imagine my surprise when my boots hit sand. Even then, I figured I'd landed on some beach, my primary concern being who had sovereignty over it.

A quick glance around under a sky full of stars told me Hitler's war machine was the least of my problems. Vast desert plains spread out in every direction, the only break in the emptiness of the land being small stony plateaus that dotted the horizon.

The cold nipped at my cheeks, and I blew on my hands for warmth. I found it odd that one of the hottest places on the planet during the day— the Libyan Desert, the only place I could be given the geography and our route even with deviation—could be so damn frigid at night.

Someone shot off a flare, and it set me to a purpose, steeling my nerves and stilling my thoughts. I headed in its direction. Others fired their weapons. I did the same, the sounds drawing us together. I came upon Hays first, then Rip. Together, we ambled through the dark, shouting and firing our revolvers, always moving toward the sounds of others.

Eight of us reunited, everyone except John. We searched for him for hours, called out to him through the otherwise soundless night, while pooling our meager supplies under a parachute shelter.

In the morning, I'm ashamed to say we started off without John. May his family find the mercy to forgive us. The sun, blinding even as it rolled over the horizon, radiated the air itself, my lungs searing as I breathed. I was sweating through my flight jacket when I woke. The heat was rising off the sand in a haze that contorted my surroundings like a funhouse mirror.

Someone—Hays, I think—had estimated our position to be about one hundred miles southeast of Soluch. I questioned that estimate but kept my silence. It gave us all a much-needed goal, a destination that, if reached, could mean survival. Northwest was as good a direction as any, and if some believed we might find salvation that way, I could propose no alternative. Though we left it unspoken, everyone knew that if we traveled even one degree off target, we'd likely miss our destination without ever realizing it.

For my part, I know my Lord and Savior shall guide us through this trial, just as he saved us from that cursed plane. The others share my conviction if not my faith. We are young and strong and doing our best to stay positive, to rally each other onward. We are soldiers, and we will persevere. Search parties must already be underway. We need to stay strong until one finds us.

The skies are clear. We are the only things alive and moving on this flat and endless expanse of sand, a splash of color on an otherwise monochrome canvas. We have flares and revolvers. Rescuers should be able to spot us easily from above. We should be able to flag down the first plane that passes anywhere near us.

Together, we will survive. But we have to move. We will head northwest. The base shouldn't be much more than a five-day trek if we have correctly calculated our bearings.

Our prayers go out to John. With any luck, we'll find him along the way.

Wednesday, April 7, 1943

We covered a lot of ground yesterday and a ton more today—miles and miles of sand. The sun is unbearable. My eyes feel like they are on fire. I must protect them constantly. I close my eyes when I walk. Sometimes I drape my shirt over my head, but that exposes skin. It seems everything is a trade-off out here—suffer one harm in lieu of another.

Eyes are useless, anyway. There's nothing to see. No planes. Where are the planes?

Too tired to write much. My skin is burnt, yet the nights are so cold I can't shake the chill. Very lightheaded. Need to rest.

Will try to write more tomorrow. Some of the men are losing hope. Others, maybe their minds. They claim something is following us. Hard to believe we've only been out here a few days. Seems like forever. Strange what the heat can make you see.

We need water. Our supply is almost gone.

How many more miles to go? I'll have to ask Hays in the morning.

Thursday, April 8, 1943

Despair, grief, dehydration, sunstroke… I know not what is causing the madness tearing through the minds of my fellow soldiers—no, my *friends*. Early on, rank gave way to democracy and communal burdens, but now, it's all the more rational of us can do just to spur the men forward. Though probably correct, our decision not to look for our plane and its supplies of food and water and its radio has led to constant bickering and irritation. The question of whether to search for it was raised again today, but our odds of finding it, miles in the opposite direction, are slim, and its contents could be completely destroyed.

So we've continued walking northwest, trudging our way through never-ending desert, shielding both sun and sand from our eyes as best we can with sleeves and cloth. But neither sun nor sand can be stopped, the heat baking our eyes when the wind-blown particles don't scrape them to shreds. Sand is an invasive species: it infests everything, creeps into your clothes, and bites like termites under bark. We cannot rid ourselves of it.

Monday, Tuesday, then Wednesday, we plodded mile after mile, oven-hot days sapping our strength, nights just above freezing tensing our exhausted muscles and rattling our bones. Sleep came in fits at best. By Wednesday, we were so exhausted we were relegated to fifteen-minute cycles of walking followed by five minutes of rest.

Having only half a canteen of water—LaMotte had carried it when he jumped—we rationed it, allowing just one capful each per day. All of us recognize the need to keep moving. We can't count on a rescue party finding us, no matter how much we thought one would. Worst-case scenario: we could walk the distance to the base, so long as we kept moving.

If LaMotte had known what he would be facing four days after he jumped, I wonder if he would have chosen to hide his canteen from us. Would I have, had it been my canteen? No one has attempted to take more than his ration, but gazes linger long and hard on that canteen, my own included.

Yesterday, we hit the dunes. They rolled out before us, first as big as houses then as big as skyscrapers. I fell several times, my legs weak under my weight. After one fall, I refused to get up, the coaxing of my fellow sufferers barely enough to convince me back onto my feet. Would that they had just left me and allowed my suffering to come to an end.

Still, we pressed on, absent the will to do so, our feet shuffling forward as if by reflex alone.

LaMotte went blind but not before going mad. His eyes were like milk.

Helping him renewed my sense of purpose, and we all took turns guiding him over the waves of sand.

Before he lost his sight, LaMotte gave us all a scare, raving about black shapes shimmering like onyx in firelight, following us through the haze. He said they moved like manta rays just under the surface of the massive sand sea, formless blots at first but always growing larger, looming closer. He claimed they reached for him with wispy smokelike tendrils, trying to ensnare him and pull him under. The fool almost seemed happy to have gone blind, no longer able to see that which spawned within him so much terror.

Of course, if dehydration and despair weren't enough to cause his hallucinations, the sun damage to his eyes might have been. Still, the way he trembled when he told us, crying without tears—and the nervous laughter he couldn't stop no matter how many times we begged him to— sent a hush over our party. Real or not, I did not doubt LaMotte believed in them. A sense of hopelessness took root, and I'd be lying if I said I wasn't succumbing to it.

LaMotte is still convinced he's being hunted. Worse yet, others seem to believe him. As if we didn't have enough problems without lunacy tearing through our minds.

There's nothing out here! Nothing as far as the eye can see. No predators! No planes! No airstrip! No USAAF! Just this goddamn sand!

Endless sand.

Friday, April 9, 1943

Though my hand is weak and my body weaker still, my mind remains sound. I have not done a good job of chronicling this horrible journey. We've plodded through endless miles of sand only to find a desert without an end. Despite our body- and soul-crushing efforts, we are going to die out here. Am I Job? Is my faith being tested by a fickle God just because He can?

Well, screw that. We don't deserve this. Our families deserve to know how He has abandoned us. Let these pages reflect what will likely be our final days in this barren, godless place—truly, hell on earth. We don't belong here.

I don't know why we've been stranded here to die. God and country took much from us already, much we gladly offered and would gladly offer again if we had to do it all over. Must they take the only thing we have left?

I've heard several of the men—brave men—praying to God to send His angels to lift us out of this oblivion, this hot expanse of nothingness that has sucked dry faith from my being as easily as it has the water from my body. Funny that as I have lost it, others have found it. But they are simply grasping at straws. They'll find no mercy from above and no death from those things LaMotte sees below.

Even now, as I write this in the icy-cold paradox of desert night, huddled under a parachute and shivering from sunstroke, I hear the others praying feverishly for escape from suffering mixed with mutterings of madness—more whispers of shadows lurking closer, of movement under the sand. I try to explain to them that there is no life here, evil or otherwise, save for the warmth in the blood boiling in our shriveled veins. Soon, that will have dried up and crumbled to dust, like our mouths, our skin, and our half a canteen's worth of that so-precious commodity we once took for granted.

Up until today, Copilot Robert Toner and I have each chronicled our doomed voyage and exile to this wasteland. Having separated from the other survivors with Shelley and Rip, I have taken it upon myself to fully transcribe the waning hours of nine dead men walking, men abandoned to oblivion by a thankless country and a willfully blind god—or a god without dominion over this devil's playground.

Were we not the righteous? Did we not heed the call to arms against a ruthless maniac set on world domination, an Axis meat grinder churning out global death and destruction? We fought for the causes of freedom and democracy, for the meek who couldn't. Yet freedom and democracy are fallacies in this prison without walls. We have become the meek, a flock without a shepherd, martyrs to some unknown cause.

Make no mistake: I am a soldier and will fight for my crew and myself so long as I have an ember of fire left burning in my body, until all light has gone out. That being so, I write this not as a gunner but as a dying and forgotten man with loved ones back at a home he will never see again—people who deserve to know in brutal honesty how I lived these final days and how I died.

In all our walking, we have not seen a single plane, heard a single engine, or been given any sign that our country hasn't forgotten us. I rage against the futility of it all, the nonchalant discarding of human life. Had we been shot down over Naples and died heroes, our deaths might have meant something. Instead, we were sent out to drop bombs on fish and fall on our swords. The enemy cannot be blamed for our deaths.

"Theirs but to do and die…"

But rage burns energy I can't afford to waste. We are beaten mentally and physically, huddling under our last parachute, where we each pray for release.

April 10, 1943

Today, we awoke to a ghostly pale Adams screaming about circling shadows. What's worse is that in addition to LaMotte, Lieutenant Hatton claimed to see them too. The three of them, together with Hays and Toner, have refused to walk any farther. I know the pain that racks their bodies, for it racks mine too—a burning ache in every muscle that shrieks against further use.

Seeing them give up spurs stubbornness in me that will drive me until I collapse—that and fear. I'm afraid that if I do stop, I'll go mad with the others. I watch the sand shift and swirl beneath me, so much like a running river plagued by rapids and whirlpools, and threaten to drown me in the dark dirt below. A chill runs down my neck as I imagine sinister figures swimming under the flowing grains, skeletal hands reaching up to grab me and make me part of their world.

And black shapes hovering like apparitions in my peripherals, shapeless forms growing larger. Coming closer.

Insanity, desperate minds playing tricks—that's all it is. No shapes, just sand. I can pick it up and let it cascade through my fingers, like an hourglass running out of time. And if, by chance, those shadows are real, then we have to keep moving. We have to outrun them.

They aren't real. Still, if we stop…

Choice has been taken from us. Our group has fallen apart. The five who are too weak to continue now rely on three—Guy Shelley, Harry Ripslinger, and me—to find help. I can see it in their eyes that they don't expect us to return. They have resigned themselves to death, and after the ordeal they've unjustly endured, I cannot fault them for it.

I will save them if I can. At least I have to try. I must fight back the gloom that haunts me. My body has all but withered. I am a fraction of the man I was only a week ago. But I must continue.

Guy, Rip, and I have said our goodbyes. We're leaving. I will write more if I survive the night.

April 11, 1943

We must have travelled another twenty miles today—nearly a hundred miles in total, if not more. Rip took us off course. He thought he saw a spring, but the only spring that spouted was one of false hope.

Just more sand. Still no signs of Soluch, no planes overhead. Is there no end to this hell?

I am so tired. I'd cut off my arm for a drink. My arms, they're like dry twigs. I could snap one with the other if I only had an ounce of strength left.

And those black devils! As if the heat, the endless walking, no food, and no water weren't bad enough, LaMotte and the others were right. We are being stalked. I've seen them too—shadowy headless banshees with vulture wings, hovering in my peripherals. But when I turn to face them, they dive beneath the sand—remaining present, though, darkening the sand above them like wicked flowing mud patches, quagmires always nipping at our heels, trying to snag our feet and drag us into their subterranean world.

Well? What are they waiting for?

I didn't believe, still didn't believe when Guy told me we were being hunted. But he shot at one again and again, until his gun clicked empty, screaming and hollering that they wouldn't die, that his bullets just passed through them. And by God, I saw it then! I followed the fear in his eyes to that malevolent spirit haunting us in our darkest hours—*in broad daylight.*

Behind it were two more, farther back but growing taller, long and towering, shadows where no objects might cast them. The way they shook, I could tell they were laughing, though they had no mouths and made no sounds. I dropped to my knees, offering what was left of me to them as night descended.

They loomed tall as houses, no longer content with hiding, their forms encroaching and bending around me as if to embrace me in forever night. Their cold indifference spoke to their evil: demons, malevolent spirits… of what type, I do not know. But I cursed the God who deserted me with them. I closed my eyes, bowed my head, and held my breath.

But they didn't take me. Like cats toying with a mouse, they were feeding off my torment. And they wanted more.

They're gone now, and Guy has calmed. He's getting some much-needed rest while I write this and stand guard. Rip, who hasn't seen them and refuses to believe, like I refused to believe, sleeps soundly beside him, huddling against Guy for warmth.

Rip will believe when they come for him. They are coming for us all. Enjoying our suffering until the last of our strength leaves us.

We have only ourselves to defend against daylight demons that cannot be touched, cannot be killed. Our only hope is to find Soluch. We must be close now. We've traveled so far. Perhaps tomorrow, the city will reveal itself if we just walk a little farther.

But for now, I lack the strength to fight. My eyelids keep closing despite my best efforts to keep them open. Perhaps I'll allow myself a moment's rest beside Guy and Rip, just a moment to shut my eyes and gather my strength.

April 12, 1943

I awoke late this morning to Rip slapping my face. I'm not sure how long he tried to pull me to my feet, but my mind and body were slow to cooperate. Together, we tried to wake Guy. We soon realized the futility in the attempt.

We lacked the strength to bury him. At least he'd escaped the clutches of our pursuers, which were with us when we awoke, always watching, sticking close to our heels. I saw them but said nothing, wanting to let Rip find comfort in his denial as long as possible. Death comes regardless.

An end to suffering. An end to all things.

Tell my family I tried. Every step I took today was for them and my family here.

I am alone now. Rip finally saw them about three hours ago. He ran in terror. One of the two specters chased him over a dune and out of sight. I hadn't the strength to follow. I wish he were here, wish we could face our ends together. But I suppose that's one journey we all must face alone.

I hope he finds Soluch or sanctuary—or dies easy, which might be the best either of us could hope for. As I sit here, back to the setting sun, I write in this journal one last time. I find I have no final words of wisdom to impart. Even if I had, they'd only fall on deaf ears. No one will find me. I'll die here without anyone ever knowing. If war has taught me anything, it's that life has no value. We live, we die, and the world goes on without us, billions of grains of sand flowing in a river of whirlpools and rapids until finally swept under.

Where serpents hide, biding their time before striking.

Only one shape remains, hovering menacingly over me, a reaper shrouded in black. It's tall and emaciated, the shape of a man stretched long and thin like taffy. A light sparkles from somewhere within its abysmal form like the gleam in the eye of a madman as he bayonets his fellow man. I shudder but do not look away except to finish these words.

My time has come. And so I'll tuck this diary away and stare at the light within the dark, waiting for a shadow to bring a long, cold night to the scorched Saharan day.

THE EXCHANGE

Ramsey covered his mouth, but the vomit had to go somewhere. It rose in his throat and forced its way through pursed lips, spraying out the cracks between his fingers. Recognizing the futility of his efforts, he gave up trying to stem the flow.

He sat cross-legged on the floor—some floor, somewhere. Darkness surrounded him. Ramsey leaned forward and planted his goopy palms on the soft carpet. After he emptied his stomach's contents, he struggled to find his bearings. Though, even in the dark, he sensed some familiarity with his surroundings.

Where am I? How did I get here? He concentrated hard. His brain pounded from the effort. He tried to scan his surroundings for clues, but the darkness proved to be all-consuming.

Wherever he was, it was quiet and warm. He dragged his fingers along the carpet—soggy, not just where he'd thrown up but also underneath his buttocks. His skin radiated heat. Ramsey went to wipe his vomit-coated hands on his jeans but discovered that he was naked from the waist down.

He grabbed his T-shirt, letting out a breath of relief, as if this minute symbol of familiarity was enough to dispel his incomprehension. It made sitting bare ass on the carpet in the dark, covered in his own puke, somehow seem a bit more normal.

Rammmmmssssseeeee....

"Huh?" Ramsey sprang to his knees, his arms slashing at the air in front of him.

Rammmmmsssseeeee... The voice, like a whisper on the wind, flowed into his ear.

"Who's there?"

Ramsey waited for a response, but none came. His head felt like a bomb had gone off inside it. Panic and the sudden urge to flee thrust his heart into overdrive. He leapt to his feet. His head connected with the ceiling, and he came crashing down. Dizziness and pain clouded his mind.

He rubbed his head where a bump had already surfaced. He reached up and touched a sloped ceiling.

My room?

Ramsey stood, this time slowly, and stumbled through the dark to where he hoped the light switch would be. Reaching out for the wall opposite the slope, taking baby steps toward it, Ramsey moved unimpeded. He followed the wall to the door and the light switch beside it. His bedroom illuminated. The light sent flashing pain behind his eyes so harsh he had to close them. After the agony subsided, he opened them a sliver, giving them time to adjust.

Gross, he thought, glancing at the remains of last night's dinner now deposited on his usually pristine carpet. The bulk of the mess pooled in front of the cutout entranceway to the attic behind the southern wall of his bedroom.

He tried to piece together the previous night, but nothing came to him. Puke clotted his short beard and stained his T-shirt. He followed its trail down to a used condom hanging off the tip of his penis.

"Where have you been?" he asked his flaccid friend. A stream of drool escaped from the corner of his mouth. He wiped the back of his hand across his lips then ripped the condom off and threw it into the pool of vomit.

I'll clean it up later, Ramsey thought, shrugging. He needed sleep, some time to give his mind a chance to reboot. He tore off his shirt, staggered toward his bed, and noticed a perfectly chiseled specimen lying atop his sheets, exposed buttocks turned his way.

"And just who might you be?" he asked softly.

Ramsey's penis stiffened despite his drunkenness, despite the pain pulsating through his body and head. His eyebrows rose as well, and he

42

turned around. He looked at the condom he'd tossed on the floor, which, after a moment's debate, he decided was beyond reuse.

He dashed out of the room, immediately regretting the sudden movement. A dry heave followed by an acidic burp forced their way up his throat. He entered his bathroom and stared at himself in the mirror. Bloodshot eyes complemented his greasy, unwashed face.

"At least you don't have bedhead," he told his reflection as he rubbed his clean-shaven scalp.

Old pipes protested with grunts as he turned on the hot water for a quick shower. The heat soothed his already warm flesh, sweat purifying his body, excreting alcohol from his pores. He closed his eyes, and by the time he opened them again, the water had gone frigid.

He turned off the water and dried himself. He picked up the mouthwash and took a swig straight from the bottle. Instantly, the memory of drinking Jägermeister flashed through his mind. It felt good to remember something. He swished it around and spat into the sink. With his towel wrapped around his waist, he half staggered back to his bedroom. He threw the towel over the filth on his carpet, turned off the light, and climbed into bed beside the enticing stranger.

Why clean up today what I can get this sucker to clean up tomorrow?

Ramsey pulled up a sheet and curled against the man. He grabbed his company's hip, excited by the feel of hard muscle beneath smooth skin, and kissed his lover's shoulder. An almost metallic scent, like iron mixed with musk and sweat, enveloped him.

"Brr," Ramsey said, stroking the man's arm. "Your skin is like ice. Poor thing. You must be freezing. Here, let me warm you up."

Ramsey's penis rested like a hot dog between the stranger's buns. He moved his lips playfully along the man's shoulder in a continuous path that led to the curve of his neck. Once there, he bit, a nibble at first then hard enough to leave imprints. The man didn't budge.

This one likes it rough.

His excitement grew, and he threw his arm around his lover and squeezed him.

"Eww," Ramsey said, withdrawing his arm from a sticky wetness. "You got sick too? I mean," he stammered, then raised his voice. "You got sick in bed too? What did we do last night… must have been one hell of a good time."

Ramsey's penis fell flaccid.

Puke on the floor is one thing, but in bed? This brings grossness of a whole new level.

"Come on, love. Let's get you into the shower." Ramsey shook the man again. "Damn, man, wake up!" Nothing stirred him. His unknown lover was out cold. Very cold.

Ramsey sighed. He stood next to his bed and flipped on the lamp atop an end table.

"Wake up," he commanded, his patience thinning.

He shook the stranger violently. The man rolled onto his back, his eyes wide open. Red stained his chest, and his neck looked as if it had been torn apart by some wild animal; strands of shredded skin hung beneath his chin, his spine visible inside the gaping hole.

Ramsey bit down on his knuckle to stifle a scream. His eyes darted from the bed to the floor and to each corner of the room, not really sure what he searched for.

"W-W-What happened?" His lips quivered as he spoke.

What do I do? What do I do?

The question repeated in Ramsey's mind like a broken record skipping at a million rotations per minute.

Oh my God, did I kill him?

Ramsey slouched, his enfeebled legs buckling beneath his weight. His heart pulsated erratically. He could never imagine himself hurting anyone. Not like that.

The fact remained: A dead man lay in his bed.

Ramsey tried to settle his nerves, to consider the evidence. He didn't recall any blood on him before he showered.

Think, Ramsey! God, it looks like a bear mauled him.

Ramsey had heard of people doing all sorts of crazy shit while they were drunk, some kind of psychotic episode during a blackout. As disturbing a truth as it was, he must have killed the stranger. No one else was in his apartment.

Unless—

Ramsey gasped. His mouth hung open. His nerves tingled on high alert. Whatever haziness had clouded his mind earlier vanished.

He crept to his bureau, pulled out a pair of boxers, and threw them on. He dashed to the kitchen and snagged a steak knife from a drawer. There, he stood breathless, listening for any sound, waiting for someone, anyone, to appear out of the darkness.

Ramsey reached for the phone, but his arm recoiled from its smooth plastic as though it were on fire.

Not yet. The police will think I did it.

Room by room, Ramsey systematically ruled out each potential hiding spot: a bathroom, a living room, a kitchen, a dining room, and a bedroom. He flicked on every light, opened every door. No one squatted within the kitchen cupboards. No one veiled himself behind the shower curtain. No one leapt from any of the closets. He made his way back to his bedroom. His closet stood open, but no feet filled the shoes inside.

Only the attic remained unchecked.

The attic door was really just a square panel with a handle to pull it open. Ramsey didn't like going into the attic. It always smelled worse than a nursing home. The air hung heavy. Pink insulation sprouted in patches from the walls and ceiling like puffs of cotton candy. Silverfish, alive and dead, filled every crack and crevice. Its sole light bulb, no matter the wattage he used, never illuminated the furthest reaches.

When he reached for the handle, he saw that the panel was cracked open. He stepped back, the knife in his hand jutting out before him.

"Who's there?" Ramsey asked. "If someone's in there, I swear to God I'll—"

The door exploded from its resting place, hitting Ramsey in the shin. He buckled from the pain. Quick to recover, he jumped back and fixed his eyes upon the exposed entrance.

"Leave now," Ramsey said, the knife shaking in his hand. "I'll tell the police I never saw your face."

A low rumble emitted from the opening, almost like the purr of a finely tuned motorcycle, but much softer, less mechanical. Ramsey backpedaled in slow motion, barely aware of his movement. His gaze never left the attic entrance.

The rumble grew louder, becoming a swishing sound, like an arrow piercing the air. A searing pain shot through his chest. He looked down. Three barbed prongs penetrated his body, their points disappearing deep beneath his skin. Cables were connected to the shafts that stretched back into the darkness of the attic.

The cords pulled taut, tugging at Ramsey's flesh. His skin tented as if he were suspended from fishhooks. He screamed and grabbed the cords. Fleshy and slime covered, they pulsated. He couldn't grip them; the more he tried, the more his hands burned.

Unable to resist the pain any longer, he let go. Deep grooves striped across his hands. He dropped onto his ass, planting his feet and pushing backward. His attacker would have to drag him every inch of the way.

Whatever tugged him didn't stop, but Ramsey matched its action with an equal and opposite reaction. His flesh split. He believed that if he didn't remove those damn prongs, his skin would soon rip from his frame.

Despite how bad it looked, the pain faded. His fear and his fight went with it. The room seemed to slant then sway. None of it—not the dead man in his bed, the prongs beneath his flesh, or the villain to whom they belonged—concerned him any longer. His lack of concern concerned him, but only briefly.

Black as space.

It was as if the attic repelled the light in his room. The intruder moved against the brightness like oil on water. The air inside the attic seemed alive. Ramsey stared at the black mass with curiosity, almost fascination. It began to swirl. He knew he should fear it.

The pain had all but disappeared. Somewhere in the back of his mind, Ramsey understood that he'd been drugged. The soft voice of his conscience still begged him to run, but his intoxication muted it, and he moved closer to the attic's entrance, falling into the euphoria.

Like a baby learning to crawl, Ramsey shuffled on hands and knees toward the door. A broad grin curled up his face. Drool ran freely from his mouth.

He entered the attic.

The darkness engulfed him with all the comfort and warmth of a fur blanket. The attic became a safe and nurturing place, a womb. His mind surged with excitement. His heart beat strong and steady. There in the darkness, he believed he had transcended to his purest self, leaving his imperfect human form on the other side of the threshold. He never wanted to leave.

§

Ramsey awoke in his bed. He scanned his room but saw no body, no blood, no disorder, no sign that a murder had occurred.

A dream?

The idea that it had all been a dream filled him with disappointment. If only a dream, how could he return to it, to feel once again those amazing sensations that had claimed his body and mind? They were gone now. Normalcy had returned, and with it, a sense of loss. He craved the euphoria. He *needed* to feel that way again.

He stared longingly at the attic, the door slightly ajar. Ramsey dismissed the false memories of the dead stranger and the murderous creature that lived behind his wall. They didn't matter. They were inconsequential figments, distractions from the euphoria that had swept him away.

Absently, he scratched his chest. His fingers came away wet and sticky. Three welts mounded over his heart, each the size of a quarter, oozing a yellowish liquid. Red striations spread like an infection from the wounds.

He stared at his attic door, hopeful and terrified.

Noooo… dreeeeam… Rammmmsssseeee, a voice called from within the darkness.

Ramsey sat up, drawing the covers to his chest. For a moment, he didn't move, not knowing what to do, then he sprang up and raced for the exit. His hand froze upon the knob.

If I leave, I may never feel it again.

He shivered and plodded back to his bedroom. Building up courage, he drew in a breath and approached the attic, his whole body shaking uncontrollably. His teeth rattled. Letting out his breath, he removed the panel from the wall.

A crunching sound came from the ceiling, like someone walking on broken glass. Ramsey's eyes adjusted to the darkness. An arm hung from the insulation… a human arm dripping blood.

Ramsey froze. He dared not move or make a sound. His muscles ached from the strain of stillness.

The arm fell to the floor, shredded at the shoulder, muscle and tissue stripped from the bone. Jagged bone fragments protruded inches above the elbow.

Two spiny black appendages, sleek and slender, slid from the insulation. Sharp talons extended from webbed hands.

Ramsey screeched.

Run. Oh please dear God, run!

All the logic in the world couldn't will his feet to move. His eyes widened, locked on this thing emerging from the ceiling.

A face breached the insulation.

Ramsey's heart nearly stopped when two small yellow eyes, cropped like a bird's on a bulbous black head, peered at him. Below poked a large upturned snout with nostrils the size of fists. Its skin was stretched thin, silvery veins coursing through it. And its smell, a foul odor, was far worse than a rotting corpse.

Still, Ramsey couldn't run. No matter how much he wanted to, his body would not obey.

The creature's lipless mouth wrapped halfway around its head. Its jaw was lined with six-inch pointed teeth that interlocked like a bear trap. Red blotches stained each tooth, and stringy chunks hung from the gaps.

The crunching sound came from the creature's mouth, those monstrous teeth gnashing and grinding, smiling wide.

Bone. This thing can chew through bone.

Hunnnngreeeee… Rammmmmsssseeeee.

Ramsey wasn't sure if it spoke the words at all or if he heard them in his head. He didn't know if it was offering to share its meal or if Ramsey was the main course.

One of the barbed cords coiled around his ankle. Its prong quivered like the backend of a rattlesnake.

"What the fuck!" Ramsey screamed. He tried to back away, tried to escape, but the cord twisted around his legs, and he fell. He smashed his chin against the floor, immediately tasting blood. The wiry tentacle squeezed like a tourniquet around his shin. His bones cracked, and a sharp, violent pain shot up his leg. His eyes blurred.

The thing tugged at him, the tentacle cutting like piano wire into his calf. Ramsey clawed his fingers at the carpet. The nail on his index finger caught in the rug and ripped clean off as he slid into the attic.

He reached for the wall and managed to brace himself for a moment. His fingers latched on each side of the doorframe. But the thing pulled harder, raising his body off the floor. The thin wooden wall splintered beneath his grasp. His fingers slipped and then let go.

"No!" he yelled. "Help!" He wriggled like a fish on the end of a line.

The creature reeled him deeper into the attic.

Ramsey came to a stop and rested his cheek against the dusty floor. A silverfish scurried away from him. The creature still gripped his leg, but the coils had loosened. Ramsey felt its presence above him, still heard it gnashing bone. The attic smelled of decay, of death.

Ramsey propped himself up on his forearms. He imagined the thing's mouth opening wide, his foot disappearing behind those rows of teeth. The gnawing would follow, the unimaginable pain of being eaten alive. Feet then ankles then shins, and so on until his body went into shock or he bled out. He closed his eyes and prayed.

Please just make it quick.

But nothing happened.

What is it waiting for?

Ramsey rolled onto his back, ready to meet his tormentor face to face. The creature stared down at him. Blood dripped from its teeth into Ramsey's mouth and onto his cheeks. Its appendages shot forward, pinning Ramsey to the floor. Then, it lifted him as though he were weightless and drew him within inches of its gaping maw.

Head first?

Sweat beaded on his forehead. Liquid warmth spread across his groin.

Something writhed like a worm along his stomach, passing his navel and up his chest. A barbed prong appeared before his eyes and rattled. The tentacle and its arrowhead-like point thrashed lightning-quick, slapping Ramsey's neck, the prong delving into his jugular.

The walls and ceiling faded into darkness. Only the creature's face remained, surrounded by swirling black pools of that dreamlike substance that seemed to be more than a liquid but less than a solid.

Plasma?

His terror became a fleeting memory. That vile weaponry the thing called teeth came close enough to kiss, and Ramsey began to feel the euphoric high. The creature had once again elevated him to Heaven.

He smiled, staring dead into the creature's mouth. "Are you going to eat me?"

Noooo… Rammmmsssseeee.

Ramsey struggled for a clear thought. It took some time, but his next question slowly spawned from the muck. "What are you going to do to me?"

Moooorrrre. The creature released Ramsey, but he remained suspended in the air, the plasma substance billowing around him. It picked up the remainder of the arm and dropped it against Ramsey's chest. *Goooodeeeeessss… forrrr… goooodeeeessss.*

Ramsey scrunched his forehead. His mind fell into a haze, but he thought he understood.

"If I bring you more goodies, you'll give me this feeling in exchange?"

Yessss… Rammmmsssseeee.

Ramsey felt superhuman, omnipotent, as he experienced euphoria greater than mortal comprehension. Human life seemed so infinitesimal, valueless.

How could I ever go back to my insignificant existence?

As the blissful tingling surged through his body, raising his senses to a higher plane, invigorating his very soul, Ramsey justified what was asked of him.

"But what happens when the drug stops working?"

Nevvvverrrr… hassss… toooo.

"Never?"

The creature nodded, and Ramsey smiled.

Ramsey knew what that meant but didn't care. He would exchange as many lives as it would take for continuous access to the creature's utopia.

Guess I'll be going out tonight.

Another prong shot from the creature and burrowed into Ramsey's chest. His eyes fluttered closed, shutting out the remainder of his humanity.

VIOLET

"**C**ome here, girl." Ed patted his thigh as he stared at the fourteen-year-old corgi struggling to shimmy out of her crate. The dog stared back, eyes swelling with excitement, big dumb smile on her face as if she didn't have a care in the world, her back legs hardly working, just par for the course.

She fell flat on her belly halfway out of the crate, still smiling, still staring up at him with her big beautiful doe eyes. Eyes full of ignorant happiness. Eyes that filled Ed's own with tears.

The dog, Violet, was old. Ed was old too. He'd named the dog after his daughter, who'd passed away some thirty years ago in a car accident. Nobody's fault, just bad weather and bad luck. He and his wife, Mara, had no other children. After his daughter had passed, then a few years later, their golden retriever, and another decade after that, Mara herself from cancer, Ed had spent so many years alone.

Struggling to live.

His daughter had clung to life for days after the accident, his wife for years after her diagnosis. Hell, even the golden had fought to live every day it could. He figured he'd owed it to all of them to keep on keeping on for as long as he could, no matter how much it pained him, missing them every day.

So he got himself a dog, and he named her Violet. The corgi hadn't replaced his daughter, but she had certainly and quickly become another daughter. And she was all he had.

Fourteen years. He smiled wanly. *That's like damn near a hundred in dog years.* He went to Violet and hefted her into his arms. The corgi licked his cheek once then rested her head against his shoulder.

He stroked the back of her neck. "Why do you even go into that crate anymore? Huh? I haven't shut the door to it since you were a pup."

Ed held her close. He knew the answer. The crate was her home, just as beside him on the couch was her home when he watched television and curled against his hip was her home when he went to bed. The one-bedroom, one-bathroom apartment wasn't much, but it was enough for the two of them.

But Violet had severe arthritis, and she was suffering. She was lucky if she could walk more than a few steps without her back legs splaying, her belly plopping against the ground. Every time it happened, she looked up at Ed with those unassuming, apologetic eyes as if she might have done something wrong. That guilt—projection, he knew, but that did nothing to soften it—burned hot in his chest, the pain deep and pure, his breath hitching in response to any inclination concerning the battle Violet was losing.

He reached for her leash then shook his head, scolding himself for his gaff. The dog hadn't needed the leash for months. She wasn't running anywhere.

With a heavy sigh, he picked up his keys and went out into the hallway. He didn't bother locking his door, the average age of his neighbors being close to eighty. He carried Violet down the three flights of stairs that led to the complex's front doors. From there, it was a short walk to the pet area, where Violet could do her business.

He placed her on the grassy earth with all the caution of a man balancing an egg on a spoon. Once she seemed to be standing firmly, he gently held her just above her hips so she could walk without fear of falling.

Violet took a few steps then spread her legs to pee. Her legs kept slipping, but Ed caught and held her as urine trickled onto the grass.

"You really need to put her down," someone said from behind him.

Ed felt heat rising in his face, some from anger and some from shame. He knew the dog's quality of life had been on a drastic decline and had battled the idea of putting her down. But every time he turned it over in his head, he wanted to scream and sob and shake his fists at the heavens for the cruelty of life's feeble condition.

It was his decision to make, though, and he didn't care for busybody neighbors butting their goddamn noses into his business. He whirled around, ready to lash out, but checked his temper and donned a phony smile before it was too late.

"Hi, Gladys." Ed hoped his face wasn't as red as it felt, though he could always blame it on the strain of bending over and carrying the dog, burdens he'd undertake for another fourteen years if it meant being with Violet all that time. "How's Kirk? Any change?"

Gladys was a hospice nurse who worked double duty, after hours caring for her husband, Kirk, who was suffering from ALS in an apartment down the hall from Ed. He didn't mean the question to sound callous and hoped it hadn't, genuinely concerned about Kirk's well-being. Kirk had always been a fine neighbor and, had his disease not debilitated him so early on in Ed's tenure at the complex, might have made a decent friend.

Gladys, on the other hand, was a bitch—a nosy, gossipy troublemaker that never knew how to leave well enough alone. A week didn't go by when she wasn't fighting with someone in the building. Ed did his best to excuse it. The woman lived a hard life made harder by unfortunate and undeserved conditions, something he knew a little about himself.

"No change," Gladys said, her mouth a thin line. "At least he didn't poop himself today."

Ed didn't know what to say to that, so he said nothing.

A gnarled finger extended, she pointed at Violet, who was now lying against Ed's sneaker. "You need to put that thing down and soon." She snarled. "If you don't, I'm calling animal control." With that, she turned to leave.

Ed clenched his teeth as he watched her go. He glanced down at his girl, who was looking up at him with tongue lolling, big dumb smile returned. He couldn't help but smile back. Like swaddling a baby, he wrapped Violet in his arms and headed inside.

Gladys's comment festered like a wound that wouldn't heal. After giving Violet some fresh water and helping her into her crate, he decided he needed some fresh air. He stepped back out of his apartment, once again leaving it unlocked, and headed for a lap around the block to clear his head.

When he got back, his front door was ajar.

His body screamed trouble. Without thinking, he ran through the door. There, Gladys stood over his dog, a long needle in her hand. In the crate, Violet's eyes were closed. Her side rose and fell rapidly as a purplish liquid ran from her mouth.

"It's for her own good," Gladys said, her mouth tight. If she felt anything for what she'd done, it didn't show. "It's mercy."

Crying, Ed pushed Gladys aside, ran to his dog, and pulled her from the crate. He raced down the stairs, taking them two or three at a time, putting tremendous strain on his own aching joints. But the pain was a distant echo, the worry and maddening dread spurring him forward at a pace he had no longer thought himself capable.

He placed his girl on the passenger seat of his car and slid behind the wheel. He drove as fast as he was able, swerving through traffic and blowing through red lights, barely able to see through the tears in his eyes.

When he screeched to a halt outside the animal hospital's entrance, Violet was already dead. Ed broke down. He didn't bother going inside.

§

A week passed, and Ed was no better off than he had been at the time of Violet's death. That night, he caught Gladys leaving on an errand. Once she was clear of the hallway, he hurried down it to her apartment, shimmied open the door, and stepped inside.

"It's for his own good," he said, almost snarling as he smothered Kirk with a pillow. "It's mercy."

COMPLEX

arrie knew she'd follow her husband, Liam, anywhere. She'd stuck by him for twenty-three years, through one-night stands, all the drinking and time spent unemployed, fad after obsessive fad, and—worst of all, though not his fault—the death of their only son. Now he was dragging both of them to early graves.

Sometimes, she really hated herself for loving him so much.

But it was easy to focus on all the bad. He had been by her side through multiple miscarriages, had tenaciously campaigned for her during her three failed runs for city councilor, and, most of all, had held her tightly every moment she needed while he grieved the loss of their son in silence.

They had married young—he twenty-one and she nineteen—and had spent nearly every day, whether good, bad, or indifferent, side by side, a pair of crutches holding each other up.

Now, Carrie was forty-two. Her back ached. Her windbreaker and jeans were damp with sweat despite the chill. She prayed for a break, dreaming of a foot massage in some St. Lucian resort spa far, far away.

But she prayed in silence. *Twenty-three years and we're going to die out here, in the middle of nowhere, miles from home.*

The sun hadn't set yet, but the thick firs, their trunks packed like cigarettes, blocked out much of the light. What remained was almost a constant twilight under a canopy of lush green darkness.

Until nightfall, when all was black. When the wolves—

Carrie shuddered then forced her mind onto other thoughts. Something jabbed into her left foot. "Hold on a second."

Liam, hiking a half step in front of her, dutifully did as requested. He tapped his five-foot, gnarled hiking staff that resembled something out of a *Harry Potter* movie and turned. "What's up? You okay?"

Carrie suppressed a sneer. She hated that staff, which served no purpose she could understand. She hated being out in those woods, and by God, right then and there, she thought she might even have hated him. She closed her eyes and took a deep breath, chastising herself for even thinking such a thing, no matter how untrue it was.

"Could you..." She grabbed Liam's sleeve. "There's something in my boot." Lifting her foot, she pulled off her hiking boot. When she upended it, bits of dead leaves and broken twigs fell onto a forest floor already full of them. Looking at her swelling ankle, she saw a fat black ant the size of her thumbnail traipsing over her sock. She scowled and flicked it off then put her boot back on.

"Better?" her husband asked, his smile sincere, warm, and full of love.

Carrie nodded. Though the stabbing pain in her foot was gone, she was a long way from better. Night was coming, and—

Again, she forced the thought from her mind, instead tucking her arm around Liam's and holding him close.

As it turned out, they hadn't much farther to go before their messiah halted the group. She took him in as he stood on a fallen tree to address his people, the fifty-four chosen who'd followed him out into that wilderness.

Jericho, the one they called *Messiah*, didn't project an aura of holiness. In a green vest over a flannel shirt, ball cap, and jeans, he looked just about as ordinary as everyone else. His short beard was dotted with gray. A spare tire circled his waist. As the story had it, he was a junkie, prostitute, and atheist until God visited him in a dream and showed Messiah his true self, the reincarnation of Jesus Christ and savior to the chosen few. He awoke cured of his addiction and clean of sin.

Carrie had to wonder if the tattoo running up the side of his neck was the new stigmata. Unlike her husband, she was skeptical of the man's authenticity as Christ rearisen. His knowledge of scripture was adequate at best, and he resembled neither lion nor lamb.

Needless to say, Carrie was dubious of the man's ability to lead them to the promised land. But her husband had seen something in the messiah she couldn't see herself. She'd at first thought it another of Liam's fads, like country music, aerobic kickboxing, and keto. So when he'd begged her to go with him on this not-so-little adventure, she eventually caved, thinking it would be a standard religious retreat filled with "Kum Ba Yah" activities and boxed lunches.

For three days straight, they walked deeper into the forest, never questioning their messiah's direction or even understanding where they were going or why. Thus far, the only positive had been that her backpack had gotten lighter, her food and water supplies nearly depleted. And each night, the wolves—at least a dozen, she guessed, from the howling that kept her awake and shivering at night—drew louder and closer.

Circling, like dogs herding cattle.

Meat.

She had read once that wolves obtained most of their water intake from the prey they consumed. The cold fact did little to rationalize her fear of tearing claws and gnashing teeth.

"Faith!" their messiah shouted, startling Carrie from her thoughts. He extended his arms as if waiting for his flock to embrace him. "Faith is what you have shown me through this ordeal, my brothers and sisters. Never have you questioned that faith, doubted your reasons for following me through this devil's playground."

He clapped, smile spreading to the ends of his cheeks. "Rejoice, for your faith will be rewarded! The time is nigh. Salvation is within our reach. Your perseverance is God's engine. Your belief in Him is righteous and beautiful. When He sings, I listen, and you, the wise, the chosen, you can hear his song through me."

Messiah threw his fists over his head. The crowd let out a chorus of cheers and amens. Carrie huddled beside her applauding husband.

After the celebration ran its course, Messiah waved his outstretched arms to quiet the most zealous of the bunch. "But our herd must be culled. There are those among us who are undeserving of what God will offer His true children." He scanned the crowd, his gaze touching on each of his followers. When it fell on Carrie, she shrank further into Liam as if trying to cram herself into his jacket pocket.

Liam smiled and kissed the top of her head, wrapping a strong arm around her. Though she couldn't put her finger on why, his comfort amplified her own discomfort.

"The devil's beasts will come," Messiah preached. "And I say, let them. They cannot touch the pure among us. They can only take the undeserving. Let your faith in Him and your prophet be your salvation."

A howl split the cold air, silencing both preacher and flock. Messiah chuckled, his teeth shining with saliva. "We camp here for the night." He clapped, and everyone broke into their individual family units to find a spot to make camp. As Carrie preferred it, they worked their way as close to the fire as possible.

§

Night descended with biting cold. Carrie snuggled against Liam for warmth, their sleeping bags keeping her from getting as close as she would have liked. The howling wind whipped into their tent, rattling it on its posts. She closed her eyes and pressed her face into Liam's chest. Her husband slept soundly, a serene tranquility written in the iron smoothness of his face.

She loved him. She resented him. She needed him.

More howls—not just the wind. The songs of night creatures were all around them, voices hungry and desperate out in the cold. The campfire cast shadows as big as mountains against the side of the tent, shapeless but sure to be full of fangs and fur. As they began to shrink with the fire, one of them definitely looked like a dog.

A very big dog—not a shadow but a silhouette. Just outside their tent.

Tears in her eyes, trembling against her man, Carrie prayed for a true savior, someone to lead her out of the woods.

And when she heard what sounded like a scream, she prayed all the more.

§

Carrie awoke to a kiss then a scream.

Her husband had just planted one on her lips and rolled over onto his back to stretch when they heard a shrill cry, full of agony and torment. It sent the sleeping camp into action.

Carrie clutched her chest, lurching upright in her sleeping bag. Her breaths came so short and fast she thought she might hyperventilate. Her body ached from sleeping on the hard, uneven earth. Exactly when exhaustion had overcome her, she couldn't remember. Ripped from her grogginess by terror, she felt as if she'd barely slept at all.

Liam was on his feet, pulling on his jeans. He had slammed one foot into a boot before Carrie realized what he meant to do.

She wrapped her arms around his leg. "Don't go out there!"

He looked down on her, his smile almost patronizing as he gently pulled her arms from his leg. "I'll be right back. I'm just going to go check it out."

"Fuck that!" Carrie scrambled out of her sleeping bag and threw on her shoes and jacket. "If you're going, I'm going." Not wanting to seem weak, she unzipped the flap and headed out into the rising sun.

The air outside was cold enough to frost her breath. She blew into her hands to warm them. A crowd was gathering around the remains of the campfire. A woman who looked to be about Carrie's age knelt beside it, the tattered remains of a sleeping bag crumpled at her knees. Blood covered the front of her jacket. Carrie didn't immediately recognize her; the woman kept keeling over and sobbing into the bag, hiding her face. When she came up for air, sucking in a gasp before bursting back into a snot-riddled wail, Carrie remembered her…

And nearly fainted. Liam caught her arm before she fell.

"Sh-sh-she had a boy." The memory of her own young son lying dead in his coffin flushed through Carrie like dirty water, polluting mind and soul. She covered her mouth with her hand and cried. "Said he was too old to be sharing a tent." She fell into her husband's arms. "He… he couldn't have been more than eleven."

Carrie stared up into Liam's eyes, searching for solace, but what she saw there made her recoil.

Nothing.

The man she had known and loved for the better half of her life seemed completely unfazed by the woman's sorrow. Had he hardened himself against grief and empathy, or did he just not care?

"Two others are missing," she heard someone say. Her eyes remained locked on her husband's.

"That older couple, the Farnsworths. Their tent's torn to shreds. Given the amount of blood, searching for them might be futile."

"We won't be searching for any of them."

The statement was made so calmly, so matter-of-factly, Carrie was momentarily stunned. When it had festered long enough to cause her blood to boil, fingers flexing in and out of fists, she slowly turned to face the speaker, his voice known to her and undeniable: their messiah.

She raised a finger, but before she could lash out at him, another launched his own complaint. An older gentleman with silver hair and a thousand-yard stare said through gritted teeth, "The hell we aren't." His right hand clamped over a dreadful wound on his left arm, just under a tattoo of a snake and the words, *Don't tread on me*.

Messiah didn't flinch. "It is exactly as I prophesized. The wolves have culled our herd, rooted out the nonbelievers." He nodded toward the man's wound. "It seems you've been given a second chance, Martin. Come, let's gather our things and walk the Lord's path together. We have many more miles to go."

Carrie stepped away from her husband, toward Martin. "Yesterday, you said we were close. Now we have many more miles?"

Messiah smirked. "The culling is not yet complete."

"A little boy is missing. Two other human beings too—good people who chose to follow you because you said you'd protect them. Promised them salvation. We can't just leave them out there. They may still be alive, and if so, they need our help!"

Messiah waved a hand dismissively. "Meh. They were nonbelievers. Blasphemers. Frauds playing at piety." He turned his back on Carrie and Martin. "They are exactly where they belong."

"That's some bullshit." Martin reached out and grabbed Messiah's arm. The crowd, all except Carrie and Martin, gasped. No one was permitted to touch their prophet. Like monsters kept away by the final flickers of candlelight in some old horror movie, they hovered close, at the ready, waiting for the dying of the light.

The contempt Carrie read in their upturned eyebrows and deep frowns caused her stomach to roil. Martin must have seen it too. His hand fell from its grip.

Messiah raised his arms, an easy smile warming his face, complementing the dazzling twinkle in his swirling mud-colored eyes. "At ease, my brothers and sisters." He stepped toward the older man and clasped his shoulders. "Martin here has lost his way. I do believe we can help him find it again."

"The only way I'm finding is the one that leads me out of here." Martin scanned the crowd. "People died last night." He threw out a finger toward Messiah. "And *he* wanted it to happen. We're all going to die if we stay here. I'm leaving. Who's with me?"

No one stepped forward. Carrie glanced from face to face, each now set with a sort of cold resignation. But the contempt was still there, directed at Martin.

Are they all insane? Carrie turned to her husband for help. He, too, stared at Martin, the corner of his mouth twitching the way it always did when he was angry,

"Liam?" she whined, her mouth hanging open in worry and disgust. "We should go too." She reached for his hand.

He pulled it away. "I'm not going anywhere."

She stared at him for as long as she could, looking for cracks in his steely armor. She couldn't figure out what hurt more: that in this, for the first time ever and despite everything they'd been through, he would not stand by her, or that she was experiencing this betrayal in front of a mob of strangers.

No, it was the former, and she thought throwing herself to the wolves might have hurt less. To top it all off, Martin was right. They were going to die out there, if not from wolves, then from exposure or starvation or any number of horrors she dared not think of. They would all die: her, Liam, Martin, Messiah, and all his followers unless someone had the courage to break free from the madness and find help.

"I'll go with you," she muttered to Martin. She turned back to her husband, filled with sorrow and hope, the emotions in her voice unmistakable. "Please?"

He grunted and crossed his arms, all the answer he would give. Didn't she deserve more? Didn't she deserve better?

She straightened her back and composed herself, no longer willing to die following a madman or watch her husband commit suicide along with the rest of the lemmings. If the stubborn mule wouldn't do it for himself, she would have to do it for him, even if it meant going it alone or with a man she hardly even knew.

Just for a little while. He'll see. By the time I get back with help, he'll have come around. And then we can go home… together.

Carrie reached for Liam again, but he refused to budge. "I'll be back with help." She pulled a small circular object from her pocket.

"I have a compass. We can find our way back with this. I've been sneaking glances at it during bathroom breaks and whenever else I can, so I know the direction we've been traveling down to the degree."

Martin smiled. "Clever. Let's go."

They started away, Carrie unwilling to give Liam a third glance for fear her resolve would melt beneath his gaze. Her heart hitched in her chest. Leaving him hurt only second to losing her son.

Carrie set her jaw. She and Martin would leave those fanatics, find their way back to a more civilized world, and never, ever put their faith in any religion or false prophet again.

"You'll never make it," Messiah said. "Your only hope for salvation is with me."

Martin stopped dead in his tracks. His face went redder than the gash on his arm. Turning on his heel, he stormed up to within inches of the savior.

"You're no messiah, Jericho." He sucked in his mucus and spat a green glob into his former prophet's face.

Messiah slowly wiped it off with his sleeve. "Have it your way." He snapped his fingers.

Martin's feet burst into flames.

He screamed as fire crept up his torso. His skin radiated an orange glow just before the fire spread over it, consuming all. It seemed to burn within him as well as without, igniting his breath as it climbed his throat. The heat intensified as the flame—and Martin with it—changed through reds, oranges, and yellows, to bright white, and finally to a brilliant blue.

The light was so bright it was blinding. Carrie clenched her eyes shut and shielded them with her sleeves. When she finally opened them again, the fire was gone. So was Martin. A small hill of fine gray ash smoldered where he'd stood.

All eyes turned toward Carrie. Messiah smiled and extended his hand. "May I see that?"

Carrie stood speechless, her mind struggling to comprehend what she'd just witnessed. Her mind slowly registered the weight of the compass in her hand. Without question, she passed it to Messiah.

"Thank you," Messiah said. The compass blinked out of existence. "I am all the guide you will need." He bowed and waved his arm outward. "Now, shall we continue our journey?"

"Yes, Messiah." Carrie stepped backward, her eyes never leaving her prophet's, her savior's, until she stood side by side again with her husband. Liam smiled warmly at her and held out his hand. She took it, and on trembling legs, she took her first step as a believer toward the promised land, where her messiah's will would surely be absolute.

DOWN IN THE DEEP, DARK PLACES

Sergeant Dinesh Patel worked the ropes binding his wrists against a jagged edge in the rocky floor. His M16 lay in a pile with the rest of his squad's arsenal, heaped up against the cave wall not more than twenty feet away, nothing between him and it except a single Taliban soldier.

He'd come to only a moment earlier and immediately recognized the world of shit he was in. He'd slammed his head against something hard during the ambush—the Humvee's ceiling or dashboard, most likely—when the IEDs exploded underneath his M1114. The last thing he remembered was the pink and purple corona over the mountains to the west as the sun set, cloaking the dusty road in twilight. Then, a deafening roar, screaming, and darkness.

As his blurry vision cleared and the pain in his forehead subsided, he found himself in a large, open cavern the size of an amphitheater. Where exactly in the vast mountain ranges of Afghanistan, he had no way of knowing. He guessed it wasn't far from his FOB in Kandahar, but without a trace of natural light finding its way into that deep, dark hell, he had no way of estimating time of day or how long he'd been out, which he might have used to guesstimate the distance he'd been taken.

That probably didn't matter, anyway. He could have been less than a mile from base, and he would have been just as fucked.

Somewhere in the dirt and rock far below my usual sandbox.

Dinesh didn't know if he should be thankful that his entire fire team remained alive and well, for the most part. Private First Class Talia Reynolds's pants leg looked as if a horde of fisher cats had used it as a scratching post. Blood pasted the tattered shreds of fabric to her leg. Her soft moaning was the only indication she still lived; her breaths were too shallow to be detected. Private Morris Branigan, just a kid and barely out of boot camp before being thrown into shit deeper than the devil's toilet, appeared to be unharmed, but his eyes had that all-too-familiar thousand-yard stare, his mind only fractionally in the here and now.

Only his driver and friend, Corporal Simon Fletcher, looked ready and able to fight, though his eye was swollen shut. And if there was anyone Dinesh wanted by his side in a fight, it was Madman Fletcher, who was fearless to the point of recklessness and always willing to draw the enemy's fire. Some said he had a death wish. But Dinesh knew he lived for the action and treated war as a way of life. Whenever they talked post-army plans, Dinesh usually did all the talking.

Seeing his corporal gave Dinesh an ounce of hope that life after service might still be a possibility. A little of the madman still shone from Fletcher's good eye. Awash in firelight, it projected a fire of its own as it glanced knowingly Dinesh's way. He gave a curt nod then looked away so as not to reveal Dinesh's intent to their captors.

Of their captors, Dinesh counted seven insurgents, but he couldn't be sure how many lingered beyond the range of the light. Each was armed with either some variant of a Kalashnikov assault rifle or a bolt-action rifle of the World War II variety. One soldier sat beside heavier weaponry—large-scale explosives and machine guns meant for mounting on vehicles. Dinesh couldn't figure why they were keeping such heavy artillery so far away from the front lines, where they could cause maximum damage.

Each insurgent wore the smug grin of an enemy who thought he'd already won.

Not so long as I live. Dinesh clenched his teeth and pressed the rope harder into the rock. He could feel strands of nylon tickling his wrists, so he knew he'd made progress. He would rather die with a bullet in his gut than force his wife and son back home in Somerville to watch some asshole cut his head off on YouTube.

The thought of his family only strengthened his resolve. With subtle but quick motions, he worked back and forth, back and forth. He would soon be free to kill or be killed. A Muslim whose family left India after the Partition and a Hindu mob's murder of his great-uncle, he offered a quick prayer up to Allah to pull off a daring escape or at least take a few of the extremists down with him. The hypocrisy of the appeal and the jihad his captors claimed to be fighting was not lost on him. True Islam promoted peace. Human ignorance and bigotry, often hidden under the guise of "politics," promoted war. Still, Dinesh would take any chance of having a god on his side.

With a roar, the entire cave trembled. A cloud of dust and dirt rose from the floor. Pebbles then larger rocks fell from the ceiling and clattered down the walls. The stalactites above cracked and shook like loose teeth.

Dinesh smiled and cheered on the USAF as they dropped their payloads from above. His celebration was short-lived, however—the blast had knocked him away from his cutting edge. His fingers groped to find it again.

Another blast came, seemingly right on top of them. One of the Taliban leapt to his feet, eyes wide with fear. He pointed at the ground and said something in Pashto that Dinesh couldn't understand. A fissure had formed in front of him, separating him and most of the other insurgents from their tied-up prisoners. It was a long crack but barely more than an inch thick, easily stepped over, but the Taliban soldier backpedaled away, mouth drawn open in horror.

The earth belched somewhere far below. The crack widened, becoming a monstrous yawning maw. Cracking rock snapped and splintered as easily as plywood under pressure. Dinesh scampered back from the crack like an inchworm on buttocks and bound heels, drawing closer to Reynolds.

"W-W-What is it?" the wounded soldier stuttered. "What's happening?"

"I don't know." Dinesh stared at the growing crack. "But I don't think it's good."

The cave continued to shudder as if it were as petrified as he was. When the first stalactite crashed down, a mere foot away from the burgeoning hole, the ground let go. More pillars plummeted to the floor, exploding against it in showers of rock and dust. Debris bit like shrapnel into Dinesh's face and exposed skin. He scooted farther away from the sinkhole when portions of floor dropped away as if some invisible man were chomping on a celery stick, while he and his squad were the insects clinging to its very end.

Ants on a log.

The campfire fell into nothingness. Next went their gear. Dinesh had just enough time to see a stalactite smash down upon a fleeing insurgent before he, too, fell into oblivion.

Dinesh fell next, and the drop seemed to last forever. He tumbled down a slope like the boulders around him. Finally, the ground flattened out, and he stopped.

Groaning, he took a quick inventory of himself. His hands had come free in the fall. Everything ached. His elbow had slammed into something and rang with pain, but neither it nor any of his other bones seemed broken. Pebbles clung to scraped skin. Blood pooled in his mouth, its taste metallic as he swallowed it. Still, his wounds appeared to be only superficial, not that he could do anything about internal bleeding if he were experiencing it. All in all, he counted himself lucky.

"Lucky, humph." He studied the pitch black. *No, not quite pitch...* Light, faint but nearby, gave Dinesh a sense of purpose. A direction. Hope. And the will to press on.

Sneering, Dinesh tore at the rope around his ankles. He might have gotten it off sooner had he been calm and collected, but the cold, damp air felt like mucus on his skin—simultaneously revolting and unraveling. A soldier through and through, he permitted himself anger before despair. The offensiveness of the atmosphere and the unfairness of his plight raised bile in his throat and ferocity in his heart. He would escape. He would find his way home.

His thrashing worked. Once free, Dinesh felt his way slowly toward the light. Serrated edges of rock jabbed into his fingertips, intermingled with the smooth, waxy surfaces of millennia-old calcium carbonate formations. Every few feet or so, he heard the tapping of not-so-tiny exoskeletal feet scurrying away like crabs over a craggy shore. Worse still were the moments when the unseen critters of that foreign ecosystem waited for his touch before squirming.

Someone sobbed off to his left, but Dinesh ignored him. His squad's only chance of survival lay with that light.

He sped up as he neared it, nearly tripping over Reynolds in the process. The capable ally had been rendered immobile, her arm buried under a boulder the size of a Smart car. Any hope of it not being ground into powder vanished when Dinesh spotted her severed hand lying on the other side.

"Sarge?" Reynolds said between coughs.

The woman—the *soldier*, his friend—was still lucid. Dinesh looked around for a means to free her, but he could see nothing in the few rays of light that reached them. "I'll be right back, soldier."

Despite Reynolds's pleas for him to stay, Dinesh swallowed hard and pressed on toward the light. As he neared it, metal glinted around a small flame. A brass canister about the size of a thermos lay in a shallow dip in the floor. He picked it up and examined it, listening as liquids sloshed in its upper of two compartments. A reflective chrome disk protruded from its side, the small flame at its center. Dinesh studied it for defects or leaks. Aside from a dent in the bottom compartment's side, the lantern had seemingly survived the collapse intact. But as it ran on fuel, its usefulness was limited by the amount of fuel it had left.

A scream broke the silence behind him, followed by rapidly spoken Pashto somewhere else in the cave. Dinesh grabbed the lamp and turned. The light shone directly on Reynolds's face, which was as white as the moon in the dead of winter. The soldier's eyes stared back, unblinking.

Dinesh took a step forward then paused. Reynolds's body jerked as if something were tugging on it, but the rock pinning her down offered little give. Dinesh reached for his sidearm before remembering it had been taken from him. He froze and listened.

Silence.

Wait. Some sort of wet squelching, like feet trudging through sucking mud, came from Reynolds's direction. Her spasms increased as the sound grew louder. Dinesh raised the light.

A shrill owlish squawk sent him staggering backward. At the last second, he found the wall, balancing himself before he could fall. But he'd seen something, only a flash. It was pale gray and smooth-skinned like a dolphin, like part of an animal. Something was alive down there in the dark. Something not human.

But built like one.

Dinesh shook his head. It couldn't have been human. Nothing human could survive down there in that vast emptiness. But the animal had vanished into the darkness, and it had dragged Reynolds's body away with it. Dinesh's heart raced. In spite of the cold, wet air, sweat trickled down the center of his back. He spun around, lamp held out in front of him in a steady hand that belied his thoughts.

Nothing. No sign of Reynolds. No sign of the thing that had taken her. Just a shoulder joint sticking out from beneath a massive rock.

Dinesh's mind raced, and his breathing quickened. He concentrated on slowing both. *Pull yourself together, soldier.* He stood up straight, oriented himself as best he could in that infernal night, and headed back to where he'd fallen, hoping he might find the weapon cache not far beyond.

Another scream came from off to his right. At least a hundred feet away, Dinesh thought, but the cavern's strange acoustics made it impossible to know for sure. The cry echoed off walls and whipped through the narrow spaces between ancient columns. The sound shook the cave, and Dinesh feared another collapse or avalanche was imminent.

Still, he swallowed his fear and pushed forward. He had to be strong, confident, and clever if he and his team had any hope of surviving or seeing their families again.

My family. Dinesh's brow furrowed. Reynolds would never see hers again.

Dinesh carried on past the hill he'd cannonballed down, stopping only briefly to see if it might be scalable. The slope's angle was severe, and he doubted he could make it without climbing equipment. If the others were injured, they stood no chance. Except maybe if they had no other choice.

If there was one thing the army had taught him, it was that desperate men could move mountains.

Assuming himself caved in, he would settle for the strength to move some very large boulders. If he were being honest with himself, he doubted there was any way out. But one thing was certain: he had to try to find one.

His light flickered in his hand as he twisted and bent, scanning the floor for a weapon, any weapon, as well as for his missing soldiers. When his toe kicked something metallic, sending it skittering across the cavern floor, his heart jumped. He ran after it.

Where he thought it had stopped, he got down on his hands and knees. "Where are you, you son of a—"

There! He set the lamp beside him, his fingers fondling the floor until they found the grip of a pistol, not his. Branigan's, if he had to guess. He searched the area and found an AR-15, which he slung over his shoulder, and several clips for it, which he jammed in his pockets. Most of what he found after that had been crushed or too badly damaged, but he picked up another assault rifle and almost cheered when he stumbled upon a flashlight, necessary backup should the lamp's fuel run out.

"Over here," a man said from somewhere not far off in the darkness. The words were in English, but Dinesh did not recognize the voice. It had been hushed and strained and could have belonged to anyone on his team if they'd been injured. Or, though he heard no accent, it could have belonged to a stranger. An enemy.

He cautiously took a step forward, pistol and lantern raised.

A shot rang out. Dinesh dropped the lantern and dove to his side. As he rolled onto his feet, he crouched, hand instinctively clutching his shoulder. Blood.

A shriek came from his left then another much closer. Several more rang off the walls, above, below, everywhere—too distinct in their pitch and gurgles to be echoes of the first. Another sound, human, perhaps a curse in a foreign tongue, came from only a few feet away. Then movement. Something scrabbling over the floor. Fast. Toward the light.

Shit! The lantern rested on its side but appeared to still be in one piece. Dinesh sprang toward it, baseball sliding on his stomach across a jagged, unforgiving floor. He came up short. As he looked up, he saw a pistol aimed at his face.

He rolled like a log as bullets ricocheted off the stone where he'd been only milliseconds prior, until he'd made it beyond the range of the lamplight.

As the lantern rose from the ground, black boots then loose white pants climbed to a camouflage jacket and a thickly bearded face and head capped with a *kufi*. The insurgent was smiling as he raised his gun and pointed it at Dinesh.

Dinesh closed his eyes when another shot rang out. He opened them when he realized he hadn't been hit. His shoulder ached, but it had merely been grazed, and that had been the result of the first discharge.

The lantern, built to withstand such mistreatment, once again lay on its side. The arm of its last possessor lay limp beside it.

Branigan? Fletcher? Dinesh started to his feet but froze when he saw another insurgent claim the lantern. His whole body trembled, his eyes wide with terror. Something down there had shaken him badly, made him need the light badly enough to shoot his comrade for it.

The man stood, swinging the lamp in a circle. He twisted a valve, and the light brightened, punching into crevices that had never seen it before, creating new shadows at the edges of the light's expanded circle.

Though the walls were close only at his front and back, Dinesh reeled from a sudden wave of nausea, the thought of his close confines smothering him under a heavy blanket of claustrophobia. The place felt like a crypt, the air stale and full of death. He fought down the panic that threatened to end him and crept backward, just out of the light's extended range. The Taliban soldier appeared not to know he was there or was too terrified of those other things moving in the dark to care about him.

Dinesh stood. He aimed. He fired. The shot pierced the man's thigh just right of his femoral artery. The shot had been meant to wound not kill, and it had done as expected. The insurgent fell, dropping his gun as his hand clashed with rock.

Dinesh ran over to the man and pinned him to the ground with his knees. He wanted the man alive, not only to question him but to force him to guide them out… or, at the least, to use him as bait. But before he could even ask his first question, the man cried out in terror.

"*Edimmu!*" The Taliban soldier's chest pulsated under Dinesh's weight. He appeared to be hyperventilating as he jerked and bucked like a bronco. His eyes gawked at something above Dinesh.

Sensing danger, Dinesh dropped to his belly atop the Taliban soldier, but he was too late. His back burned as if a flaming rake had dug trenches across it. As he rolled onto it and looked up, inadvertently knocking the light away so that it no longer reached his or the insurgent's feet, he saw nothing but darkness.

Blood, no doubt his own, dripped in a pitter-patter down onto his chest. He shot at the source. The animal above howled. Its talon-like nails clacked across the ceiling.

"Fuck!" Dinesh shouted. "What are you?"

The Taliban soldier beside him shrieked and clawed at Dinesh's pants as another creature pulled him out of the light. The insurgent caught his boot, and Dinesh began to slide. He stomped the Taliban soldier's face to get him off. The Afghani disappeared into the sounds of screams and tearing flesh.

Whatever those things were, they were feeding on the soldiers. The remaining insurgents had become the secondary concern.

Find my men. Find my way out. The plan sounded so simple. Dinesh grabbed the lantern and stood, then he scanned the ceiling. Finding it clear, he allowed himself a breath. One of the rifles lay at his feet, its strap cleaved through. A few threads held together the other's strap. Dinesh stuck the pistol down the front of his pants and carried the broken-strapped AR-15. Four scratches, each about an inch apart, ran in rows across its stock.

With the only light source resonating from his hand, Dinesh knew he made an easy target. He saw no sense in playing things quiet. "Fletcher? Branigan? If you hear me, stay where you are. There's something down here with us… something predatory… but it seems to fear the light."

He held up the lantern. "For the rest of you out there, if you can understand my words, lay down your weapons and come into the light when I give the signal. You have my word, you will not be harmed."

The silence was deafening. If his men were somewhere around him listening, so were those things. He raised the AR-15 to his shoulder. "When I say go, stay low and move fast. If they live down here, they probably hunt by sound or smell, and if it's the latter, you're probably already dead. So move as quickly and quietly as possible, and I'll provide cover. Now… Go!"

The sound of pebbles skipping over the stone floor came from three directions. An Afghan spilled into the light, a Russian machine gun in his hand pointing at the ceiling. Dinesh aimed at the man, shouting for him to drop the weapon, even as another man slid into the light at his left. Dinesh caught the familiar pattern of US Army fatigues in his peripheral vision and kept his rifle trained on the insurgent.

The hand and boot toe of a third man made it to the light's outer perimeter, but he was yanked backward before Dinesh could make out who it had been. He vanished in a whirlwind of thrashing and screams.

"What are you waiting for, Sergeant?" The voice clearly belonged to Corporal Fletcher. "Take him down."

"No-no-no." The Taliban soldier dropped to his knees and placed his machine gun on the floor. "I surrender. I surrender."

Fletcher circled Dinesh and picked up the weapon. He aimed it at the Afghani's forehead.

"Stand down, soldier," Dinesh ordered.

"Come on, Sarge." Fletcher maintained his position. "You promised not to harm him. You never said *I* wouldn't. Besides, you know he'll stab us in the back the first chance he gets."

"That may be, but do you know what those things are? 'Cause I sure as hell don't. Maybe this asshole can shed some light on the subject. Maybe he can show us a way out."

Fletcher lowered his weapon. His injured eye was swollen shut and looked even worse than it had before the collapse. Dried blood flaked between folded flesh. He grunted. "I hope you know what you're doing."

Dinesh chuckled uneasily. "I'd be lying if I said I wasn't winging it."

Fletcher laughed. He grabbed the Taliban soldier and stood him up. "Turn around." When the Afghani complied, Fletcher patted him down. He pulled a boot knife from a sheath around the man's left calf.

He flipped it in his hand. "See? Stab you right in the back. Speaking of which…" He circled Dinesh. "Something got you good. Let me—"

"I'm fine." Dinesh pulled away. "We'll worry about it if... *when* we get out of here."

Fletcher nodded. "How sure are you those things won't enter the light?"

Dinesh shrugged. "We're still standing."

A frothy-white liquid spattered Fletcher's shoulder and the ground around his feet. The Taliban soldier ducked, burying his head under his arms. The American soldiers followed suit.

"What are they?" Fletcher asked.

"Don't know. I haven't gotten a good look. You?"

"I can hear them scurrying about on all fours, climbing over rock, the walls even. And smell them too. God, they stink—like some of the guys do when we don't find their bodies right away, and something else... unwashed, unclean." Fletcher poked the Taliban soldier with the Kalashnikov's barrel. "Hey, you." He circled a finger in the air. "What are they?"

"*Edimmu,*" the insurgent muttered, the word whispered through cracked and quivering lips. He stared blankly at the ground as if the mere thought of those creatures was a burden he needed to escape.

"Eddy-moo?" Fletcher raised an eyebrow. "The fuck is that?"

The Taliban soldier curled his index fingers over his top lip, their tips pointing downward to resemble fangs. "*Edimmu. Ekimmu...* Demons? Devils?"

"Bullshit." Fletcher spat. "Do you think he means some animal like—I don't know—the Tasmanian devil? Some nasty critter they just happen to call devil?"

"No," Dinesh said quietly. Though he didn't believe in monsters, the vibe he was getting from their new Taliban pal was enough to make his skin crawl. The word was somehow familiar, but he couldn't put a finger on where he'd heard it before. "I don't think that's what he means."

"Aw, hell." Fletcher slapped his sides. "So what's the plan? Find Reynolds and Branigan and get the hell out of here?"

"Reynolds is gone." Dinesh raised the lantern and stood. "If Branigan's still alive out there, we have to find him." He turned to the Taliban soldier. "Do you know a way out of here?"

The Afghani pointed to their right. "If there is a way, it would be that way." He threw a thumb over his shoulder. "That way, deeper into the mountains."

"Okay," Dinesh said. "You lead. We'll be right behind you."

The man nodded and stepped forward.

Fletcher leaned in. "You sure we can trust this asshole?"

"No, but what choice do we have?" Dinesh fell in behind the Afghani. He pointed to the urine staining the soldier's pants. "Besides, he wants out of here just as badly as we do."

"All right." Fletcher stepped in close behind Dinesh. "Hand me that spare AR-15. I don't trust this Commie crap." He looped the Kalashnikov over his shoulder and peeled the rifle gently off Dinesh's back.

"Take the flashlight too." Dinesh stepped easier without the weight in his back pocket.

In a single-file line close enough to do the conga, the three men walked blindly into the dark, a circle with a diameter of roughly fourteen feet their only protection against an unknown enemy.

After about a hundred feet, they reached a wall that spanned out as far as they could see in both directions. The Taliban soldier indicated left, and Dinesh followed.

They'd gone barely a few steps when they came upon Branigan. He was ashen white and unconscious, splayed out against a tilted slab of smooth stone. Something about it reminded Dinesh of a sacrificial altar.

"He's wounded." Fletcher stepped forward to help his brother-in-arms, but Dinesh held him back.

"Something isn't right about this." Dinesh examined the scene. Branigan's pants had been all but torn off. A chunk of flesh and muscle had been removed from the side of his thigh. Crescent-shaped incisions marred the rest of his leg. Row upon row of deep punctures resembled something between shark bites and what humans might leave if all their teeth were filed into fangs.

Branigan's eyes burst open. His fingers groped for Dinesh's sleeve. "H-H-Help… me…" He collapsed against the slab, whatever last bit of life he had been clinging to all but spent. A rivulet of blood ran out of the corner of his mouth.

"We've got you," Fletcher said, stepping forward.

"Wait," Dinesh ordered.

The ground cracked and gave way beneath Fletcher's weight. The stone in front of Branigan was as thin as a plate of glass. He turned and reached for the ledge as he fell.

Dinesh dropped his lantern and rifle and dove onto his stomach, swinging his hand forward and catching Fletcher by the wrist. His grip slipped when his hand smacked against the side of the pit, but he recaught Fletcher in a firm handshake.

Then Fletcher's weight seemed to double. "Something's on my back!"

Dinesh drew his pistol and shimmied closer to the trap. Peeking over Fletcher's shoulder, Dinesh saw nothing in the dark.

A hand swiped at his face, and he flinched backward, just out of reach. Still, he held onto his friend. "Climb, goddamn it!" Dinesh grunted as he prepared to fire over Fletcher's shoulder, but an arm as thin and reedy as a bamboo shoot hit him in the wrist with more force than its sinewy, skeletal frame should have been capable of.

The pistol flew from Dinesh's hand and spiraled off into the cavern. His grip was slipping, so he used both hands to pull Fletcher upward. The veins in his biceps bulged as he attempted to curl the soldier's weight and that of the thing on his back. A power surged through him, adrenalinelike, hot, and full of vitality. Alert, alive, and suddenly full of rage, he felt the sensation's raw fuel give him the strength he needed to make progress.

"Next time," he seethed through gritted teeth, "follow orders, soldier."

But there wouldn't be a next time, not for him or for Fletcher, if he couldn't end that creature latched to his soldier's back. Hands preoccupied, Dinesh could think of no way to kill it without dropping Fletcher, which wasn't an option. Adjusting to the weak light, his eyes made out the creature's toothy grin, a mouth so full of needlelike teeth and so unnaturally wide, it could only belong to a predator. But the smooth, pale-gray face, tiny upturned nose, and large oval albino eyes looked too human not to be so... or to once have been.

The creature reared back, its jaw unhinging as it opened its mouth impossibly wide. The human parts Dinesh saw then were the bits of meat stuck between the gangly abomination's teeth. He couldn't raise Fletcher or let him fall even he wanted to—Fletcher's grip was too tight around his own. All he could do was die bravely, in a way that would make his wife and daughter proud. He hoped that when their times came, they would join him wherever he was heading. Moments with them and their smiling, beautiful faces played like a rapid-fire slideshow behind his eyelids as he sealed them shut and a bear-trap mouth snapped toward his face.

Purple spots burned through the images. The darkness took on a pinkish hue then became bright yellow as he opened his eyes and the onslaught of light seared his retinas. The creature squealed. A barrage of bullets unloaded into its face silenced it. Its limp body fell from Fletcher's back. Two full seconds later, it hit bottom with a sickening crack.

Head ringing from the gunfire so close to his ear, Dinesh lifted Fletcher halfway out of the hole before he realized what had happened. Once certain Fletcher had his footing, he stood slowly, arms raised, and turned.

The Taliban soldier pointed Dinesh's AR-15 at him. He clutched the lamp tightly in his other hand and motioned with it to his right. "*Imshi*. Tunnel. This way."

Dinesh nodded but made no sudden movements. "What about our friend?"

The Afghani's brow furrowed. "Him?" He glanced toward Branigan and grunted. "Too late for him." He raised the gun and shot Branigan in the head. "He not come back."

Fletcher raised a fist. "You son of a—"

Dinesh blocked the corporal's path. He pointed at Branigan's body, which was slouching forward, peeling away from the rock. As he fell forward into the pit, the soldier's back came into view. The meat had been stripped away, revealing Branigan's shoulder bones and part of his spinal column.

"He was already dead," Dinesh whispered.

"This way," the Taliban soldier urged. "We must hurry."

Fletcher growled. "If you think I'll follow some towelhead into—"

"He hasn't asked for our weapons or fired at us. My guess is he thinks he'll need us to get out of here, and I'm guessing we may just need him too." Dinesh shrugged. "Besides, he's got the lamp." He reached for the AR-15. "Now give me that. You get to use the Commie crap as punishment for not obeying your commanding officer."

Fletcher smirked and handed over the rifle. "Yes, sir."

As they fell into line behind their circumstantial ally, Dinesh wondered what would happen if all three of them made it out alive. They walked a hundred feet in silence then another hundred. The air got warmer, the walls closing in on them. After about ten minutes of walking, the tunnel narrowed to only eight feet wide, the ceiling only eleven or twelve feet high.

"He's leading us into a dead end," Fletcher whispered.

Dinesh said nothing. Everything was awash in the lantern's light, everything defensible, except whatever lay beyond the lamp's range in front of them and behind. The lantern flickered.

The Taliban soldier fiddled with a valve, and the lamp burned brightly again albeit with a shortened range. "Carbide lamp," he muttered. "Needs car—"

He let out a long, slow breath. A flash of metal and blood spewed from his mouth. A rusty hook protruded from the back of his neck. Before Dinesh could react, the Taliban soldier vanished through a hole in the ceiling. The lantern went up halfway with him before falling from his grip. It landed with a loud crack and flickered like a dying strobe light. Both Dinesh and Fletcher aimed and fired at the hole, the flash from each shot adding to the strobe-light effect. But they soon stopped, realizing they were wasting precious ammo.

The lantern flickered then went out. For a second, all Dinesh could hear was his and Fletcher's heavy breaths. The air seemed to freeze around them, the quiet as fragile as thin glass.

Then the shrill owl-like screeches of one of those monsters shattered it. The noise sounded like a battle cry.

"Run," Dinesh whispered. "I'll lay cover. Go!"

Dinesh backpedaled as fast as he could, praying for a flat surface behind him. He opened fire down the tunnel, bullets sparking off the ceiling, walls, and floor, ricocheting unpredictably. In the flashes, he saw them coming, saw them hit and still coming: humanoid creatures with clacking clawed fingers and toes. The hairless, skeletal frames charged like big cats on all fours or skittered like monstrous roaches across the walls. Their teeth dripped with saliva and the remnants of their last meal.

At Dinesh's back, Fletcher cleared the way forward with bullets and the flashlight's beam, which he methodically waved behind him, suppressing the charge and giving Dinesh some breathing room. Dinesh had no idea where they were heading or if they should stop and make their final stand. A way out seemed unlikely, but he wasn't ready to concede defeat. The air was warmer. They did seem to be making their way along an incline. Maybe they would make it out. Maybe, if they could just find dayli—

Dinesh tripped. His elbow smacked against the ground. Pain jolted up his arm like an electric shock, but he held onto the AR-15. He blew away the first creature as it tried to leap upon him, smattering teeth and brain all over the ceiling.

The second's body seemed to absorb the rifle fire. It fell on top of him, oozing black coagulated blood from a half dozen bullet holes. Dinesh kept its biting jaw away by jamming the rifle into its neck.

Damn, but did he feel strong and the creature so light! He held it back with ease. Sitting up, he pulled the gun away and caught the creature around its neck. Seeing those teeth, he remembered the word the Taliban soldier had called it and where he'd read it: one of those monsters of the Old World, of myths and legends—like sea dragons and cyclops, ghouls and werewolves, and… *vampires?*

Or something more akin to a vampire. Not real. Or at least they hadn't been real an hour ago.

Whatever the damn thing was, its scrawny neck cracked easily within his grip. Its head collapsed sideways, suddenly too heavy for its weakened support beam. Smiling, enjoying the thing's suffering, Dinesh grabbed it by the arm and whipped it onto the floor.

A flashlight's beam scattered the approaching horde. "I've got you, Sarge," Fletcher called as he dragged him by his collar through a narrow opening into a circular antechamber with a roof so high that he couldn't see it.

But he could see something. Either his night vision had improved, or light was trickling in from somewhere high above, refracted through a tunnel or several of them. He felt as if he were below a lake's surface, stuck in that hazy gray area where only a few of the sun's persevering rays dared to venture before dying.

"It's a feeding chamber," Fletcher said. "We can't stay here."

As Dinesh got to his feet, he first noticed the dead creatures around the corporal's. Fletcher constantly spiraled the light around the room and up the walls. When the corporal rotated around one segment, Dinesh saw not only the dead bodies of Reynolds, Branigan, and several insurgents, but also heaps of the creatures themselves, adults and young, all chewed down to the bone. Several pregnant females, looking like sticks with stomachs distended as if grotesquely malnourished, lined the pit, their heads blown off.

"They're cannibals…" Dinesh covered his mouth. The thought of the creatures breeding for a food supply caused his stomach to roil. Still, he snatched Reynolds's dog tags from around her neck. He couldn't find Branigan's tags on what remained of the corpse.

Pebbles trickled down the cave walls.

"Sarge?" Fletcher grabbed his shoulder. "We need to move."

Dinesh gnashed his teeth. He suppressed the urge to crush Fletcher's fingers. He'd always been even tempered, kept his cool in the most harrowing situations wartime had to offer. But something about Fletcher's touch sent waves of anger and hostility surging through his muscles. Fueling them.

"Where?" he snapped, pointing at the narrow entranceway. "We can't go back that way. There's gotta be a swarm of them on the other side of that opening."

"I don't see any other way out of here unless you want to start climbing."

Dinesh sighed. "I guess this is it, then?" He slapped in a fresh clip. "It's been an honor, Madman."

"The honor was all mine, Sarge." Corporal Fletcher turned, planted his feet, and brought the sight up to eye level. The time to fight and die like warriors had come. Back-to-back, the soldiers opened fire.

Creatures scurried down the wall in droves. For each one that fell, two more took its place. Headshots seemed the only certain way to make sure they stayed down, not a difficult task for two expert marksmen in close proximity to their targets, growing closer and closer by the second.

Naked albino bodies tore at each other to be first through the room's entrance, only to fall to Dinesh's torrent. Their dead clogged the pathway in.

Behind him, the corporal's barrage of gunfire trickled down to a one-bullet-at-a-time approach, as he was no doubt trying to conserve the last of his ammo. Each time the AR-15 fired alone, Dinesh's breath hitched. The question of whether the rifle's Russian cousin had gone the way of the musket repeated endlessly in Dinesh's mind. And if Fletcher had already fallen, how much longer did that leave Dinesh, ammo or no ammo, with no one watching his back? He considered saving a bullet for himself.

Maybe he picked up more ammo, and I just didn't see it. Maybe—

"Sarge!" Fletcher shouted over the blasts. "I think I've found a way out!"

"Lead on. I'm right behind you."

Fletcher grabbed the back of Dinesh's fatigues and pulled him toward the far wall. Dinesh laid down some suppression fire, the faces of a hungry horde snapshotting in muzzle flashes barely his barrel's length away.

He backed into the cavern wall. Fletcher had gone, leaving him there to die. After everything they had been through—

Dinesh jumped as a hand grabbed his shoulder and yanked him into a narrow crevice barely wide enough to fit a man and as dark as an unlit closet. Instinctually, Dinesh fired straight up the wall above the opening he'd squeezed into. A creature fell dead at his feet. As he continued to back away, he could hear others of its kind feeding on it.

Dinesh couldn't walk backward without his shoulders slapping into the walls. His head scraped along the ceiling. The creatures would have had an easier time maneuvering in there with their wiry, lanky limbs, but even they couldn't fit more than two at a time. Still, the chances of a ricochet hitting him or Fletcher increased infinitely in those close quarters.

"There's a light up ahead... It's the outside!" Fletcher groaned. "But it looks really tight." He passed back the flashlight. "Here. I'm going for it. They won't be attacking from this way."

Dinesh chanced a glance over his shoulder. Fletcher was pushing himself up onto a ledge no more than a foot and a half across. It led into a twenty-foot shaft that got narrower and narrower the closer it got to the outside and a small square of light. It reminded Dinesh of a gun port on a pirate ship.

He turned away from it and shone the flashlight back the way he'd come. A creature cried out, leapt onto the ceiling, and scuttled away. He had no doubt another was ready to take its place as soon as he took the beam away. He resolved not to do that.

The light at his back vanished. "I'm close," he heard Fletcher's muffled voice say, "but I think I'm stuck."

"I'm coming in." Dinesh hesitated, looking for a place to rest the flashlight so that it covered his back. He settled for the ledge as he hopped up onto it. The flashlight rolled back and forth on its side then came to rest, perched precariously on the jagged surface.

Satisfied his backside was covered, Dinesh scrambled up to Fletcher's feet. "I'm going to push. You ready?"

Fletcher mumbled something that Dinesh took as a yes. He grabbed Fletcher's boots by their soles and pushed. Nothing happened.

He planted his toes against crags jutting up from the floor, trying to brace himself, but all his strength needed to come from his shoulders and arms. He roared and pushed again, military pressing the corporal forward.

Fletcher screamed. Dinesh slipped. He slid backward, his foot kicking something loose. It skittered off the ledge and onto the cave floor.

The flashlight! Dinesh looked and saw the way forward clear. He shuffled forward on knees and forearms as fast as he could toward the light. "Almost there, almost there," he chanted, his movements increasingly difficult in the cramping space.

Fletcher's face appeared in the hole. His hand reached out for Dinesh.

"Almost there. Almost—" Dinesh hollered in agony. His ankle flared with pain. He kicked at whatever had it, panic sending him into spasmic jerks, always forward. His hand found Fletcher's. His face felt the first rays of a morning sun. He spilled out onto an Afghan mountainside. Instead of warming him, the rising sun chilled him to the bone. He fought against an instinct to climb back into the hole.

He stood, and Fletcher embraced him. "We did it, Sarge!" He let Dinesh go, his smile wide. "We..." He looked down at Dinesh's ankle.

Dinesh followed his gaze to the cavity where his Achilles tendon used to be.

"How are you even standing?" Fletcher asked. He crouched. "Here. Let me get that wrapped—"

"I'm fine." Dinesh glared at his fellow soldier. In fact, he *was* fine. The pain was already dulling. He just needed to get out of the sun before it rose too high. That and a warm meal would heal everything—he was sure of it.

He looked at the blood crusting around Fletcher's eye. Could he smell it? Yes, he was sure he could. Coppery, mixed with sweat, it smelled divine.

"Lead the way," he said, smiling, his incisor stabbing into his lower lip. "Don't worry. I'll be right behind you."

A BOY AND HIS DOG

(and Zombies)

Benny growled.

Jack hugged him tightly. "Easy, boy," he whispered. "Easy."

The German shepherd stretched out his front paws and snarled at the door. Benny was good like that. He always knew when *they* were outside, the sick who shuffled down the hallway, looking for a way out.

Looking for food.

Jack was only seven, but he was no dummy. He knew that when Benny growled, he and Daddy had to be quiet. *It's Dad*, Jack scolded himself. *You're not a baby anymore.*

Slowly, quietly, his father crawled toward the door and rested his back against it. His eyes met Jack's, and he placed a finger over his lips.

"No," Jack mouthed, but all that came out was a soft whine. He reached for his father, a towering, muscular man who gave the best hugs and smiles despite werewolf-hairy arms and tombstone teeth, wanting to grab his hand and pull him away from that door and the sick people roaming behind it.

They're my neighbors. Mrs. Sampson, the Baker twins... Gabriel. Jack cried, the thought of his best friend having turned into one of those monsters, those... *Zombies*. His father didn't like when he called them that. "Technically," his dad had said, "they're not zombies because they're not dead. They're just sick." The sickness began when some dumb people had eaten snails that had lots of really small bugs eating them. Why anyone would want to eat snails, Jack couldn't figure out, but Dad said that when people ate the sick snails, the tiny bugs crawled out and started living in the snail eaters. The bugs ate their brains and their bodies, making them crazy and gross-looking. Eventually, they died, like Jack's grandpa had died, though that was because he'd been like nine hundred years old.

Dad had told Jack that when all the sick people finally died, things would go back to the way they were. Jack never wanted to get old or die. And since those bugs lived all over the sick people's bodies, even in their mouths, he couldn't let them bite him.

For two weeks, Jack had been trapped in his second-floor apartment, separated from his mother, all because some stupid people ate something they weren't supposed to eat. His cheeks flushed as he remembered all those cookies he'd taken when Mom said he couldn't.

But that was different. The sick people, or the first sick people anyway, had eaten something that turned them into mean, hungry monsters. It was hard for Jack to think of them as anything but zombies. They looked like zombies, acted like zombies, and even *smelled* like zombies, or at least what Jack thought zombies smelled like: used diapers and rusty pipes.

They are *zombies. Zombies eat people.* He shook his head and clenched his teeth. *So what? Grow up. Be strong, like Daddy.*

Dad.

Jack wiped his eyes with his sleeve. His father smiled, but his eyes were wide open and his hands were shaking. "It's okay to be afraid," his father had told him. "It's how you handle your fear that matters."

Jack wasn't afraid. His hands curled into fists. *No way. I'm strong.*

His father nodded at the window. Jack backed away from Benny and crawled to it. The fire escape was clear. They kept the ladder up, since even stupid zombies were smart enough to climb. When people started getting sick, his father had made them an escape route by laying a mattress in the narrow alley below the fire escape for them to jump down on. Jack had hoped he would never have to.

The morning was quiet. Litter and puddles spotted the pavement below, but the alley was otherwise empty. For a moment, Jack allowed himself to believe that he, his father, and Benny could leave that place, go get Mommy—*Mom*—and find a new place to live.

A thud came at the door—probably just some stupid zombie bumping into it. Benny barked.

The banging at the door came again, then faster and louder. Jack pulled his shirt up over his nose, the dirty-diaper smell growing stronger. He could hear gurgling and wondered if the zombies had blood in their throats then whether if it was their own blood. He wondered if Gabriel was out there, too, trying to get in, wanting to eat him.

Back firmly against the door, Jack's father slid up to his feet. "They won't stop coming now. They know we're here. We have to leave."

The door rattled. Jack heard a crack.

"Go!" his dad shouted, then softer, smiling, he said, "Be strong."

Jack threw one leg over the window sill then the other. He looked back at his dad, who had his arms out to his sides, balancing himself as if his weight alone could hold back the bulging door and the frenzied crowd behind it.

"Go!"

Jack checked the alley but saw no one. Behind him came a loud bang. His dad screamed. Benny barked and growled.

Holding his breath, Jack jumped off the fire escape. He fell flat onto his butt and back just like Dad had taught him.

Above, Benny whimpered as he slid onto the landing. Trembling, the dog took a few steps toward the edge.

"Come on, boy," Jack whispered as he tapped his thigh.

Benny backed away, stepped up to the edge again, backed away again. The window filled with hands, then arms, then faces, none of them healthy or belonging to Jack's father. A fat man in a gray suit fell face first onto the landing.

Benny turned and barked. As the sick man rose to his feet, his gnarled fingers reached for the dog. Benny turned, pattered to the ledge, and jumped. He landed with a howl and fell onto his side.

"Benny!" Jack ran onto the mattress, threw his arms around the dog, and helped him stand. Benny held up his front-right paw like he did when Jack asked him for it.

"Can you walk?" Crouching, Jack stared into the dog's chocolate-colored eyes. He examined the four-year-old shepherd, who was almost as tall as he was. Last time they'd taken him for a checkup, the doctor said he weighed eighty pounds, which had to be more than that big pumpkin Jack had picked up last Halloween and got in trouble for dropping even though it was only an accident. That thing had been super heavy, and Benny was like five times as big.

"I... I don't think I can carry you." He looked at the injured paw, but he didn't see any blood or bones sticking out like some of the zombies had.

As Benny limped off the mattress, a flash of color whizzed by his tail, just missing him. A zombie, the old woman from the apartment down the hall from Jack's, was lying face down on the mattress. As she started to get up, the man in the gray suit landed on top of her.

Jack gawked as two more fell, the zombies pig-piling on top of one another. Benny licked his hand, and Jack snapped out of his daze. "We have to go, Benny." He fought back the tears as he waited a few more seconds for his dad to appear in the window. *But where do we go?*

The zombies were dragging themselves from the pile. Jack could wait no longer. He ran down the alley with Benny at his side. With every step, the shepherd put more weight on his paw. Soon, his limp was barely noticeable. Jack thought his dog was going to be okay.

"Am *I* going to be okay?" He stopped at the end of the alley and peeked out at Third Street. He saw his old bus stop, where Mrs. Crawford had picked him and Gabriel up for school about that time every weekday, back when things were normal. Everything had changed so much in just two weeks. Jack's mom had been at work when the sick people overran the city. He hadn't seen her since. Now, he'd lost his dad, too.

"It's your fault," he hissed, grabbing Benny by the scruff and squeezing. "Why'd you have to bark?"

Benny whimpered, and Jack let go. He sniffled and wiped his nose on his sleeve. "I'm sorry, buddy."

Jack looked back at the ten or twelve zombies that had fallen from the fire escape. He wasn't too scared of them. They were the slow ones—

outside, he and Benny could easily outrun them. Those who had just turned were different. They moved fast and were always hungry. Still, if he just stood there, the zombies would get him eventually.

He turned in a half circle. All directions ahead seemed clear. But it was impossible to tell what hid behind the next corner or the one after that, and no buildings were safe, their skinny hallways clogged with the sick.

"Where should we go, boy? Do you think—"

He gasped. The answer was so simple. "We're going to find Mom!"

Benny tilted his head up at Jack then stuck out his tongue and panted. Jack started down the road, heading the way he saw his mom go to work, his dog padding alongside him.

A woman screamed somewhere in the distance. A car alarm blared much closer, drowning out the footsteps of whomever had set it off. Still, he saw no one.

"We need to find someplace to hide. We're not safe out here." He couldn't help but wonder if they would be safe anywhere.

Benny looked up. Jack thought he saw agreement in his eyes.

"It'll be okay, boy. I'll protect you."

He picked up his pace. Soon, he was sprinting with only a vague destination in mind. Benny matched his speed, the injury to his paw seemingly forgotten.

Jack ran by one zombie, who he easily avoided, then another. After that, he passed them more regularly. In the park to his left, a group of them fed on what looked like a brown carpet covered with lasagna. They paid him no attention as he passed, their mouths gorging. A hoofed leg jutted out of the gathering, and Jack guessed it belonged to one of the police horses he saw in the park back when all they had to worry about were crackheads and purse snatchers. Dad wouldn't let Jack play in the park alone, not even before the world got sick. He wondered what Dad would have thought of him out alone now.

Dad...

He forced himself not to cry, not until he and Benny were safe. That's what a brave boy would do, what Dad would want him to do. He would make his dad proud.

As he reached the end of the park, where the big buildings gave way to smaller ones and old, worn houses with rusty gates lined the side streets. They used to be homes, but their owners had either evacuated the city or now prowled its streets.

He remembered seeing all the buses on TV, back when TV still worked. He had hoped to see his mother getting on one of them but never had. His father hadn't been able to get him out. The sickness spread too fast. When they first learned of it, one of the infected was already roaming their hallway, attacking anyone who stepped into it. His father had locked and barred the door then called the police, but no one came. When the electricity went out and the phones stopped working, the hallway filled with sick people.

We should've put the mattress out sooner. Maybe then, we would have made it to Mom.

Jack hadn't heard from his mother since... "Mom!" he shouted, remembering his plan. "We have to find her!"

All the times he'd been late for school and Dad had to drive him, they'd drop Mom off at work first. She worked at a bank, though he wasn't sure what she did, except that she was some kind of writer. He knew what the building looked like—reddish-brown brick with those white cloth things hanging over the windows, sort of like eyebrows. He just needed to figure out where exactly—

A shrill cry came from the park, and he turned to see a runner heading straight toward him. He'd already closed half the distance between them. Benny started to growl. Jack turned to run.

He sprinted as fast as he could, his arms swinging like that scary pirate ship he was finally tall enough to ride at the carnival. He couldn't hear Benny next to him or the zombie behind him but was too terrified to turn around and look. The runner would catch him. He was definitely faster than Jack.

I need to hide.

A metal fence as high as Jack's chest enclosed the house at his left. He had jumped fences like that before, like when he and Gabriel would go swimming in the public pool after it had closed for the day. He grabbed the top of it, pushed himself up, and swung his leg over it so fast he lost his balance and crashed down on the other side.

Unhurt, Jack sprang to his feet and raced to the front door, praying someone was inside. He pounded his fist against the wood.

No one answered. His dog barked. "Oh, no! Benny!"

The dog was on the other side of the fence, snapping and snarling at the sick man and dodging his attacks. Jack ran to the gate, unlatched it, and pulled it open.

"Benny, come on!"

The zombie straightened and made a noise like soda when Jack blew bubbles into it. He turned Jack's way and grinned—or at least Jack thought he was grinning. His teeth gnashed, exposed between thin lips drawn back.

Benny bounded into the yard. Jack slammed the gate shut behind him and latched it, but the runner was quick. He grabbed Jack by the arm.

"No!"

In a flash of fangs and fur, Benny's teeth clamped around the zombie's wrist. The dog whipped his head violently from side to side, and between that and Jack's squirming, the zombie lost his grip, tearing Jack's shirt.

Jack ran to the side of the house. A small window sat at ground level, leading into a basement. He kicked it in then slid his sneaker along each edge to break off any remaining shards. Feet first, he shimmied inside.

Benny appeared in the window frame, trying to squirm through. He howled in agony, a sound Jack had never heard from his pet, and he knew the zombie was attacking him.

"Benny!" Jack ran to help just as Benny kicked himself inside. The dog fell on top of Jack, knocking him to the ground. He hit his head hard enough to cry out, but when he felt the bump that had formed, it wasn't even bleeding.

But Benny was.

The black fur on his lower back was slick and matted. A small patch of hair was missing. He looked sad and afraid, or maybe that was just because Jack was. The runner was crawling in through the broken window. He fell head first onto the cement floor.

Dizzy, with darkness creeping in at the sides of his vision, Jack fell, too.

§

When Jack woke, he was lying in a big bed, twice the size of his own but without his superhero sheets. This was a grown-up bed. It smelled clean and was soft and warm.

Benny was curled up beside him, snoring. The dog's loud snore usually made him laugh. Occasionally, it annoyed him when he was trying to sleep, but right then, its steady beat slowed his own.

Do dogs turn into zombies? Jack didn't think so. At least, he hadn't seen a zombie dog running around the city. Cats were just mean. He didn't think he'd be able to recognize a zombie cat.

He wondered if the zombie had gotten them, if he was dead and in heaven and his body was lying around back on Earth, finally done trying to bite normal people. His fingers combed through Benny's fur. Gabriel had told him dogs didn't go to heaven. He said they didn't have souls. Jack didn't believe him. Mom used to play an old cartoon that proved all dogs went there, even the mean ones.

Gabriel will know the truth soon. Jack hoped Gabriel would make it into heaven so that he could see his friend again. God just *had* to let Gabriel in.

Being dead won't be so bad. Maybe I can see Daddy again and… maybe Mommy too. It's not so bad to call him "Daddy" every once in a while, is it?

As he petted his dog, his fingers ran over a stiff cloth. His dog's wound had been wrapped, the fur around it soft and clean. Someone had washed Benny and taken care of him.

But all Jack could think about was his parents. He started to cry and rested his head on Benny's side. The dog jolted awake but lay back down without complaint.

Jack sobbed. "We wouldn't of had to leave… Daddy wouldn't be dead, if you didn't bark. You stupid dog. Stupid, stupid dog."

Even as he said the words, he didn't really blame Benny. He knew his friend was just trying to protect them. He stroked the dog's side, being careful not to brush up against the fresh bandages. "I know it wasn't your fault." He sniffled. "It was an accident."

His head rose and fell with Benny's long, slow breaths. Soon, the dog was snoring again. "I love you, Benny," Jack whispered as his eyes drifted shut.

§

"Wake up, sleepyhead. You gonna hog my bed all week?"

Jack woke with a start. He sat up and scrambled away from a man wearing a plaid shirt and olive slacks held up with brown suspenders. With wrinkles rolling like waves down his forehead and dark spots that looked like birthmarks easily visible under thin wisps of white hair, he looked old enough to be Jack's grandpa's grandpa. Benny lifted his head, sniffed, then went back to sleep.

"Are you a zombie? Are you going to eat me?" Jack knew zombies didn't talk, but the questions came out before he could think.

"Whoa, easy there, feller. I ain't no zombie, and I sure as heck ain't gonna eat ya." The old man raised his hands and backed away a step. He sat down at the end of the bed. "The name's Ted Witherspoon, but you can call me Gramps. Most kids your age call me that, anyway. Least they used to." He looked away.

"Am I dead? That zombie... he got in through the window. He bit my dog and—"

"It's okay, it's okay. I took care of that rascal. And you ain't dead, but you sleep like it. You've been out for over a day! That dog of yours too. Won't leave your side."

"My dog..." Jack's chin fell. "That zombie, he bit my dog and... I don't know if dogs turn into zombies like people do. Do you know, Mister..."

"It's Gramps. Just Gramps. Don't need no 'Mister' in front of it." He patted Jack's hand. "I think your dog's gonna be just fine, young man. Ain't no diseases I know of that are communicable between humans and dogs."

"Commun-sickle?"

"It means sicknesses that humans get, dogs can't get them."

"So Benny's going to be okay?"

Gramps smiled. "Suppose so. And he's a brave one, that dog of yours. Let me clean out that bite and wash him and wrap him up real nice. He's probably hurting some, but you know what? I think he's gonna be good as new in a day or two."

Jack took in the room. A bureau sat along one wall and a dresser having a big mirror and one of those weird snowflake cloths on top of it rested against another, but the space was otherwise empty. It smelled like furniture polish. "Where are we?"

"My bedroom. What's the last thing you 'member before waking up?" He slapped the blanket. "Never you mind that. Do you remember breaking a basement window?"

"Yeah."

"Well that's my window, what's left of it, anyway. Not much of a window now, what with the board I hammered over it. I haven't boarded up all the windows, but I keep the shades drawn. Don't want them sick fellers seeing me and thinking I'm breakfast. Speaking of which, you hungry?"

Jack's eyes widened, and his stomach grumbled. He frowned. "Mom says I'm not supposed to take food from strangers."

"Your mom sounds like a smart woman. Is she... around?"

"I think she's at work. My daddy... he died. I'm going to see Mommy now."

"I'm real sorry to hear about your dad, kid." Gramps stared silently at the blanket a moment then stood. "Well, why don't we have some breakfast, and we'll talk some more. I've told you my name, fixed up your dog, and you've slept safely in my house for more than a day. I think we're no longer strangers, but if you'll be needing a more formal introduction"—he stuck out his hand—"put her there."

Jack studied the man's hand. It had really boney knuckles and lots of veins, and Jack didn't want to touch him. But he grabbed Gramps's hand and gave it a firm shake just like Daddy had taught him.

"Whoa, kid, that's some grip." Gramps laughed. He waved his hand in the air as if Jack had crushed it.

Jack laughed, too. "You're funny. And you talk funny."

"Well, where I'm from, you're the one who talks funny."

"Where's that?"

"Oh, way south of here. Seeing that this is the End of Days and all, I came up here to try and reconcile with my daughter, see my grandkids one last time, but... I was too late."

"They're dead?"

"Yes... er, no. I mean, I think so. What I mean to say is, uh, I haven't seen them."

"Don't give up hope. That's what my daddy says. He says Mommy's still out there. We can't give up hope, 'cause that would be like giving up on Mommy." He sat up straight and stuck out his chest. "I'm never giving up on Mommy."

"You know what? Sounds like your dad is just as smart as your mom. Must be, to have raised such a smart whippersnapper like yourself."

Jack straightened. "I am smart. I know how to multiply."

"Oh yeah? I'm not even sure I remember how to do that, but I can heat up a can of SpaghettiOs over a fire, if that'll do ya. If not, I got some beans, some soup—"

"SpaghettiOs!" Jack smiled.

"You got it." Gramps stood. "When you're ready, come on down the hall, and we'll have ourselves some breakfast. I 'spect you're gonna need to use the bathroom. It's the first door on your left."

"Gramps?" Jack called before the old man could leave.

"Yes?"

"I'm Jack." He pointed to his dog. "He's Benny... in case you were wondering."

"I was. Just figured you'd tell me when you were ready. Nice to meet you, Jack. You too, Benny." He winked and left the room.

As soon as he was gone, Jack sprang out of bed. His curiosity got the better of him, and even though he knew it was wrong, he snooped around the room, opening drawers and the closet door, scanning the things Gramps kept on the dresser and bureau. He found nothing of much interest, so he stepped out into the hall.

There, the walls were lined with pictures. In most of them, a mom posed with her two kids, both boys a little older than Jack. At least he thought she was the boys' mom. *Why would she take pictures with someone else's kids?* The pictures were all the same: the mom with her two kids smiling at the park or the soccer field or the beach or whatever. She seemed like she'd been a good mom, doing all those things with her kids. Jack loved it when his parents took him places like that. The zoo was his favorite.

He didn't see any animals, though. He didn't see the boys' dad or

Gramps in any of the pictures, either. A fingerprint smudged the glass over one photo, much too big to have been made by someone Jack's size.

He wondered if Gramps had gone to any of those places. *Maybe he took them all.* He frowned. *Probably not if he was in, like, Florida. That's way south.*

"Be sure to wash your hands!" Gramps called.

Figuring he had stuck his nose far enough into where it didn't belong, Jack found the bathroom, used the toilet, washed his hands, and made his way into the kitchen. A hot bowl of SpaghettiOs awaited him at the table.

He rubbed his hands together and pulled out the chair at the spot set for him. "Mmmm. They're my favorite!"

Gramps snorted. "I'm glad. Can't stand the things myself."

Jack shoveled canned noodles and sauce into his mouth, saving the tiny meatballs for last. His stomach grumbled the whole time, and he bet he could eat a fish tank full of the stuff. He'd eaten SpaghettiOs lots of times before, but for some reason, they tasted better than ever that day, he guessed because of the way Gramps had cooked them or how badly his stomach had wanted them. Halfway through the bowl, he realized Gramps wasn't eating. The old man just sat at the other end of the table, reading a book that was four times as thick as anything Jack had read.

"How come you're not having any?"

"Hmm?" Gramps looked up from his book, his glasses perched at the end of his nose like Santa's in a Christmas card Jack had gotten last year. "Oh, I ate a bit while you were sleeping. We've got plenty of food, but that won't always be so. Figured I'd better start rationing it, try and make it last as long as I can."

Jack looked down at his bowl. It had been filled with SpaghettiOs. Gramps must have given him the whole can. He pushed it toward the man who'd saved him from that mean zombie. "Here. Let's save the rest... or you have it."

Gramps put his book down. "Hogwash. I didn't mean it like that. Eat up."

But Jack couldn't take another bite. Taking Gramps's food, knowing that he'd just be leaving soon, made the fork heavy in his hand. "Thanks for breakfast, Mister—"

"Gramps."

"Thanks for breakfast, Gramps. If you're not gonna eat it, can Benny have it?" He didn't feel right about giving Gramps's food to his dog either, but Benny needed to eat.

"I don't see why not, if he can stomach them."

"Gramps?"

"Yessir."

"Is that your family in those pictures on the wall?"

Gramps smiled. "Sure is. My daughter and her two boys, Adam and Michael. Wonderful kids."

"How come you're not in any of them?"

Gramps folded his hands behind his head. His eyebrows curled toward his nose, and his forehead crinkled. "Well, you see... life's about making mistakes... oh heck, son." He slapped his thighs. "Don't spend your life regretting what you should have done. Go out and do it before it's too late."

Jack had no idea what Gramps was talking about and didn't know how to respond. "Thank you," he said after a long, awkward silence. He rose from the table, pushed in his chair, and carried the bowl into the bedroom. He could feel Gramps watching him as he left.

Benny's head lifted as Jack entered the bedroom. His nostrils fluttered as he sniffed the air. With his ears perked up, he drooled as Jack set the bowl in front of him on the hardwood floor. The dog slid off the bed and began to eat. A moment later, he licked the bowl clean.

"We have to leave here," Jack said as he scratched Benny behind his ear. "Gramps seems real nice, but we have to find Mom."

Benny licked the sauce from the sides of Jack's mouth.

"Gross!" Jack laughed. He wiped his face on his sleeve.

"I can't let you go out there, son." Gramps stood in the doorway.

Jack jumped then pouted. "I have to find my mom."

"It's too dangerous to go out there."

Jack balled up his hands. "I gotta go! If I don't go, that's giving up on Mommy!"

Footsteps sounded above. Jack looked up at the ceiling. "Someone's up there? Someone alive?"

Benny bowed his head and growled.

Gramps lowered his gaze. "Someone's up there, but no one alive."

"How do you know? They might need our help!" Jack started out of the room.

"I know." Gramps stepped in front of Jack. "I've... been up there."

Jack's shoulders drooped. He understood and sighed. "Are we the only ones left?"

"I don't know, kid. Seems that way sometimes." Gramps stared into space. His eyes shimmered. "World's a cruel place."

"Are we safe down here with them up there?"

"Huh? Oh yeah, kid. We're safe. Them dummies don't know how to open doors. Even if they hear us, they won't know how to get to us. Just walking around up there, bumping into furniture."

"Did you know them?"

"Oh yeah, I knew them. I knew them very well. Good people, all three of them. Better than I ever was."

Gramps stared off into space again. After a moment, he cleared his throat. "Anyhow, you see why I can't just be letting you mosey on out of here, don't you? Them dummies are all over the place out there, and not just them slow ones. Don't know if it was fate or chance that brought you here, but as God is my witness, I'll let no harm come to you, not while I'm still breathing."

"Then... will you take me to find my mom?"

"I think I ain't much for traveling. I can get around the house here just fine, but walking long distances is hard on this old man's joints." He crossed his arms. "And running? Humph! I'd run myself into an early grave. I ain't no use to you out there, kid. Best we stay here, anyhow. Wait for help to come to us."

"No. I have to find my mother." Jack's lip quivered. He didn't want to cry. Babies cried, and he wasn't a baby anymore.

Gramps threw up his hands. "All right, all right. I'll make a deal with you. I'll take you to see your mother in one week—"

"A week!"

"Listen. You've seen them, right? They're fastest when they first turn, but the longer they're, uh, *sick*, the slower they get. It's like the disease is eating away at their muscles and bones, or they're just rot..." Gramps paused. He ruffled Jack's hair and smiled.

Jack hated when adults did that. He pulled away.

"What I mean to say is... I figure that the longer we wait, the safer we'll be. Eventually, they'll all be like snails."

Jack scratched his chin. "What if they make new ones?"

"Kid, I really don't think there are many new ones left to make. I mean, you were out there. Did you see anyone else? The army?"

"No." Jack stared at the ground. "Just them."

"Okay, so one week, assuming you know where we're going."

Jack nodded. "One week."

§

Jack spent the rest of the day helping around the house. He did chores willingly, bringing out the garbage and guarding Benny while the dog ran and dug up Gramps's fenced-in yard when he was supposed to be pooping. Jack wondered if the dog even remembered how close he'd come to being zombie food.

Benny didn't bark or growl, so maybe he did remember. Jack walked outside on tiptoes and opened and closed the door as silently as he could. A city full of people had just up and vanished. It was so quiet, he thought he could scream at the top of his lungs—and a big part of him wanted to—and no one would hear him, except maybe Gramps and his dad up in heaven. He missed Daddy so much.

Gramps watched him each time from the doorway, holding a gun like those Jack had seen in the cop shows his mom liked, but why Gramps had named it "Smith Weston," Jack didn't understand.

Inside, Jack couldn't find much to do. Gramps didn't have a working TV or any video games, so Jack let the old man read to him. He liked the sound of Gramps voice and the funny way he talked, but he didn't understand much of the book Gramps was reading: something by George Steinbrenner, who Jack—being a huge baseball fan like his dad—knew had once owned the second-best team in baseball, the New York Yankees.

He yawned and tried to listen, tried his hardest. Why a baseball guy had written a book about angry grapes didn't make any sense. And the book was so boring, Jack couldn't keep his eyes open.

When he woke back up in the chair, Gramps was gone.

The front door was open. It led out into a stairwell where another front door separated them from those who would eat them. The stairs led up to the second floor.

Jack crept toward the open door. Through it, darkness spilled into the kitchen. A stair creaked.

Jack gasped then held his breath. Footsteps. They grew louder. He slowly backed away from the doorway.

Gramps emerged from the darkness, holding Smith Weston. He was frowning, and his eyes were puffy. Jack thought he might have been crying. He'd never seen a grown man cry before.

Gramps sniffled then smiled. "Hey there, kid! Sorry if I woke you."

Jack could tell Gramps's smile wasn't real, that he was just pretending like Jack did when Gabriel got a new toy that he wanted. He would give up all his toys for another chance to play with Gabriel or any of his friends from school, even the girls.

Gramps closed and locked the door behind him. "Just… taking care of a few things, is all."

Jack heard footsteps above. "Did it work?"

"Did what work?"

"The things… taken care of?"

Gramps's legs shook. He stumbled toward the kitchen table and fell into a chair. His face was white. Sweat dripped from his forehead. "I… I couldn't. I'll try again tomorrow." He propped his elbows on the table and rested his face in his hands. His body began to shake.

Jack didn't know what to do, so he called Benny and headed into his bedroom. He jumped up onto the bed, his dog following and curling up against his leg. Benny was so warm, but Jack liked feeling him close.

He missed his parents. "I wonder what they're doing right now." He stroked Benny behind the ear. "Do you think they miss me like I miss them?" His eyes filled with tears. "Do you think they even remember me?"

His tears fell. Benny sat up and started licking them off his face, which made Jack laugh.

"At least we're still together." He hugged Benny tightly. "Don't ever leave me, okay?"

§

Bang!

Jack sat up, gasping for air. He'd fallen asleep again. Benny lay next to him. The room was dark. The dog sat back on his haunches, his ears standing up.

Was I dreaming? Jack patted his shirt, still wearing his day clothes. The bed remained made under him.

"What was that noise?"

When the loud blast came a second time, Jack nearly fell out of bed. The noise came from above. It sounded like a gunshot.

He slid down and crept to the bedroom door. Benny walked beside him, whimpering and watching the door.

Jack yanked it open. Moonlight shone in from a window in the kitchen. With his hand resting on Benny's back and his heart thudding in his chest, he walked toward the light.

The door to the stairwell was open. More pale light poured in through the glass panes on the outer door.

A scream echoed down the staircase, and Jack froze. A voice, *Gramps's* voice, said through sobs, "I'm sorry, Adam."

A third gunshot, and Jack instinctively covered his ears. Benny barked. Jack tried to shush him, but the dog wouldn't be shushed.

"I'm sorry... so, so sorry." Gramps said again. A fourth gunshot, followed by a loud thud and something like the sound his baseballs made when Jack dropped them on his apartment building's stairs, seemed to shake the building. Or maybe Jack's body was shaking. Those sounds got louder until the something spun by him, cracked against the wall, and clanged to a stop at his feet.

Jack crouched to see what it was. "Smith Weston..." He picked up the gun.

"Gramps?" He called up the stairs. "Gramps?"

Gramps didn't answered. Jack started up the first step. "Ow!" Benny's teeth had sunk into the cuff of his jeans and tugged. "Hey! No biting!"

Jack gulped. He looked at his dog but saw no sign that Benny had changed into a zombie.

Benny whimpered and scratched at the front door. A thud came against the back door, then another. The noise had brought guests. The dog scratched more feverishly.

"Gramps?" Jack called one more time, too afraid to climb the steps and see what had happened after Benny had warned him against it. The dog pawed at the welcome mat, trying to dig under the front door. A gurgling noise came from upstairs.

Jack unlocked the door and threw it open. He and Benny fled into the night.

§

Jack had no idea where he was when he finally stopped running. The sick were everywhere. He had easily outrun them at first, but his body had run out of fuel. He looked back. They were still coming after him, though he'd left them in his dust.

"I," he said between wheezes. "Just need a minute… to catch my breath."

Benny looked up at him. The dog wasn't even panting. In fact, he looked like he was smiling, like instead of running for their lives, they'd just been playing. Benny loved to play.

They were out in the open, at night, with no place to go. Not only that, Jack was lost. "Gramps's house was over there." He pointed over a herd of zombies ambling toward him. "Or was it over there?"

He took deep breaths. His eyes teared. "Be strong. Be strong." He stroked his companion. "Any ideas, buddy?"

Benny growled even before Jack heard the footsteps, sneakers thumping on pavement, coming his way fast. He hadn't had time to catch his breath or rid himself of the stitch in his side. His legs and arms felt heavy, his right arm weighed down by—

"Smith Weston!" In his panic, he'd forgotten the gun.

The runner grew closer. He was a big one, probably a grown-up, but from that distance, he looked like a shadow. With shaky arms, Jack raised the gun.

"Jack!" the runner shouted.

Jack gripped the gun tighter. *He knows my name. How does a zombie know my name?* He shrank away in fear until a thought exploded in his head. "Dad?"

The runner was almost upon him. "Oh my God! Jack!"

Jack started to cry and laugh, and he didn't know why. The gun fell from his hands moments before his father's arms embraced him.

"Oh my God! Jack! You're alive!" His father peppered his head with kisses. "Are you hurt? Are you bitten?"

"I'm okay."

"I thought I'd lost you!" Jack's father was crying and laughing too.

"I guess dads do cry."

"What?" His father pulled back and grabbed him by the shoulders as if he were afraid to let go. "I have been looking everywhere for you since you left. When I saw a kid your height run by with a dog at his side, I allowed myself to hope and followed as fast as I could. I didn't know for sure it was you, but I had to try. When you rounded that corner a few blocks back, I thought I'd lost you all over again." He pulled Jack into another hug. "Damn, son, you're fast!"

Jack pinched himself to check if he was dreaming. The pain made him smile big. But it didn't make sense. He saw the zombies coming out of their apartment window. His dad never had. "How did you get out?"

"The zombies broke the door down on top of me." He laughed. "They trampled right over me, and I couldn't get up. And a good thing too! They couldn't see me under the door. So I stayed there until I could find an opening and came out looking for you."

Benny snarled. A zombie staggered nearer.

"But we can talk later, when we're someplace safe."

Jack nodded. He picked up the gun.

"Holy… moly," his father blurted. "Where'd you get that? On second thought, never mind. You'd better let me have it." He took the gun in one hand and Jack's hand in his other.

"Come on. I've found Mommy. She's at the compound. That's the first place I looked for you. She's safe, and she misses you dearly."

The compound! Jack had forgotten all about it. The place where they were bringing all the normal people who couldn't get out of the city. His chin flattened against his chest. He felt dumb then, with another thought, worse than dumb. "She didn't want to come look for me?"

His father crouched down and looked him in the eyes. "No, son. She wanted to more than anything, but where she is, it's safe. They wouldn't let her out and risk bringing the sickness into camp."

"Are we going to see her now?"

"Yes. She's going to be so happy to see you. I know I am." His dad ruffled his hair, and that time, Jack didn't mind it so much.

He frowned. "Benny got bit. He's not a zombie, though."

"Is that right?" His father reached for Benny, but the dog backed away. "Well, I'm glad you two were looking out for each other."

"He didn't mean to bark, Daddy. Back home, he didn't mean to."

"I know, son."

They hurried in silence, zombies shambling everywhere around them, none of them fast enough to keep up. They'd all been sick too long and were close to giving up.

Jack hadn't given up. Not on Mommy. And he was on his way to see her.

His dad's hand felt cold and wet, like the outside of a soda can. Jack looked at it then up the arm above it. His dad's sleeve was caked in dried blood.

"Dad?" He let go of his father's hand. "Are you okay?"

His dad was sweating. His face looked so white under the moon, the same color as his teeth as he smiled down at Jack. "I'm fine, son. Just worked up a sweat running after you."

"But there's blood—"

"It's not mine."

Before Jack could ask another question, a runner came at them fast from behind the corner of a building, only a few yards in front of them. Jack froze. He closed his eyes, threw his arms over his head, and screamed.

A gunshot thundered close by. He peeked out from the cover of his arms and saw the zombie lying in the street at his feet.

"Time to go," his father said. "We need to hurry. The shot will bring more of them."

So would Jack's scream. He was glad his father left that part out. Together, they raced down the street, turning where his father said to, drawing more and more unwanted attention with every step. Runners filed in behind them. Some were gaining fast.

"This way," his dad shouted. "It's not much farther."

Following his father's gaze, Jack saw where they were heading. Four tall buildings sat across an open square that had been the bus terminal before the buses had all left. In front of the buildings, a huge fence stood, topped with barbed wire and lined with watchtowers. People with guns manned the towers and the spotlights on their roofs. Jack assumed they were soldiers, given all the big army trucks and Humvees parked along the fence.

Their guns were pointed at him and his dad.

"Don't shoot! Don't shoot!" his dad yelled. "He's not sick!"

The *rat-tat-tat* of machine gunfire filled the air, and Jack skidded to a halt.

"Don't stop." His dad grabbed his wrist. "They're not shooting at—oomph!"

His father toppled over, he and another man rolling across the pavement like clowns in a circus act. No, his dad and a zombie. He started over to help when another zombie—a young girl—charged at him. He put up his hands to defend himself.

Benny took the girl down before she could reach him.

"Run to the gate!" his father shouted. He was on top of the zombie that had tackled him, pointing the gun at its head.

Jack heard the shot as he ran to where soldiers were filing out of an opening in the fence. Some kneeled and aimed their guns. Others spread out. He covered his ears as shots fired from everywhere.

At last, he made it to the gate. Benny padded up beside him, looking unharmed. His father was coming too. They were all right. They were all going to be all right.

The soldiers aimed their rifles at his father. "That's far enough," one of them said.

"What?" Jack ran over to the soldiers who aimed their guns at his dad. Another soldier grabbed him by the shoulder, but he twisted free. "That's my daddy. He's not sick. He's not one of them."

His father raised his hands and stopped twelve feet away from the row of armed men. "It's okay, son." Then, to the nearest soldier, he said, "Can I at least say goodbye to him?"

The soldier nodded. He lowered his weapon. Jack ran to his dad.

His father crouched to hug him. "I have to go, Jack. I'm sick."

"No," Jack whined. "You can't be. You said it wasn't your blood."

"I am, Jack. I'm sick. I was bitten. It happened when I forced my way out of our apartment. I don't have much time, so—"

"No!" Jack was sobbing, and he didn't care who thought he was a baby. He knew what it meant to be bitten. He knew his father was going to get sick and become one of the runners. And that wasn't fair.

His father pulled away. "Go inside now, Jack. Your mother is inside, and she misses you deeply."

"I don't wanna go inside! I want to stay with you!"

"I know, and… I love you, Jack. Take care of your mother. Be strong." He nodded at someone behind Jack. Before he could fight it, Jack felt himself being pulled away. He stared at his father, his eyes full of tears, until the soldiers dragged him behind the gate and slammed it shut.

Another pair of arms encircled him, and he struggled to be free.

"Jack?" a soft voice called. He turned into the arms and saw the face of his mother. "Hush," she whispered. "You're safe now, Jack. I've missed you so much. Oh, God, how I've missed you."

He collapsed into his mother's arms, too weak to fight her. They both cried. Benny licked the tears from his cheeks. It didn't make him laugh like it usually did. He wanted his father and his mother, for things to be like they were before the stupid world got sick.

"Be strong," his dad had told him. And he had been. He had never given up on Mommy and had found her at last.

He wiped the tears from his eyes and stood up straight then looked out past the gates. *I will be strong. And I'll never give up on Daddy either.*

JUST LUCKY, I GUESS

Kevin Rego scoffed as he read the tabloid's cover. "Bull sharks swim up river, swarm vacationers." He snickered, imagining a flock—*a herd? A gaggle?*—of fins swimming upriver and circling a helpless, wholesome American family. The visual was horrible but ludicrous, since sharks didn't generally swim that far upstream into fresh water.

He scanned the gossip magazines featured at his favorite sidewalk kiosk a block away from his inner-city, cubbyhole apartment. Celebrities were having affairs, divorces, or babies, or having affairs resulting in divorces or babies, but Kevin dismissed those headlines. He preferred his soap operas with more action and danger. An article claiming Bigfoot sightings briefly piqued his interest, but his thoughts returned to that undoubtedly fictional family featured on the *Winston Cable*'s cover that had allegedly survived a likewise fictional swarming of sharks.

Do sharks swarm?

Kevin read on, his voice amplifying with his skepticism. "Sources say the Violets escaped their perilous encounter thanks to some quick thinking and a few roast beef sandwiches." He shook his head. *Why would they eat their sandwiches in the river?* He rolled the tabloid into a thin tube, obscuring his guilty pleasure from any busybodies his reading aloud might have attracted. Warmth filling his cheeks, long brown hair flopping over his downcast eyes, Kevin approached the cashier.

The clerk, a sunglasses-wearing baby boomer with nose hair that sprouted into an oily mustache, grunted as he seized the tabloid, unrolled it, and scanned its barcode. "Beautiful day, huh?"

"The sun is shining, and the birds are singing." Kevin closed his eyes, basked in the ultraviolet rays, and sucked in the fresh air... then began coughing. The city's usual wet-dog and foot-fungus scents were only two of a plethora of foul odors that invaded his nostrils, and he hadn't even made it to the subway yet, where his odds of breathing in anything pleasant would plummet.

Fortunately, he'd started early enough on a Saturday morning that the city's usual music—the stray-cat sex yodel, mixed with a duet to domestic violence, followed by the motorist-curse-and-honk festival—had yet to begin. He couldn't remember the last time he'd actually heard birds singing.

He smiled awkwardly. "Well, the pigeons are shitting, anyway."

The clerk put out his hand. "Two-o-six."

As Kevin sifted through some change, the ground began to rumble. A soft vibration coursed through his body, not all that unpleasant until his mind registered its cause. Coins shimmied and fell from his hand. Kevin didn't dare move.

After a moment, the tremor ended. With the nonchalance of a nudist disrobing, the clerk eased his glasses up the bridge of his nose. "There goes another one." He snorted. "Bet it didn't even register."

Somehow ten degrees colder inside his leather jacket, Kevin released his breath. "Let's hope it stays that way."

"It's all the drilling. We've poked so many holes in the planet's infrastructure that its support beams look like Crocs."

Kevin squinted. "Doesn't it have something to do with plates or tectonic... whatevers?"

The clerk frowned. "Which sounds more plausible to you?"

Kevin shrugged and paid the man. He would leave the reasons behind the recent uptick in seismic activity to those wiser than himself. Instead, he focused on his reason for waking up so early: all the many splendid things he would eat at the food truck festival in Galahad Park, just a quick subway ride and short walk across the Palisades Bridge.

As he left the kiosk, three teenage boys brushed past him, their braying laughter reminding him of all the trouble he caused at their age. Memories swirling, he chuckled, but the target of the boys' mischief squelched his mirth. An old, cloudy-eyed bag lady, struggling to push a crippled shopping cart over the sidewalk, seemed oblivious to their approach.

Kevin grimaced at the sight of her. Her skin was the color and texture of worn leather, full of fault lines chronicling a hard life. A tattered shawl hung from her shoulders over a sweat-yellowed nightgown. Her big toe jutted from one of her mismatched loafers. Together with her cut-off gloves and the plastic-bag cap tied around her chin, her clothing offered little protection against the dying year.

Still, she was plenty dressed for the autumn heat wave. But neither her clothes nor the smorgasbord of trinkets in her cart—a wooden clock, a doll missing an eye, all sorts of plants Kevin didn't recognize, and what looked like a necklace of bones glued together like macaroni art—shielded the street denizen from the wickedness of pubescent boys.

Sure, Kevin had been a troublemaker, but he hadn't bullied those less fortunate than him. It was... *unsporting?* His breaths seethed through his teeth. A low grumbling emanated from the back of his throat.

The teenagers—Moe, Larry, and Curly, he decided—fell on the woman, dancing, prodding, and playing keep-away with what likely amounted to all of her worldly possessions. She fought back, but her feeble swipes had no effect. When Curly, the biggest of the three teens, kicked over the cart, the woman shrieked and scrambled to collect her things.

Kevin snapped. "Hey, assholes!" He charged at the boys, booting Moe in the ass so hard the kid popped into the air. Curly threw up his arms as Kevin pummeled him with the rolled-up journal. Larry, mouth agape, shrank away from the action.

"What the hell, mister?" the first boy shouted, palms pressed against his buttocks as if he were trying to hold in his poop.

A between-jobs stunt double for several B-movie action stars, Kevin had the muscle and the endurance to take on ten stooges but could seriously hurt them if he didn't check himself. He snarled and raised a fist. All three boys took off running.

He crouched beside the woman, righted the cart, and scooped up the spilt items, wishing he'd worn gloves. Oil oozed onto his fingers from a braid of hair speckled with gravel, and he wondered why she would keep such a thing. The half-eaten sandwiches he placed in the carriage's basket looked like cultures for penicillin.

Once everything was back where Kevin supposed it belonged, he stepped closer to examine the woman for injuries. He recoiled, a sour-milk-and-soiled-undergarment potpourri sending him reeling like a punch to the nose. Lice hopped through her patchy gray hair, those beneath the plastic bag bouncing against it like microwave popcorn. Other critters weaved in and out of the fabric of her shawl.

Swallowing his revulsion, Kevin forced a smile. "Are you okay, ma'am?"

The old woman looked past him, around him, and everywhere but at him, her expression as blank as starless night. Kevin was considering whether she might be blind or senile when she lunged at him with speed unbefitting one who looked as though she might dissipate like a dandelion in a slight breeze. She latched onto his jacket then fumbled down his sleeve. Finding his hand, she clasped it in hers.

"Jonah!" Her toothless maw of rotting gums curled into a smile.

"Uh... it's Kevin, ma'am."

She leaned closer. "Jonah! You saved me from those brutes!"

"I'm sorry, but I'm not—"

"If I had just a bit more of the old juju in me, I'd have turned those snot-nose brats inside out!" She cackled long and hard, punctuated by a rippling fart.

Kevin's eyelids fluttered. The sulfuric air turned his stomach. He pulled away, but the woman only squeezed his hand tighter.

She sighed. "Oh, how I long for the old days, Jonah. The old country, too. The caravan, the families, the magic... but I suppose we were lucky to get away when we did. Always someone after us, out to hurt us..." She lowered her voice. "You don't think those boys knew, do you? Sent by Wallachia?"

Kevin's smile wavered. The woman was beyond his help. A pang of guilt shot through his chest as he yanked his hand free. "Well, if you're okay—"

"You look so good, Jonah." She stroked his arm then massaged his shoulder. "So young, so full of life! The old power... you've found it again, haven't you? How'd you manage it? Huh?" She tugged Kevin's sleeve. "Tell me. I must know."

Starting to sweat, Kevin again pulled away, but the woman clamped her hand around his wrist. "Tell me!"

Her fingernails dug into his skin, and he dropped the journal. He pried off her grip. "I... am not... Jonah."

As Kevin pushed her away, the bag lady buried her face in her hands. Her sobs, however, were short-lived, replaced by a guttural moan that crescendoed into a roar. "You always had it all, Jonah! You were always the lucky one. Even when Rory cursed you with wasting, you recovered." She glared at him with pupilless eyes, white canvases with tendrils of red branching in every direction. "Always so lucky!"

Spittle flew from the corners of her mouth. She shook with rage. Her eyes grayed then darkened into black whirlpools that exploded with light like galaxies surging into life.

Kevin raised his hands in defense. He wanted to run, but the woman's gaze was like a tractor beam pulling him into endless space. Sweat beaded on his forehead. His skin prickled.

"I'm not powerless yet, Jonah!" the old woman raved. "I'll show you what it is to be lucky. I'll show you luck like you've never seen her before!" She sneered and began muttering words in a language Kevin didn't recognize. Clouds passed in front of the sun. The air sizzled with electricity, standing up the hair on his neck.

As the bag lady chanted, her hair grew longer, and her skin cracked. Like a comic-book villain revealing her dastardly plans, she cackled madly, convulsing as if in the throes of a powerful orgasm.

When she finished muttering, her skin was the color of bone. Her eyes were clear. "Luck be your lady, Jonah," she whispered, her body shriveled like a juice box drained of liquid and air. "But she demands... sacrifice."

Free of her hypnotic gaze, Kevin backpedaled. The bag lady didn't move. Her ragged breaths gave way to wheezing then silence. She collapsed onto the pavement.

Kevin hurried to her and shook her gently. "Are you okay?" When she didn't reply, he rolled her over. Her eyes were billowing clouds. Her nose trickled blood, and her jaw hung slack.

He placed his watch's glass surface over her mouth, hoping it would fog up like he'd seen happen in the movies. But looking back at the watch, all he could see was the time. Shoulders tensing, he stood and looked around to see who was watching.

The clerk at the sidewalk kiosk cleared his throat and hid behind a newspaper. Kevin tiptoed away, forgetting his tabloid in his desire to be anywhere but there. Part of him knew he should call emergency services, but the woman's craziness and sudden death had him shaken out of his wits. By the time he came to his senses, he'd wandered several blocks away. He couldn't help her then. The weight on his shoulders was real enough to hunch them.

Like someone or something sat on the back of his neck.

But his paranoia relented as he continued his trek. Stress leaked from his muscles as his adrenaline rush dissipated. Soon, he was half himself again, and his lizard brain had kept him on course to the festival.

A woman had died, though. At least he thought she had. He considered turning around, heading home to relax and put the awful morning behind him. The other voice inside his head—logic, he assumed—suggested that the best way to forget about it was to keep to his plans and enjoy the day.

He took a deep breath. *It can only get better, right?*

As if bidden by his thoughts, a crumpled paper tumbled across the pavement ten yards ahead where the sidewalk cornered around a tall building. It scraped over the cement, a slight breeze sliding it closer to the curb. If the paper—*the money*, Kevin thought, noticing its greenish hue—made it onto the street, he wouldn't risk traffic for what was probably a dollar.

Or one of those stupid ads made to look like money so idiots like me will pick it up. Still, Kevin wasn't rich, and the stint between gigs had been long—too long to pass up free moolah. So he picked up his pace.

As he reached it, he squatted, snagging the bill just as it slid off the curb. A bony knee thumped him in the side. Someone toppled over his shoulders.

A man rolled off the sidewalk and got up cursing. He puffed out his chest and stepped into Kevin's space. "What the fuck, man?"

The lean figure wore a tank top, gym shorts, and a visor that made him look like an old bookie, though he was only in his twenties. Sweat dampened his shirt and darkened the visor's rim. On his feet were worn running shoes. As Kevin read the clues, the man had been jogging before Kevin entered his path.

Kevin had tangled with bigger and meaner folks than the peacocking Tony Little look-alike, so he wasn't a bit intimidated. Still, he had caused Tony Two's fall. "I'm sorry," he said with as much sincerity as he could muster. "I should have been watching where I was going."

The jogger pushed him. "Yeah, you should have, asshole."

The man's hands on him spawned something feral inside Kevin. He feinted forward, fist raised, but caught himself before he did something he could, but probably wouldn't, regret. The man cowered as he slunk backward, into the street.

"You're not worth it." Kevin turned and walked away, head held high for being the bigger man. His peripheral vision caught a twinkle of green light. It reminded him of the green he held.

"Oh shit! A Benjamin!" He smiled and stretched the bill between his fingers as he continued toward the subway. His mind barely registered the screech of tires or the thud and wailing that followed as he considered his good fortune.

He walked through a broken turnstile then filed in among the throngs awaiting the next train. *Now, if I could just avoid any more drama.* He sniggered and sent up a silent prayer, half in jest. The incoming train screeched to a halt, its doors opening directly in front of him. The mob engulfed him, everyone vying for the open seats.

The train was crowded. Pickings were slim, but Kevin got a bead on an orange, no-cushioned beauty. Just as he was about to plop down into moderate discomfort, an elderly lady appeared below his buttocks as if she'd materialized there. The smirk across her face suggested she knew what she'd done.

Despite his quick temper, Kevin was mostly a gentleman. He would have offered the woman his seat had she been forced to stand, but the shady tactic, the sleight of hand—*the outright thievery*—rankled him. He grimaced, turned away, and grabbed the handrail, his window to claim another seat having already closed.

Just two stops. He huffed. *Let it go.*

The train squealed and jolted as it barreled along the tracks. It sounded like a mining cart, metal wheels grinding against steel rails. As it screeched to a stop, Kevin imagined sparks flying.

The doors opened, but no one got out. The incoming flood filled the car to capacity, humans packed together like a box of straws. Body heat drove up the temperature. At least three of those bodies pressed against Kevin. A frat boy's beer breath wafted over his neck, the kid's wallet—or so he hoped—pressing hard against his ass. The unwashed aroma of the fat guy to Kevin's right added to the bouquet. And rounding out the scents was the perfumed shampoo of the attractive businesswoman in front of him. That, he could live with.

He looked down at the seat-stealing wench. Her smirk grew, and she gave him a wink.

Kevin festered as he took in a fourth smell that sparked a doughnut craving. *Coffee? Definitely coffee.* The scent grew stronger as Ms. Business opened the lid on a Styrofoam cup and took a sip.

"Mmph!" Her eyebrows shot up, and she covered her mouth with her hand. "Hot!"

Kevin smiled. "You okay?"

The woman nodded and smiled back. When she didn't look away, Kevin's cheeks warmed.

The train jerked forward. The coffee flew from Ms. Business's hands. The elderly lady howled.

She was still screaming as Kevin tried to blot the coffee off her face with his sleeve. The droplets that got on his exposed wrist scalded his skin, so he could imagine the depth of pain the seat thief was feeling. Blisters surrounded by blotches of deep red formed on her face, pus bubbling under the growing domes.

Through racking sobs, she batted him away. "Go!" she yelled, as if her injuries were somehow his fault.

So when the train stopped again, he did go, leaving Ms. Business to assist her burn victim. A twinge of guilt came and went when he considered his luck in not getting the seat.

He reached into his pocket and pulled out the hundred-dollar bill. The bag lady's words echoed through his skull. *Luck be your lady… but she demands sacrifice.*

What does that even mean? He shook his head, refusing to give any more credence to the ravings of a lunatic. He'd been a bit lucky that day. Nothing too unusual. A hundred bucks was nice but not exactly life-changing.

Something fell off the back of the bill. He bent to pick up a small laminated rectangle. A picture of Ms. Business smiled up at him. *Maria Richardson, Realtor.* Realizing she must have slipped it into his pocket, he beamed.

Now that's unusual. Kevin did all right with the ladies, but rarely had they made the first move. His brow furrowed. Had there been a cost to his good fortune? The man who'd tripped… The woman's burn…

"Nah!" He laughed away the ridiculous notion. *Anyway, at least I'll probably get a date out of it. Hopefully, not for coffee.*

Still, Kevin couldn't shake his uneasiness. The coincidences were racking up, and the weight on his shoulders seemed even heavier than before, draping over him like a wet blanket. He couldn't dispute he was having a weird day. People were getting hurt. Again, he considered going home, but the food truck festival only happened once a year.

He climbed the subway steps to the street. A traffic jam of vans and trucks blockaded the road. At first, Kevin thought the festival had extended to his side of the Palisades Bridge, but the mounted cameras, satellite dishes, and call signs of the local news stations clued him in to his mistake. A series of flashes turned his attention to Diane Westbrook of Channel 8, who stood in front of a large dais as she spoke into a microphone.

A crowd of reporters circled the platform upon which stood two adults and two children, all wearing T-shirts featuring a lizard wearing sunglasses, the logo for Rancho Chanchero's Roast Beef. What a lizard had to do with a sandwich shop serving cow products was a mystery to Kevin.

The dais stood in front of the cliff. Behind it was nothing but blue sky and a forty-foot drop onto rocks. A river cut through the ravine, nearly one thousand yards wide at the bridge Kevin meant to cross.

"Ha!" Kevin recognized the people on the stage: *the shark family*. He snagged a picture with his phone. The banner propped over the family read: *The Violet Family Can Attest—Rancho Chanchero's Roast Beef Satisfies Even the Hungriest Carnivore.*

Must be a slow news day. His amusement draining, Kevin squeezed through the crowd. He'd barely made it a few steps when he came to a convenience store with a sign in its window. *Play the lottery. Win up to $1,000,000 instantly!*

Kevin rolled his eyes. *Okay. Let's see if I'm really lucky.* He walked into the store.

A bald man with eyebrows as thick as hedges sat behind the counter. His beady eyes coursed over *The Winston Cable*, his lips moving as he read. Apparently finished, he sneered and tossed the tabloid onto the counter. "Not even a shark would eat that roast beef."

Kevin clapped. "That's what I'm saying!"

"Huh?" The clerk's head rose. "What can I do for you?"

"I'll take a ten-dollar scratch ticket and..." He studied the candy racks for anything that might call to him. "That's it."

Lottery tickets hung like accordions from miniature plastic cubes behind the clerk, who turned to face them. "Which one do you want?"

"The one with a million-dollar payout."

The clerk tore off a silver card and presented it to Kevin. "Ten dollars." When Kevin tried to pay with his credit card, the clerk refused to take it. "Cash only. Lottery rules."

Kevin sighed. His billfold was empty. He dug into his pocket for the hundred-dollar bill.

The clerk tapped a sign plastered to the counter. "No bills larger than twenties." As Kevin's smile shriveled, the clerk said, "Never mind. Give it to me." He counted out Kevin's change. "If you're heading to that food truck thing, you're gonna need cash. Most of the vendors won't accept credit cards."

"How'd you know—"

A rumble like an airplane landing shook the ground. Kevin caught himself on the counter. Before the word "earthquake" popped into his mind, the rumbling subsided.

"Just a little one," the clerk said. "No worse than trying to stand on the subway."

Kevin thanked the clerk and left. He patted his pockets for something to scrape the covering off the numbers, which were—he chuckled—sure to be winners. He sat at the curb and, with the metal edge of his apartment key, revealed his winning numbers. He then read the rules aloud. "Match any of your numbers to any of the winning numbers, win prize shown. Reveal a bell symbol, win prize automatically." He nodded. "Sounds simple enough."

He pressed the key against the first of four rows and scratched off all five spots without finesse or expectations. His heart skipped as he uncovered a twenty-three, thinking it a match to his winning numbers. "Nope. Twenty-four."

He shrugged and scratched the second row with less zeal. A bell symbol appeared in the fourth slot. "Shit." Kevin revealed the prize beneath it. "Two fifty." Trying to decipher the meaning of the *K* after his prize amount, he barely noticed the ground vibrating or the pebbles jumping like fleas onto his jeans. "Two hundred fifty... thousand? No way."

Pulse quickening, he continued on to the third row and, finding nothing, completed the fourth. Two more bells appeared. The prizes under each bell were *250K* and *500K*, respectively.

"A million dollars?" He leapt to his feet. "A million dollars!" The ticket trembled in his hand. Energized by his amazing stroke of luck, he wanted to jump and scream and dance but kept it bottled up for fear of attracting anyone who might try to steal his ticket.

He looked around. No one paid him any attention. The reporters at the back of the press conference were hopping into their vans. Those closer to the dais were crouching and covering their heads. The shark family huddled together, moving like rugby players slowly toward the dais stairs.

The rumbling intensified. Kevin threw out his arms to steady himself. A car alarm went off. A loud crack came from the platform. The ground beneath it gave way, and the dais tilted over the cliff. It began to slide, with the shark family still on it.

One of the children toppled over the drop. Kevin sprinted forward to help the remaining three. As the angle of the tilt increased, the father slipped. His back braced him against the remnants of a barrier fence. He looked as if he might hold on until the dais tipped further, nearly vertical, sending his wife and daughter airborne. They slammed into the father, knocking him over the rail. He hooked one arm around the rail and the other around his wife, who in turn had hers hooked around their child's. But the railing cracked, sending the three tumbling into the ravine.

Kevin skidded to a stop. The dais disappeared over the cliff, and the rumbling grew louder. Sounds of glass breaking and people screaming filled the air. A car crashed into one of the parked vans beside him. The cliff's edge moved closer to his feet as if some invisible giant were chomping away the earth. A telephone pole toppled into the approaching abyss. Wires crackled and swung wildly. Cracks split the pavement under Kevin's feet. Still, he didn't move.

At last, Kevin forced his shaking legs to heed the alarm blaring in his brain. Bursting forward, he fled the devastation. Nine steps onto the bridge, he realized he was still heading toward the festival. Twenty-two steps in, he considered whether a bridge was the safest place to be during an earthquake. Thirty-nine steps in, he stopped to turn around.

A suspension cable snapped and whipped by his face. Gasping, he watched as it exploded through a car window then reemerged coated in gore. A roar, followed by a cloud of dirt and dust, came from the head of the bridge. When the air cleared, the convenience store, its neighboring buildings, and the bridge's connection to the mainland were gone. Cars, people, and huge chunks of concrete plummeted to the shallow riverbed below.

A screeching mob ran toward him like linemen looking to sack a quarterback. A large woman, parts flopping like a bulldog's jowls, beat him aside with her purse, shouting, "Move, you idiot!"

Kevin joined the footrace toward the center of the bridge, climbing its arch ever higher, pavement cracking and crumbling at his heels, then overtaking him. The bridge split, jutting a three-foot wall into his path. The portion below Kevin tilted forward, scraping against the still-erect segment as it slid under it. Kevin pushed off his toes and propelled himself atop the growing wall.

Once up, he chanced a look back. The section he'd left was falling like a hammer in slow motion. In seconds, it would strike the still-standing pillars.

A cry for help halted his flight. The woman who'd struck him—he must have passed her during his mad sprint—hung from the wall he'd just climbed. A U-Haul skidded down the slope behind her. Her fingers clawed for purchase, her legs dangling unseen off a deadly precipice.

Kevin dove for her arms and latched on. He strained to pull her up, unable to lock his fingers around her thick wrists. The U-Haul picked up speed as it slid. Kevin braced himself with his heels and pulled with all his might.

He'd drawn most of her upper torso onto higher ground when he heard bone crackle like porcelain underfoot. The woman's eyes rolled back. She became weightless as the U-Haul pinned her in place. Blood gushed from her mouth. As the U-Haul fell into the river, only half the woman's weight returned.

Kevin let her go. The collision of the falling segment against the pillars sent jolts through his funny bones. He held his breath as he waited to fall, but the supports held. The rumbling had stopped. Aside from the alarms, sirens, and wailing chorusing from all directions, the world had settled. He stood, hoisted upon a steel and concrete pedestal, with both ends of the bridge missing.

It's over? Kevin took deep breaths. He and a handful of survivors were on terra firma, a man-made island standing against all odds. He dusted himself off. "Now, *that* was luck—"

The ground fell away.

Thrown outward, Kevin kicked his legs as if he could run on air, but gravity did its thing. His butt and thighs slapped the water. The tingling he felt didn't yet register as pain, his racing mind only comprehending that he was sinking, plunging into someplace dark, cold, and suffocating.

He shot downward until reaching soft mud. Pushing off the riverbed, he swam toward light and air. He gasped as he breached the surface then began to laugh, amazed he was still alive.

A teenage girl surfaced nearby and was soon laughing with him. Her mirth ended abruptly when a chunk of cement smashed her back under. Kevin yelped and looked up. Piece by piece, the bridge continued to fall.

He closed his eyes as debris splashed around him, each impact jostling him in a new direction. He cleared his eyes and searched for the shore even as waves relentlessly slapped his face. Reasoning he was halfway across the bridge when he fell, he headed for the first shoreline he saw, knowing only that whatever remained up would soon be coming down.

A few wet and shivering survivors stood on the bank, helping others out of the water. A man was shouting and pointing at a food truck rolling down the steep earthen cavity where the cliff walls of Galahad Park used to be.

Another survivor was flagging Kevin. She pointed to an overturned truck in front of him, only visible between waves. Its service window faced up, water lapping over it and cascading in little waterfalls into the truck's interior. A lizard wearing sunglasses was painted on the cab. The Rancho Chanchero truck must have fallen off the bridge on its way to the festival.

Something brushed against Kevin's right arm. He jerked it back then scanned the water for what had touched him. A black dorsal fin sliced through the surface, moving away. Kevin counted four more dorsal fins circling the truck. A plastic-wrapped torpedo roll, undoubtedly stuffed with roast beef, floated past Kevin. A shark snapped at something floating near the truck and disappeared underwater with it.

"This can't be happening." Treading water, Kevin couldn't decide whether to turn around or chance the sharks for the closer shore. Every muscle ached. His breathing hitched. Drowning sounded a whole lot better than being eaten alive.

A hollering man still riding his motorcycle crashed into the water. Another person hit the water near the truck. A dorsal fin passed in front of Kevin and dove under, heading toward the second splash. Neither the person nor the shark resurfaced.

"Swim!" The sound of his own voice was all the encouragement Kevin needed. He kicked toward the shore beyond the truck, pink water beading on his arms with every stroke.

Nearing the truck, he slowed and dog-paddled into the circle of fins, disturbing the water as little as possible. The sharks passed him by, too close for comfort, but seeming more interested in beef than human.

His hand smacked into something, and he squealed. He twisted and thrashed like a man amid a wasp swarm. His breaths hissed, and his heart thumped so hard it hurt.

A high-pitched laugh escaped his throat. Tears squeezed from his eyes, more from pure exhaustion and disbelief than from the many other emotions swirling inside him. "It's only seaweed or-or-or... plants. Yeah, just plants. There's no seaweed in fresh water."

His inner voice jeered. *There's no sharks in fresh water, either.*

Kevin flailed at the object, but it coiled around him like the tentacles of some Lovecraftian monster. The biker swam by to his left. Sputtering out water, Kevin called for help. The last thing he saw before going under was the biker shake his head and turn away.

Kevin needed to compose himself if he wanted to live. He needed to *think*. The vinelike material pressed against his face, smothering him. But he saw it then for what it was: not some wicked beast but a net of some kind.

Rope. That, he could deal with. Perhaps it was the bridge's suicide-prevention mechanism since there had been nothing to catch him. Its gaps were too big for fishing but too small to squeeze through.

Still holding his breath, he concentrated on where he was caught. His movements purposeful, he slipped his legs and arms free. But when he tried to surface, the net loomed over him, popping up only enough to allow him a breath. He dove in search of a way out of his trap.

The netting closed around him like a shroud. Square by square, he swam along it as the current whisked it about where debris hadn't pinned it to the bottom.

Surfacing for air, Kevin stifled a scream as a dark-gray body glided by him. The net's bulk pulled him down again. He searched for a silver lining. *If this net's trapping me in, it's probably also keeping the shar—*

Two rows of sharp triangular teeth clamped together inches from Kevin's cheek. Shreds of the shark's last meal hung from the top teeth like beef in a meat locker. The predator's nose butted his head as it tried to gnash its way through the rope. Kevin shrieked, expelling the rest of his air. As his bladder let go, he could do nothing but stare at the source of his impending doom.

Unable to chew its way through, the man-eater continued on its loop. Kevin wheezed as he breached the surface. As the weight of the net drove him under again, he forgot about escape and looked everywhere for the shark.

A dark blur, growing bigger, slowly came into focus. Teeth exposed, the shark appeared to be smiling. Kevin tried to recall if he'd learned any shark-repelling techniques from *Shark Week* on The Discovery Channel. *Poke it in the eye?* That seemed right. Kevin clenched his jaw as the shark shrank the distance between them. *I can't even see its fucking eyes!*

He gritted his teeth and prayed. *Please, rope, don't fail me now.*

As the shark attacked, Kevin threw out his hands to block the blow. Realizing his action was a good way to get his arms bitten off, he jerked them back. The net lingered where he'd pushed it just long enough for the predator's jaw to close around it. The shark shook its head like a dog playing tug. The net caught in its teeth.

The rope tore as that massive jaw chewed. A hole formed. Soon, the shark would dine on something meatier.

Kevin closed his eyes. After a moment, the water settled, and he chanced a peek. The shark was gone.

And it had bitten him a way out. Wasting no time, he swam through the hole and kicked for shore. Passing the food truck and what remained of the biker, he soon reached shallow water. Still, he kept on, never looking back, never wanting to see what might be following him. In waist-high water, he planted his feet and staggered toward shore.

A paramedic waded out to him. "You're a lucky one! Those sharks have been picking off people left and right."

"They're bull sharks," Kevin said, delirious from exhaustion. "They like roast beef."

"I can't believe... Look out!" The paramedic pushed Kevin just as a huge form lunged out of the water. Its jaw clamped down where Kevin had been standing and the paramedic's arms then hovered.

Kevin fell onto his butt and crab-walked away from a monster with a mouthful of rope and human limbs. As the paramedic screamed, Kevin scurried to shore. After several minutes with his face in the sand, he summoned the strength to sit up.

A soft beeping—a ringing in his ears maybe—needled his tired brain. Not remembering what he'd done with the lottery ticket, Kevin found it in his pocket, wet but still intact. He started to laugh, amazed by how little importance the ticket had just then.

He was still laughing when he uncovered the source of the noise—a rusted and half-buried metal detector. As his fingers dug shallow graves over it, lightning-laced clouds darkened the sky.

GLIMMER

I am heading there to die.

We are heading there to die. A laugh escapes me, an almost hysterical cackle, for I recognize the madness in the notions of wanting and seeking death. I know I should be careful what I wish for, but wishes have a way of dissolving on the tongue.

My daughter needs this, and I need her. I'm pressing the pedal to the floor, urging my SUV faster and faster, risking the danger for fear of the alternative. Of being too late.

The dotted lines separating the lanes tick by so fast they become a solid streak. The engine revs higher and higher. Should a deer... No, nothing else matters. Only Kylie. To hell with anyone or anything foolish enough to get in our way.

The remains of the hotel are close now, a charred husk, black against a black night—a megalith to opulence reduced to condemnation and obscurity. I hear my daughter's breathing, shallow as she lies on the back seat, her lungs forcing breaths through dry, colorless, cracked lips, each accompanied by a whistling wheeze or a short moan. I want to scream, to tear out my hair, but I can't give into despair. Not now. Not when we are so close. So I force a smile despite her pain even though no one will see it.

"Hang on, baby," I say, unsure if I'm talking to my daughter or myself. "Just one more minute."

My knuckles whiten as I squeeze the steering wheel tighter. In slowing to look for the entrance, I notice the fence around the property. *Stupid!*

How could I have forgotten about the gate? And what will I do if it's locked?

I'll ram the fucking thing, that's what I'll do.

My breaths stop hitching, then stop altogether as I turn the wheel and fishtail onto the path leading up to the hotel. Half of a massive, wrought iron gate is open, while the other half is missing, and I lose a wing mirror as I squeeze through the opening. Tall grass and weeds smother out pavement and clear passage. Once, the beautiful lane had circled an ornate fountain, cherubs splashing at play. Now, grass and brambles as high as wheat obscure my way. But I will not be swayed.

I plow through the brush, my SUV more than a match for the growth, letting my memory guide my way. Metal squeals as thorny fingernails scratch lines into my doors as if trying to peel their way inside the vehicle. I am not for them, however; I offer myself only to what awaits inside.

As I pass the fountain, tires treading too quickly over unseen ground, I see that the cherubs are gone. Instead, an empty pedestal guards over black stagnant water, while a mosslike fungus eats its way into the stone.

Behind it, cracked steps rise out of untouched earth to the mausoleum that once catered to the freshest stars and brightest up-and-comers: a hotel, speakeasy, and hedonistic playground that out-roared the roaring twenties itself. It was even rumored that Calvin Coolidge had often frequented the hotel. I chuckle despite the fluttering in my stomach and the clutter in my mind. *Too bad he didn't die here. It might have been nice to meet him.*

No levity can erase the terror that seizes me as I look upon those front doors. I freeze, heart thumping and car slowing, my cowardice immobilizing me when I'm mere feet from my goal. My throat goes dry. I cannot stop the memories from swirling.

I had been there once before, when the lawn was only thigh high. A childhood dare, boys challenging boys. We'd all heard the stories. What dies there stays there. It was true enough that the hotel had gone up in flames, more than a hundred souls trapped inside, the exits barred from within as if its occupants had formed some kind of suicide pact. Even though none of us had believed in ghosts, none of us were brave enough to spend the night.

Until I answered the dare. I walked in to a carnival of lights, something alive that should have been dead. People talking, laughing, having drinks at the bar, smoking cigarettes, all dolled up in the fashion of the time—their time, an age decades before my birth, before the Great Depression and a second world war, Johnny Carson and Vanna White. Before the world became a place only explored through a screen.

An invisible guest walking among echoes that time forgot, I watched in awe as a tuxedoed maestro's fingers danced over eighty-eight keys, the song like an echo carried on the wind. The spirits seemed so happy, locked forever in timeless bliss, that something inside me longed to commune with them.

To be like them.

All at once, the conversation stopped. The pianist halted his melody, his last note hanging like a bell toll in the still of night. And everything was still: spirits frozen in impossible poses, drinks being perpetually poured into never-filling glasses, cigarette smoke like cotton-candy puffs billowing in the air.

I looked closer, marvel relinquishing to unease, to knees buckling. Smiles had become strained, too big, lecherous. Mouths that had been laughing contorted into silent screams. The air weighed heavier upon me, icy cold and raising goosebumps on my crawling skin as I backed slowly toward the door. My elbows pressed against it and I tried to push it open, but it wouldn't budge.

My heart leapt into my throat. I pushed harder, put my back into it, but the door still wouldn't open. My breaths came short, my thoughts frenzied. I had to get out of there. I turned around to find the door barred and chained, a padlock holding the barricade in place.

Eyes tearing, I searched for something to break the lock or for another way out. My chin quivered; I could feel the scream building before it bellowed from my mouth. All eyes were upon me then, alien and unnerving, black liquid orbs filled with incalculable darkness, voids that, had I dared to gaze into them too long or too deeply, would have sucked me into their abysmal oblivion.

They *saw* me. The lights went out. Screaming, crying, warmth running down my legs, I turned to run. The door, no longer barred, gave way easily as I crashed through it. I kept on running, past my friends, out the gate, down the road, and into the night.

My parents picked me up some time later. I had no idea where I was, how far I had run, or how they'd been able to find me. I was still screaming when they tried to coax me into the car, screamed until my vocal chords bled.

But that was then. I was a terrified kid, moods too easily subject to fancy. I step on the gas. I am not that scared little kid any longer.

Still, my daughter… I have to consider her fear. I shake my head. *No. This is the only way.*

A loud crack as my front wheel mounts the steps and my bumper collides with stone. I yank up the emergency brake and climb out. Long reeds bend under the door then whip up to hit me like the rap of a belligerent father's belt. Its door ajar, keys still in the ignition, the vehicle chimes as I circle it. The night is eerily dark, starless, my high beams and the dome light providing the only illumination, creating a brilliant igloo connected to a tunnel showing me the way forward, a path up to the hotel's massive oaken doors.

My headlights flicker, and the hairs on my neck stand on end. The SUV is near mint, the bulbs fresh. I frown. *Could I have damaged it that badly…* No, the ghosts are already at play.

I will not be swayed.

I pull open the back door and offer a smile to my daughter, her chest still rising and falling albeit faintly. By now, my wife is probably aware of our absence, but I never told her of this place or my plans. She wouldn't understand or believe. But she's smart and curious, and I truly believe that once the SUV is found, she'll want to peek inside for herself, and maybe then we can all be together. Yes, I'm sure that's how it will play out.

It has to be.

Gently, I lift my daughter from the seat. She stirs as I cradle her in my arms, careful not to let my tears drop onto her favorite Dora the Explorer pajamas, the kind with the feet. Allowed to come home to die, as the so-compassionate doctors had put it, she at least gets to wear these PJs again, not those awful hospital gowns that made her look so…

Sick.

I chuckle and stifle a sob, remembering how much she loves… loved sliding over the kitchen floor on those feet. Her mom… she would get so worried about Kylie falling, but the two of us would share a laugh, a mischievous thing that was all our own.

She shifts but does not awaken. She barely weighs more than her pajamas, the leukemia having eaten away everything but her soul. Something lodges in my throat, and I choke on it before I can force it back down. As I plod up the steps, I shake off my reverie, wondering how I might open up the doors with my daughter in my arms.

They creak open as if caught in a breeze I cannot feel, though the temperature seems to drop twenty degrees all at once. In the slowly widening opening, a column of impenetrable darkness invites me in.

The hotel is welcoming us. I step inside.

I jump as the doors slam shut behind us, shrouding us in pitch black. No turning back now. I must be strong, for Kylie and for myself. I will not be scared away this time.

I take a hesitant step forward, and my shoe crunches something that sounds like cereal but is probably wood or—I swallow something bitter—exoskeleton. But without light, I cannot see. And for the first time, I begin to doubt my plan. *What if the spirits have left this—*

In a flash, the hotel comes to life. I flinch but quickly take in the scene. Round wooden tables are set about a tavern to my right. Men wearing sharps suits with tight vests, black shoes, and ties line barstools or sit with women wearing everything from double-knitted cardigans or cocooning furs to thin, loose silk dresses, sometimes tiered or with fringe. Most of the women and many men sport headwear, felt hats and bonnets for the ladies and fedoras and newsboy caps for the gents.

At a piano to the left of the bar, a man with slicked-back black hair hammers away a jovial tune. Though his back is to me, his aggressive, almost manic style of play recalls within me my first visit to the hotel, and I recognize him as the same tuxedo-clad piano player I had seen in my youth.

Everyone wears smiles. The biggest belongs to a man in the corner, sitting alone and flicking the lid of a lighter.

To my left is the hotel lobby. Filled with red-velvet and mahogany Bergère chairs and matching sofas on polished hardwood, the sitting area reeks of posh elegance. Besides a young bellhop in a red uniform and a man in a suit standing behind the reservation desk, presumably the night manager, the lobby is empty.

Ahead is a grand stairwell adorned with red carpet and banisters that appear to be solid gold. At its first landing about twelve steps up, additional stairs continue to the left and right, up to the hotel's rooms.

The giant candelabra over my head flickers. I look to the stairs then the sitting area, opting for the latter for fear I will not be able to get into the rooms above. Or that the stairs, in their true form, or the floor above may not be able to support our weight.

I laugh at the ridiculousness of my fear. After all, I am here to die.

I head for a sofa and sit, laying my daughter atop it with her head resting on my lap. Stroking her hair, I wait, unsure what exactly I am waiting for. Kylie's breathing to stop, I suppose. I pray I have timed our flight well.

What an odd thing, to pray for my own daughter's death. But it is an end to her suffering and, selfishly, I admit, my own as well. Taking deep breaths, I compose myself, gripping the armrest for steadiness and steadfastness. *We are where we need to be.*

The music stops, and the lights go out.

A woman, beautiful and ethereal, appears as if out of nowhere, seated with legs crossed in the chair in front of me. She illuminates the space around her, her form somehow radiating bluish light like that at the center of a flame. Like the others, she is dressed in 1920s fashion: a dark, sequined dress hugging her curves, her lipstick and eyeshadow a matching shade. In that light, *her* light, there were only blacks, whites, and blues, her pale skin like cream under the light of a full moon, matching the pearls around her neck. Unlike the others, she does not play at being alive.

My breathing quickens as she slowly rises and approaches me, pausing only to puff from a cigarette holder that resembles a magic wand. In her dark, deep-set eyes, I see only sadness, grief as deep as my own. She walks closer and crouches before me. Her hand covers mine in a gesture of solace, as if across the planes of life and death, a bond of mutual empathy is forming.

I snarl with anger and pain as her nails dig into my hand. I look down to see a chuck of skin and tendon missing from the space between my thumb and forefinger then back up in time to see the woman grinning maniacally, her clothes now tattered, face skeletal, empty black pits where her eyes had been. Ripcord flesh stretches thinly over bone as she raises her cigarette like a knife over my daughter's forehead. I leap up to tackle her as her arm swings down but instead pass through her, never making contact. She disappears at my touch, but her light remains like pixie dust in the air.

I scramble to my feet to check on my daughter. Her head is now on the sofa, and an eight-inch rat—twenty with tail—is nibbling on her earlobe. Kylie cries out as the bastard bites down and comes away with meat.

Seething, spit hissing through my teeth, I snatch the rodent up by its tail and slam it onto the ground. Before it can roll onto its feet, I crush its head under my heel.

Something moves under my daughter's pajama bottoms, the fabric tenting near her knee. I reach into them and feel another leathery hairless tail. "How dare you violate my daughter!" I seethe with rage and raw hate for the vermin. As I pull it out, it squeals and shrieks, its claws and teeth seeking purchase in my daughter's flesh. I raise it in front of my eyes, snapping and twisting and pulling as I tear the animal in half. After dropping its remains to the floor and even though I know it's dead, I stomp on it again and again until my rage can subside.

Only then do I do what I should have done first: I check my daughter for other vermin. I see none, and my daughter still sleeps, or if she'd ever been awake, she must have fainted. I cradle her closer and wait for the next attack.

I set my jaw and settle in for a long night. I will not be swayed.

The lights snap on and with them, a cacophony of voices. I throw my hands over my ears. The murmur of conversation has crescendoed into the roar of a freight train. The brightness, too, is amplified, so much so that I am momentarily blinded. The atmosphere is that of a carnival or maybe a funhouse, with spinning floors, swirling walls, and strobing lights. That wretched piano man slams away at the keys, producing only noise. The rest of the guests seem not to notice.

He sees us.

The words are not spoken, yet I hear them through my ears as clearly as if they are. I look around for the speaker, but none of the spirits, caught up in their revelry, seem to know I exist.

The music stops, and time halts, just as it had when I was a kid. One by one, each head turns my way, a smile impossibly wide on each face, glistening, sharpened teeth in each mouth. The man in the corner flicks his lighter, the only sound and motion remaining in that ghostly party. *Chink-chink, chink-chink.* He stops.

And we sees him!

I clench my fists and stand, letting my daughter's head fall upon the couch. "I'm not running! Not this time. I will not be swayed!"

The faces, undaunted, continue to leer at me, silent and unmoving. I scan their drawn, pale expressions for any motion, the slightest twitch, but receive nothing but steady salacious grins. I step forward. "You hear me? I will not be swayed."

A clink comes from behind the bar. A bow-tied bartender polishes glasses behind a sea of mannequin stillness. He turns to face me, his bushy handlebar moustache and crow's feet crinkling as he raises a bottle of what appears to be brandy. He points at Kylie, then waves me over.

I creep closer, weaving in between patrons frozen in place, doing everything I can to avoid touching them. They reek of cigarettes and booze, but those odors mask something fouler, ashy and acrid like bales of burning hair. Their beady, black-pit eyes follow me as I pass, never blinking, making me feel as if I'm stuck in a giant still-life painting with only the dead to keep me company.

And my daughter. *I'm doing this for her.* The lie tastes bitter on my tongue, and I hadn't even spoken it aloud. I've soured everything. It doesn't matter. All that matters is that we can be together now. Our time will never end.

The bartender places a glass on the bar and pours from the bottle. The liquid is dark and syrupy and is certainly not brandy.

"What will it do?"

The bartender again points his long narrow finger at my daughter then slides it across his neck.

The gesture speaks as well as any words. It hits me in the chest like a boulder, and my resolve nearly crumples beneath its weight. It's one thing to let my daughter die naturally—if there's anything natural about a five-year-old being stolen from the world before she even has a chance to experience it—but to be the means to her end…

"It's better this way," I say as much to myself as to the bartender and Kylie.

The bartender nods and offers an earnest smile that lights up even his albino-white complexion. I take the drink and return to my daughter. Lifting her head, I place the glass to her lips. "Drink, baby," I say through sniffles and tears. As I slowly tip the glass, she responds as if by reflex, taking the liquid into her mouth.

With half the glass emptied, I lay my daughter's head back down. I stare at the liquid, sloshing it before my eyes. The lights go out as I toss it back.

I cough and choke, spit the contents from my mouth, not liquid but solid. And moving. A centipede drops from my lips and lands on my shirt. In the bartender's glow—he's standing much closer now, body shaking with silent laughter—I can see the critter squirming toward my neck as if it wants to return to where it had just been. I yank it off and throw it to the ground then remember my hand and the glass it still holds.

Gasping, I drop it as many-legged things crawl over the lip. The bartender continues to mock me in silence, his head tilting farther and farther back as he cackles like a madman until, with a finger across his neck, nail carving a slit through the skin, his head falls back permanently. Crawling, skittering things spew forth from the gaping hole.

I pick up the glass and hurl it at him, but it passes through the wall behind him and vanishes without a sound. "I will not be swayed!"

The lights snap on, and I shrink beneath the stares of the patrons. They circle my daughter and me, looming taller, closer, stretched thin like taffy and bent at the waist to glower down at me with lewd sneers and salivating mouths. Their eyes are like looking down train tunnels, those faraway specks of light at their ends twinkling with malice, sparkling eyes of cats toying with their prey. They are all around me, claustrophobically near, enclosing me in a ring of slender men and slenderer women, with no safe passage out.

He sees us, voices say in unison from tongues that don't move. *And we sees him.*

And though I cower, I still find strength. I have not forgotten why I came. "Do your worst." Eyes follow my movement as I sit beside my daughter. She coughs, the liquid I poured down her mouth sputtering over her lips. It looks like blood.

Her eyelids flutter. "Daddy?"

I press my hand over her mouth and squeeze her nostrils shut. "It's better this way," I whisper, my eyes filling with tears, my body wracking with sobs. I can't expose her to more harm from those malevolent spirits. It's clear the place wants us, but it's enjoying our torment first. My daughter is no one's plaything. Her passing should be as swift and as painless as possible.

So my mind justifies as I clamp down harder. She is squirming now, her eyes wide open, staring at me accusingly, not understanding that what I do is for her own good. My strength is tested in that moment, and I hold firm. She will understand. Soon enough, she will understand.

Her body falls limp. The lights go out. Again, I am swallowed by the dark.

Chink-chink. Chink-chink.

That twisted man and his infernal lighter. It echoes through the hotel lobby so that I cannot determine where it comes from, so loud that it is more like the rattle of chains along pavement than the flip and closure of a lighter top.

A blue light appears close by, and I drop to my knees, crying fiercely and yet smiling. My daughter, my Kylie, has found her way. Enveloped in a bluish aura, she steps toward me in her Dora the Explorer pajamas, sweet smile on her face, arms out to comfort and be comforted, as perfect in death as she was in life.

The other spirits, still in their circle, appear around me, so many of them now that they bathe the entire lobby in their bluish glow. In their radiance, I can see the true state of the hotel: the charred husk I had seen on my way in filled with burnt and toppled furniture, exposed walls, and a patchwork roof that somehow fails to let in any light despite its many holes. Rats and other things scurry about, looking for their next meals. Cobwebs bridge gaps between railings and awnings and hang from fixtures. Anything cloth, carpet, tapestry, curtain, or wallpaper has long since burned or rotted away, leaving only ant mounds of ash and dust.

Kylie's new home and soon to be mine. I will not be swayed. With a shaking hand, I draw the pistol from my jacket pocket as my ghostly daughter steps closer. Her brow furrowed, she stares at me with doleful eyes, a world of compassion blessed with the innocence of one so young. But in those eyes, there is also understanding. She smiles softly then nods her approval as I raise the gun to my temple and pull the trigger.

Nothing happens.

I moan as I pull it again and again. Still, nothing happens.

My daughter reaches her tiny hand out, closes it over mine, and gently, tenderly pulls my hand toward her. She examines the gun with curious, fascinated eyes, then my hand, as if the feel of mortal flesh has become foreign and remarkable to her, the memory of her human form beginning to fade. She draws my fingers to her sweet, tender lips and kisses my hand.

Then bites off my thumb.

I scream and back away, covering my wound with my other hand. The pain shoots up my arm and into my brain, causing it to reboot. I fumble to understand what's happening, make sense of my mistake.

The spirit spits out my finger and grins that same leering, sharp-toothed grin the others wear as blood trickles down her chin. She is not my daughter. However much like my daughter that thing pretends to be, it cannot be her. Only a malicious reflection, a cruel manifestation of this wicked place.

Which means my daughter is gone. And I...

I killed her.

The circle of wraiths closes.

And we seize him.

I run for the door, a spirit in a flapper dress dissipating as I barrel through her. The door is barred and chained, the house apparently having decided to keep me this time. But the walls are dilapidated, the structure infirm. There has to be a way out.

I race through the lobby, around the stairwell, searching for a back door, only to find one barred in the same manner as the entrance. I check the windows, try to pry back the boards that cover them, while the spirits jeer and holler as if I am sport. They move in close, brush against my arm while licking their lips or smiling their awful grins. But they do not block my path, and I sense I am a mouse in a maze full of cats.

I head up the stairs, thinking to find a breach in the wall or an unbarred window from which to jump. Though I know the structure is unsound, the forces at play create an illusion of solidity that supports me as well as if it were real. The hotel is as whole as it was before the fire, at least when whatever controlling force is at play wants it to be.

Except, not quite. As I climb the stairs to the left, I find myself impossibly back in the lobby, the spirits forming a corral between me and the stairwell. My gaze darts about, looking for answers as my mind tries to comprehend how I could be standing where I am. I turn to see the entrance, still barred, then again bolt up the stairs, this time turning right.

Only to find myself back at the entrance. My cheeks are wet, and it takes a moment for me to realize that the sobbing I hear is my own. The hotel has me, and it won't let me go. Worse, it won't let me die. I drop to my knees and bury my face in my hands.

At last, I summon the courage to raise my head. Nothing stirs. Lines of specters stand at my sides, silent and solemn. Before me, the Kylie-thing waits alone with outstretched arms. "Be with me, Daddy. Be with me forever."

The hotel is offering me an out if I have the courage to take it. I stumble toward her and drop to my knees. "I'm sorry, baby." Blubbering, I reach out to accept her embrace. "I'm so sorry."

I feel her teeth as they bury into my collar. Before my eyes roll back, I see the others coming. Hot, searing pain triggers from everywhere on my body at once. As I am ripped and shredded and torn asunder, I hear my scream, loud at first then as if from afar.

Then nothing. I arise whole and unblemished, radiating a bluish glow. My daughter is beside me, and she takes my hand. Looking up at me, she bares a bear-trap grin, and I recoil, an expression of an instinct that would soon fade.

I am no longer sad, no longer afraid. Instead, I am hungry. Ravenous, even, so much so that if I had to bear it long, I would surely go mad.

But I rejoice as I retake my daughter's hand and stand with her facing the entrance, the others forming a half circle behind us. She is smiling, and I am smiling, bigger than I ever have before, for I know my SUV will be found and others will enter.

The house will be fed. My daughter and I will live on, and I have no doubt her mother will join us soon.

DICHOTOMY

Men scream as they die. The sound of my heart thumping in my chest drowns them out. I have not yet seen the enemy beyond outlines and shadows in the dark, their shapes monstrous, things children believe hide under their beds or in their closets, not creatures of true flesh and blood.

We're dying, and I don't even know where to aim. I hug my face against the dirt, low in the trench, rifle tight against my chest. The night above veils the carnage on the battlefield, an empty landscape between two civilizations. We know nothing of the Others or why we fight them. Just what we are told: that they are monsters, evil; that they must be killed so we might live.

My brother has fallen, so I need little reason to fight. Still, a tingling in my gut tells me this is all wrong, that we should keep to our side of the barren field and them to theirs, where both may live in peace and prosperity. But who am I to question my superiors; them, educated and wise beyond my years, me, but a simple soldier knowing no more than a simple life filled with farming days and family nights? I am a fool to question them.

The stars above twinkle across a still plain, their tranquility offering hope. They shine for all, even the Others. But they are too far away to hear our screams.

The enemy's banshee wails have my comrades shaking. My hands tremble as I hug my rifle closer. I see my face, white and ghastly, in the shine of my bayonet, wondering if tonight will be the night I die.

Our men are fleeing the front line, but our captain orders them back. Those who refuse are executed. With numbers dwindling, it'll soon be my squad's turn to march. Fingers fumble as I check and recheck my bayonet stud, bolt, and safety. *I am ready*, I lie to myself. I don't want to die.

A horn blows, our signal to move. I stand, but my weapon falls from my shaking hands. I suck in air, my breaths having come too fast and too short. I search inward for strength, the memory of my brother, the love of my family awaiting my return. It is not enough to steel myself for what is to come, but it will have to do. *Courage comes from hidden places*, I tell myself, chuckling awkwardly as if I could convince myself I'd find it.

Most of my squad has climbed over the lip. Cries of pain, death wails, come from everywhere. I pick up my weapon and dig my boots into the wall, climbing into hell before I lose my nerve. On unsteady legs, blinded by darkness, I charge. The enemy is in front of me, somewhere unseen.

Waiting.

The path before me is littered with the dead. I step over bodies, some of men I recognize: the baker from Dunbury Street, an old schoolmate from my youth—people with wives and children, just like me, who will never share in their families' love again. Their faces are still, watching the stars as the stars watch them back, neither caring about those still alive on the ground.

I think to retreat, to run home and hide. But something inside me compels me forward. Whether it's fear of being slaughtered by my own comrades or of being labeled a coward by the ones I love, I do not know. Courage is the lesser of two evils. I must do this for my family, to protect them from the teeth and claws of monsters they'll never see, though being a husband and father seems more important than foreign sacrifice.

Even as I conjure the soapy smell of my daughter's hair all those times I cradled her in my arms, I step forward, closer to the enemy, the sight unseen. My boots squish in the blood of wasted heroes. Shots are fewer now. Screaming has been replaced by soft whimpering and prayers for help. I look to my left then to my right and see no one. Am I all that is left?

A massive shape, one of *them*, races toward me out of the black. I struggle to steady my rifle as I take aim, the enemy frightful, unnatural, instilling panic into my every nerve. My weapon shifts in my sweaty palms.

I release my breath and close my eyes, the enemy's wails driving a spike of terror into my brain. Opening my eyes, I fire.

The shot goes wide, and my enemy lurches forward—smaller now, shadows and distance having played tricks with my eyes. I can almost see the beast, not much taller than me, but still with murder and wickedness in its soul.

It leaps. No time to aim and fire. I steady my arms, strengthened now by righteousness. I will deliver this evil from our world.

Seething and hissing, the monster strikes. Metal glints in its raised fist, a knife it means to plunge inside me. Its face is pale like death itself, contorted with rage—or perhaps, fear—horrible to behold. I crouch and spring upward, thrusting my bayonet into its gut. The blade falls from its hand as it slides down into mine, blood sputtering from its coughing mouth. Its weight is heavy in my arms. I flick my rifle to my side, tossing my enemy to the ground.

The beast sputters before gasping its final breath. I feel nothing as I check the horizon for others. The field has gone silent, and I am still alive.

Hesitantly, I crouch beside the slain creature, not wanting to see but needing to know whom or what I fight. Kneeling in the dirt, breath hitching in my throat, I see no monster at all but a man. His dead glass eyes, empty of soul, stare at the stars. I lean closer, his face familiar even in the dark night.

It looks like mine.

AKIN

"**W**here's Papa going with that ax?"

Jesse swung his leg over the bench to follow, but as he rose, Mama's strong hand on his shoulder sat him back down. She dug her thumb and forefinger into his cheeks and pinched so hard his mouth made fish lips. "Jesse Merle Haggard Foster! How many times do I need to be telling you to mind your own business?"

Jesse tried to turn his head, but Mama pinched harder. Papa always asked Jesse for help chopping firewood, and Jesse could too. He could split at least three or four—okay, at least two—logs right down the middle before his arms got all sorts of sore. Not like Papa, who could chop a million gazillion—

"Are you listening to me?" Scowling, Mama crouched beside him. That close, he could smell the fruity lotion on her skin and something else on her breath that reminded him of that stingy stuff she poured on his knee when he skinned it chasing a possum under the porch. But Mama had on her mean face, all frowny and glaring, and Jesse knew he was in trouble even if he didn't know why.

He tried to nod, but Mama's hand held his chin up. "Yes, Mama."

She softened then and massaged his shoulder. "Never you mind what your daddy's doin'." She smiled. "Now eat them pancakes before they catch a cold."

He giggled. "Pancakes can't get sick." Mama only sometimes said funny things, not like Papa, who had to be the funniest person Jesse had

141

ever met in all his life. But the distraction only lasted a moment, his mind drifting back to his father, who had disappeared around the front of the house. *We don't need no wood. It's hotter than blue blazers.* He didn't really know what blue blazers were, but he bet if he could touch one, his finger would melt right off.

A fly landed on his plate. "Git!" He swung down his hand, stopping himself just in time before smashing the bug into a syrupy grave. Stuck in the molasses, the fly buzzed and twitched.

"Mama? Billy Jo says every time a fly lands, it throws up. Is that true?"

Mama had sat across from him at the picnic table and was chomping on an apple. She wiped juice from her chin and, still chewing, said, "Don't rightly know."

Jesse sighed and flicked the fly off his breakfast. "Do you think I'll get the AIDS or something from—"

Thump.

Jesse froze, plastic fork in his hand hovering over the table. Whatever Papa was doing didn't sound like no wood chopping. This had less *thock* and more *squish*. And he ain't never heard no wood scream before.

He swallowed. "Is Papa okay?"

Mama smiled and leaned across the table. "Papa's fine, baby. Now finish them cakes. You love pancakes."

It was true. He did love pancakes, and he loved eating outside on a sunny morning—except for the flies... or when the outhouse was stinking too much. But the day was so perfect, he wondered what they might do later. *Go for a swim in the lake? Maybe—*

Another *thump*. Another *squish*. Another scream.

He turned on the bench, peering at the corner of the house and willing it to vanish.

Mama huffed. "You know how I feel about wastin'."

"I'm sorry, Mama." He stared down at his pancakes, no longer interested in them. "It's just that... If I finish my breakfast, can I go help Papa?"

Mama stood and put her hand on her hip. "You're beginning to try my patience." Her gaze rose. "And anyhow, it looks like he's all done."

Jesse spun around to see Papa crossing the yard in long strides. His shirt sleeves and overalls were yucky, covered in something dark and wet. Mama was gonna be cross if he left those clothes lying around the house.

"Well, well," he said, wiping the back of his hand across his forehead and leaving a streak. "What y'all havin' over here?"

Jesse cringed as Papa tousled his hair. He was too old for that, and besides, Papa's hands were dirty. He tried to run his fingers through his curls, but they caught on something sticky. Mama would have to brush out the snarls if he'd gotten syrup in it somehow.

"Pancakes?" Papa said as Mama slid a plate in front of him. He nudged Jesse with his shoulder, his big white teeth shining through a bushy beard flecked with bits of meat. "I do love me some pancakes. Thanks, Mama."

Jesse giggled and pointed at Papa's beard. "It looks like you already ate."

"Oh?" Papa laughed his big, hearty laugh that always made Jesse laugh too. Growling like a bear, he snapped at Jesse's finger.

Jesse shrieked as he pulled back his hand then giggled some more. "You can't get me!"

Papa ran a napkin over his chin, barely cleaning it, then poured a half jug of syrup onto his towering stack of pancakes. Jesse wished he could eat as many pancakes as Papa when he got older.

"Who was it this time?" Mama asked.

"Oil company, I think. Maybe insurance… I don't know," Papa said, pancakes stuffing his cheeks.

"Eeee!" Jesse laughed. "Talking with your mouth full!" Even though he'd seen Mama do it a moment ago, he couldn't tease her about it. She wasn't funny about it like Papa, but she would join him in the teasing.

Papa swallowed and threw up his hands, little red snowflakes falling from his cuffs. "Ya got me."

But Mama wasn't laughing. "What we gonna do with the car?"

"I figure I'll take it apart and sell it down at ol' Leroy's. Should be worth sumptin, it being one of them fancy kinds with the computers."

"What in the hell do you know 'bout takin' apart a car?" Mama leaned toward Jesse and tapped her temple. "Your father… I love him, but sometimes, he don't know how to use his brain."

Jesse snorted and looked at Papa, wondering what he might say to that. But Papa just stuck out his tongue, which with the stuff on his chin was just about the funniest thing Jesse had ever seen, especially when Papa added his googly eyes.

Mama was a spoilsport, always the first to stop playing. "I'll take care of it." She nodded in the direction of the front yard. "What are you going to do with... the rest?"

"I was thinking same thing we did with them hikers last winter." He lowered his head and stared at his breakfast.

Jesse wondered if Papa was sad. He rarely saw Papa sad, and he never didn't eat his food. He didn't remember any hikers, but he did remember last winter having been a good hunting season and good eating.

Papa tugged his beard. "It's not like we ain't got no signs, Loretta. It's their own damn fault."

"Ronald Hank Williams Foster! Don't you be cussin' in front of the boy."

Papa turned to Jesse, his mouth and eyes opened wide like he was scared of Mama, but Papa wasn't really scared of nothing. Jesse stuck his tongue out before his father could, and he and Papa started laughing all over again.

"Boys will be boys," Mama said, crossing her arms and shaking her head. But the corner of her mouth twitched, and Jesse knew she was trying not to smile.

She sighed. "All right. Salt and ration it, but no jerky this time. Gave me the sh... the poops like you wouldn't believe."

"Poops!" Jesse couldn't think of a funnier word. Mama was being really funny that day. Not Papa funny, but—

"So how you feel 'bout drivin'?"

Jesse looked at Papa, but both Papa and Mama were staring at him. He gasped. "Me? We're getting a car?"

"We're *borrowing* one," Mama said. "It's out front. But you'll have to sit on my lap. Don't think them scrawny little legs of yours are gonna reach the pedals."

Jesse wasn't keen on sitting on Mama's lap—he was a big boy, and big boys don't do that—but if it meant he got to drive an honest-to-God automobile, he'd skin the rats in the crawlspace for a whole month.

"Go on, then," Mama said, shooing him. "Put on your suit, and we'll drive on down to the lake for a swim."

Jesse stood and froze, staring at his half-eaten breakfast. He pouted. "But... I didn't finish."

"It's okay, this time. Looks like Papa's gone and caught us some extra provisions."

Jesse didn't know what *provisions* meant, but he smiled at Papa all the same. He turned to leave.

"Hold it, mister." Mama squinted at him. "Plate?"

"Oh, yeah." Jesse picked up his dish and headed over to the wash basin, scraping the leftovers into the raccoon trap before scrubbing the plate clean. It took him longer than usual because the syrup didn't want to come off. When it was finally clean, he went inside, got changed, and ran back outside.

His parents were no longer at the picnic table. He hurried around front, where Papa was skinning some kind of animal that didn't look so right on account of it not having that much fur. He hoped it wasn't sick, 'cause then it might give them the AIDS. But he trusted Papa, who was such a good hunter. He wanted to be just like Papa someday.

When he moved closer, a honk scared the bajeebies out of him. Mama sat behind the wheel of their brand new, honest-to-God automobile. "Times a' wastin'."

Jesse sprinted for the front seat, filled with love for Mama and Papa, thinking he must have the bestest parents in the world.

ELEANOR

Father Stuart McKenzie had been forgotten. His father was a minister, as his father's father had been before him, serving God while their Church of England broke further away from the tenets of Rome. Stuart shocked his family and friends when he'd converted to Catholicism, and they had shunned him for it, even though they professed to worship the same God Almighty that he did.

And so God had become his only friend. Sent away to a small, West Sussex church in a largely Protestant district, Stuart passed the time writing sermons for the two or three folks who would listen. Even on the weekends when no one attended his mass, he diligently provided his sermons, reasoning that duty required it of him. Mass was an excuse to escape his tiny chamber, a dreary space furnished with nothing but a desk, a dresser, his bed, and a few old books, his apathetic companions through the quiet hours of night.

His room sat above the nave. Across the hall was a larger room, with greater space offering greater comfort but requiring less humility. It was grand compared to his confining quarters but still modest by most standards, adorned only with a bed, a dresser, and a desk, much like his. A window was the room's only source of light. It looked out to the garden below, where Stuart alone toiled. It was a room without a soul, barren of life. He had never entered it, not until Eleanor arrived at his door.

Since the day he'd found the baby on his threshold, Stuart had loved her. At first, he didn't know why he loved her, when all those who should have loved her did not. He didn't know who had placed her there, discarding her without regard for the life it would impact. He wondered if he loved her because she was a gift from God; or perhaps she'd been sent to test him, an offer to prove himself worthy of the Kingdom. More likely, though, Stuart loved her because, like him, she was all alone.

Yes, that was closer to the truth. Stuart loved her because no one else would, *and* because she was all he had to love.

Stuart had found the child, newly born and starving, outside his tiny parish church's arched wooden doors. He'd opened them expecting to find his delivered groceries but instead found her sitting in a milk pail. Horrified by her appearance, Stuart nearly retreated, slinking back behind the door. He soon realized that his instant rejection of an innocent child was far more horrifying. Muffled sobs emitted from the steps outside.

He wondered how many people had cast the little girl aside and was ashamed that he'd almost been just like them. His hands hesitant, his mind unsure, Stuart lifted the pail and carried the baby into the warmth of his church and his heart.

She hadn't so much as a blanket to warm her. Naked and abandoned, the child persevered against incredible odds, particularly given her extreme deformities. A young man at the time, Stuart had declared it a miracle and God's wish for him to take in the child.

Someone had tied a string around her ankle. Affixed to it was a note that read *Eleanor R.* Stuart considered that the name might be a pseudonym, but he liked it all the same. Whatever else there was of Eleanor's origins had been buried along with her real name.

That was fifteen years ago. Since then, Stuart had done the best he could by Eleanor. He bled dry his meager congregation to help raise her, and when that wasn't enough, he begged from merchants and passers-by and any charitable sorts he could find, all under the guise of raising money for the church. He sacrificed his own well-being and personal comforts for a baby girl who was not kin. All the while, he kept her a secret, knowing too well how intolerant the world could be.

Now, fifteen wonderful years later—happy years, he liked to think, for both of them—the world still was not ready for Eleanor. It would never accept her.

With a heavy sigh, thinking himself more a jailor than a father, Stuart knocked then opened the door to her chamber. She stood in front of her bed, her back toward the door.

"What mask is it today, Eleanor?"

She turned and faced him. A mask made of stiffened linen, bleached to a fine white, covered her face, a broad smile stretching across it. Stuart had picked up the twin masks of comedy and tragedy on a trip to Greece long before he had parenting responsibilities. Leather straps held the mask in place, hooked into one of the ridges lining the back of her head.

Once, Stuart had given her a whole slew of masks, their expressions marking a full range of human emotion, but variety had led to confusion, and Stuart had decided to simplify things by ridding them of too many options. Only the original two masks remained: one happy face and one sad. Eleanor always wore one of the two. She kept them on a small table by the door and would put one on whenever she heard him coming up the stairs. She wore them always; Stuart hadn't seen her true face in many years.

Not that her face was something he could ever forget.

He struggled with the memory then remembered his company. A sweet girl, fair-natured Eleanor was undeserving of scorn or ridicule, especially from he who loved her. And when she spun around, all doubt and misgivings vanished. He had raised a wonderful child.

Stuart beamed at the sight of Eleanor in her happy mask. He took her in. Even dressed in a dull brown frock, Eleanor might have passed for a beauty if not for her patchwork, matted hair, her misshapen cranium, and that abomination that could not rightfully be called her face because it wasn't a face at all. *That* hid behind her masks, and Stuart was thankful for it. He had offered her several wigs to hide her remaining deformities, but Eleanor never took to any of them.

For a child who had been given no chance, who by all rights should have died at birth from any number of complications if not from her abandonment, Eleanor had sprouted and grown strong. Tall and lithe like a dancer, she moved with grace, confident in her steps even though she was blind.

She walked a straight line up to Stuart and threw her arms around him. The bag of groceries he carried beneath his arm crinkled. With his free hand, he pulled her closer. Her body seemed to complement his. Her breasts heaved against his chest.

When did you become a woman? She had grown so much under his watchful eye. Her appearance suggested that Eleanor had come of age, but she was still a child in so many ways. She needed him, and he needed her.

Stuart stared into the empty white eyes of her mask. They, too, were smiling. He hoped that Eleanor was truly smiling behind them, that the life he had provided her was enough and would always be so.

"Give me a moment, dear. Let me put these groceries down." He gently pushed her away, but she resisted and snuggled in closer. He gave in. "Are you hungry? I've brought apples, the kind you like best."

Eleanor's hand slid gently along his side, found the grocery bag, and reached inside. When she withdrew her hand, it was holding a plump red apple. Stuart had no doubt that, somehow, she had plucked the finest specimen from the bag. She always did.

"Would you like me to cut it up for you?"

She cocked her head then scurried into a corner like a dog that thinks its master might take back the treat it had been given. She turned her back to Stuart, her custom when she ate.

It was another of Eleanor's quirks for which Stuart was thankful. He could never get used to that slit down the front of her neck and how it opened into a cavern when she ate. Somewhere in that hole were teeth and only God knew what else. Eleanor had nearly died the first week in his care before Stuart could summon the nerve to stick a bottle in that hole and see if it would take milk. He shuddered whenever he thought about it.

But Stuart never revealed his repulsion. Eleanor couldn't see it on his face, and he was careful to never let her hear it. He wondered why she hid herself. How could she, a girl who had spent her entire life limited to a single room in the care of one who cherished her, know shame?

Stuart suspected, though he could not understand how, that Eleanor was tuned in to his emotions. It was almost as if she could sense what he was feeling.

Always.

The face she chose that day and every other day mimicked his mood.

Stuart tried his best to be happy as much as possible, for her sake. Eleanor had already suffered her fair share of misfortune.

"What shall I read you tonight?" he asked when she'd finished her apple, core and all. "The Good Book?"

Eleanor faced him. Juice ran down the front of her frock. The mask stared blankly.

Stuart laughed. "I didn't think so. How about Homer?"

Nothing.

"Dickens? Yeats?"

Eleanor balled up her fists and straightened her arms by her sides. She snapped her head left and right and tapped her foot. Stuart was teasing her now, and she knew it.

He laughed. "Okay. How about Chaucer? Shelley?"

Eleanor rose up on her toes. Stuart didn't believe the Catholic Church approved of either author, but Eleanor seemed to like them. Her head cocked to the side. He knew he had piqued her interest, but she hadn't given him a solid sign of approval.

"Dumas?" Stuart paused, awaiting her reaction but saw none. He sighed. He knew what she wanted. "Swift?"

Eleanor clapped and nodded repeatedly. Stuart figured that was as sure a sign of approval as any.

"Swift it is. One of these days, I hope I come to understand your fascination with Gulliver and all those silly Lilliputian fellows."

Eleanor traced the wide smile on her mask with her finger. A gurgle rose from her throat.

"What? Lilliputians? They make you smile?"

Eleanor nodded. She crouched and hovered her hand over the floor.

"Yes, I know. They're small."

Eleanor sprang up. She grabbed the sides of her dress and twirled.

Stuart couldn't help but laugh. Eleanor was good company. She filled all his empty hours, staved off the voracious beast that was loneliness, a constant predator in the life he'd chosen. A twinge of guilt came with the selfish thought. He hoped he offered Eleanor some comfort in return.

And what will she do after I'm gone? Stuart forced the question out of his mind. For now, Eleanor seemed happy. They'd face tomorrow when tomorrow came.

"Okay, silly," he said. "Get cleaned up. Dinner will be in one hour, if you didn't just go and spoil it. Afterward, we'll go visit those Lilliputians you like so much."

Eleanor ran to the closet and picked out her nicest dress, a blue one that Stuart had bought her for her thirteenth birthday. It was too big for her then, but she hadn't stopped growing. The last time she wore it, Eleanor had filled it out nicely.

With her mask on, it was sometimes easy to pretend she was pretty. The hole in her neck was barely visible when she closed it. As he looked upon Eleanor, Stuart couldn't help but feel the sin of pride. He had done right by her. He had done right by God.

§

When the hour had passed, Stuart carried Eleanor's dinner—porridge and a bit of leftover lamb from Sunday's supper—up to her room. He set the tray down and knocked on the door, giving her time to make herself decent before entering.

When he opened the door, he jumped, startled to see Eleanor standing just inside it. She wore her blue dress. It clung to her curves, revealing her shapeliness, except where the neckline had been ravaged. Shreds of fabric hung down over her breasts, baring her cleavage.

She wore her sad face.

Stuart frowned. He entered the room and placed the tray on her nightstand then returned to where Eleanor stood fidgeting. He took her hands in his. "What's wrong, dear?"

Eleanor pinched the front of her dress and pulled it. Her chin dropped, and she shuffled her feet.

"Too tight?"

Eleanor nodded slowly.

"Couldn't breathe?"

Again, she nodded.

"Well, there's nothing to be done for it," Stuart said. He released her hands and slapped his own together. "We will just have to buy you a new dress."

Eleanor cocked her head at that then fell against him, squeezing him tightly. Stuart's fingers drew soothing circles on her back. After a moment, she slipped from the embrace and ran toward the door. She picked up her happy face then paused.

"Don't worry. I won't look."

And Stuart didn't. He turned away, wanting to believe, wanting to deceive himself that Eleanor was beautiful lest she ever sense from him otherwise.

"You will always be beautiful to me," he muttered. "God's little miracle."

Her happy face on, Eleanor clapped and skipped back over to him. She started to pull her dress over her head, raising the hem high enough for Stuart to glimpse the milky skin of her thigh. He stopped her.

"Wait a moment. I'm still here, silly goose. Your dinner is on the nightstand. When you're finished, if it pleases you, change into your nightgown and hop into bed. I have to work on next weekend's sermon. I will return with Gulliver as soon as I've finished."

Eleanor nodded and raised her head. She sniffed at the air and bee-lined toward her dinner, but she waited for Stuart to leave before eating. He said goodbye and returned to his room to pen his next homily.

After an hour, Stuart stared down at a blank sheet of paper. He couldn't wipe the image of Eleanor in her blue dress from his mind.

§

Stuart finished reading the last word of the Book of Genesis then stood to stretch. He slid a finger along the novels on his shelf until he came across a ragged tome. *Hello, Gulliver.* Eleanor's fondness for the story reassured him. Her body might be growing up, but Eleanor still had the mind and heart of a child.

With the book and a candle in hand, he crossed the hallway to her room. He found her sitting up in bed, waiting in the dark for him. He wondered if she'd been sitting like that since he had left her. She had dolls and toys enough but had outgrown most of them. What did she do when he left her alone?

He shook his head and paused before stepping into the room. Again, he wished there was more of a life he could offer her. Her room was all she knew, all she would ever know, beyond what he read to her in his paltry collection of books. *I will have to ask for more donations soon.*

But the worlds in his books were not real. The world outside her window was, and it would destroy Eleanor if given the chance. Out there, happy endings were things the less privileged could only read about. And with her deformities, Eleanor would end up a toy for the damned.

People fear and hate what they do not understand. Could Stuart blame them? He had feared her once too.

He donned a shaky smile and shed the weight from his shoulders. Eleanor clapped as he approached. She slid over on the bed and patted the mattress, offering him a place to sit. Stuart settled in next to her for what would likely be a marathon journey through Swift's work, skipping certain parts he knew would upset her. Eleanor hated when he stopped before the story was complete. He broke the binding and began to read.

Midway through the sixth chapter of Gulliver's exotic journey, a strange purring sound emanated from Eleanor. She had long ago given up on sitting, her head sunk deep into her pillow. At first, Stuart thought she was snoring. He closed the book and rose quietly. That's when he noticed her hand making small circular motions beneath the sheet.

"Eleanor!" Stuart gasped. This was something new, something he had never considered. His face must have spanned every shade of red. He was unprepared. "Are you... You can't do that."

Eleanor didn't stop. Her body and mind seemed locked in a rhythmic trance in tune with the motion of her hand. Her purring turned to moaning. Embarrassed and not knowing what else to do, Stuart ran from the room.

§

Over the next several days, Stuart couldn't shake Eleanor from his thoughts, his mind endlessly replaying her sinful behavior. Such thoughts were unbecoming of any man, let alone a priest and the girl's guardian.

He felt filthy, vile, lowly. He kept his distance from Eleanor, leaving her to her own devices except to deliver her daily meals. Stuart had never been with a woman, and these ungodly visions ruminating in his brain filled him with shame and disgust. He prayed to God every hour on the hour for forgiveness.

Day in and day out, Eleanor wore her sad mask. Did she understand why he kept away? She pawed at Stuart during each brief visit, hugged him tightly, clung to him so that he wouldn't leave her. She'd worn a different dress each time he had brought her a meal. He could tell she was trying desperately to find the one that would please him, make him stay, convince him that she was still beautiful.

Stuart knew all this because he knew Eleanor. Her sadness made him weep. His heart ached with hers. *It isn't your fault, Eleanor.* He wanted to tell her as much, but how could he explain to her the kind of thoughts that were festering inside him, the feelings they stirred? They were unnatural, ungodly even. If he tried to explain them to her, how would she ever be able to love him again?

At last, he broke down and went to her with wet cheeks. "You know why I have stopped reading to you, don't you?"

Eleanor lowered her chin. The sad, melodramatic frown of her mask, together with the single tear forever emblazoned on its cheek, somehow didn't seem melodramatic at all. It fit Eleanor perfectly. It matched what he felt.

"Well?"

She nodded slowly.

"Do you promise never to do it again?"

She nodded.

"Very well," he said. "I'm sorry we did not have this talk sooner. I was… uncomfortable, and I apologize for making you wait and even more so for making you sad. I will come back later and read to you tonight, something other than Swift. Would that please you?"

Eleanor dropped down to her knees and wrapped her arms around Stuart's leg. She rubbed the side of her head, a smooth surface where an ear should have been but where only an open cavern existed, against his thigh.

Stuart stiffened. "Get up." He ripped himself free and stormed out the door, slamming it behind him and no doubt leaving her to contemplate what she had done wrong.

But he kept his promise. That night, he returned to Eleanor's room with a book he selected at random, something by Sophocles. He read, and she listened, and for the moment, they were content. Eleanor even wore her happy face again.

He returned to his room, relieved. Things seemed to be returning to normal—on the surface. But a fire burned within Stuart that no amount of prayer could extinguish. That didn't stop him from trying. He got on his knees and prayed that the Devil would not tempt him again.

His prayers failed him. Temptation had taken residence. It slept across the hall.

§

Months passed. Stuart went about his routine as he always had. But something wasn't right. Life had been difficult, solitary before, but now all joy had left it. The empty space Eleanor had filled had sprung a leak. The contents of his mind and soul spiraled in a whirlpool of doubt and depression. She was still with him the same as she had been, but Stuart had changed, and he didn't know how to change back. So instead, he suppressed his urges toward Eleanor by keeping her at arm's length. The intimacy they once shared had broken.

She must have sensed something was wrong. Though she wore her happy face, it no longer seemed genuine, at odds with body language she'd quickly correct, but not before Stuart took notice. Clinging her arms around her knees while he read, sleeping with a doll again, turning away each time Stuart looked at her with sadness in his heart—Eleanor couldn't hide her feelings from him. At first, Stuart had thought he was only projecting his inner turmoil upon her. But when he visited her this time, Eleanor had on the same frock she'd been wearing for the last three days. Her hygiene suffered, too. A foul odor, faint but persistent like a rotting carcass covered in lye, filled her room. She'd lost her girlish bounce; her energy had gone flat.

"I brought you your favorite," Stuart said, desperate to lessen the rift that had grown between them. He smiled, but his brow furrowed with worry. "It wasn't easy to get them. They're out of season."

Eleanor took two quick steps toward Stuart, then halted. She cocked her head and waited.

"It's okay."

She skulked toward him and reached out her hand. Stuart placed an apple in it.

"Shall I cut it up for you?"

Eleanor started to turn but pounced back to his side and latched onto his arm. Stuart jumped but did not pull away. She followed the length of his arm down to his hand, where he held a long, serrated kitchen knife with a dull but effective point.

She snatched it from him.

"Now be careful with that—"

Eleanor jabbed the knife into the apple near its base and made a horizontal slit through its peel. The apple oozed, bleeding juices from an open wound. Above the line, she dug out two tiny pits roughly level to one another. Then she stabbed the knife at Stuart's face.

He stepped back. He gasped but was not afraid. He didn't believe Eleanor was trying to harm him, but he didn't immediately understand the message she was trying to convey either. Then it struck him.

"What is it, Eleanor? You gave the apple a face?'

She nodded. She placed the knife and the apple atop her dresser and approached him, standing closer than they had been for months. He could feel the heat of her body against his, the warmth of her breasts and the heart beating behind them. Her breath tickled the hairs on his neck. The sweet scent of ripe fruit entered his nose as her fingers danced across the contours of his face.

"Is it my face, Eleanor? Is that apple supposed to be me?"

Eleanor shook her head and stomped a foot. She poked Stuart's cheek, then ran her fingers across the lines of her mask.

"Eleanor." The word came out as a plea—not to ask the question she had asked too many times before, each time causing Stuart more pain than the last. Some questions were better left unanswered. Others, like this one, couldn't be answered.

She wanted to know why he had a face and she didn't.

His voice fell to a hush. "We've been through this, dear." As a child, she had spent hours studying his face, comparing it to her own. She wanted to know why he had a voice and she could only sputter. Ears, nose, eyes: all had been matters that spurred her curiosity. But the answers Stuart had given never seemed to satisfy her.

How does she know that she is the oddity? Maybe I should never have given her the masks.

Eleanor grabbed her mask beneath the chin. The action startled Stuart from his memories and sent his heart racing.

"Leave it on!" he shouted more sternly than he had intended. Eleanor slid her fingers beneath the mask, groping at the disfigurement behind it. Again, she went to take it off.

"Please," Stuart said, grabbing her wrists. "You are stunning with your happy face on. I want to see you happy, always." He faked a smile, not sure if he was trying to reassure himself or the other who could not see it.

Eleanor twisted from his grip but made no further attempt to remove the mask. A sound akin to a growl emitted from her throat. She pushed past Stuart and stamped her way to the table beside her bedroom door. With her back to Stuart, she ripped the mask from her face and threw it against the wall. She replaced it with her sad face.

"Eleanor, I—"

She stormed past him again, got into her bed, and hid beneath the covers, cradling her knees. He walked up to her bed and placed his hand on her back, trying to soothe her. She scooted away.

Stuart winced. A hollow pain stabbed at his stomach. His sadness swallowed him, commanded him to retreat. "I will leave you alone, then." His voice fell quiet. "I'm sorry, Eleanor."

He turned and plodded out of her room. His head hung low, he headed down to the sanctuary, where he would pray for God to deliver her the peace he could not.

§

The moon was descending when Stuart finally made his way back upstairs to his room. He stopped at Eleanor's door to check in on her. Her door was open a crack. Had he left it that way earlier? He couldn't recall. Eleanor never left her room, so it seemed the most likely conclusion.

A low moaning came from inside the room. *I hope she hasn't injured herself.* He moved in closer. He would just have a peek to make sure she was okay.

His eyes widened as he spotted Eleanor atop her bed. Her nightgown circled her waist, everything beneath it exposed. She writhed as if she were feverish, her hand working between her legs with dizzying speed as her moaning intensified.

Stuart began to sweat. His mouth filled with saliva, and he choked it down. He felt his penis stiffening before his mind could register the error in its ways. As he leaned closer, the floorboard creaked with his shifting weight.

All went quiet inside Eleanor's room. Ashamed, he stepped back, and the floor creaked again. He froze, afraid to make even the slightest movement that would alert her to his peeping, his degradation.

After a moment, the moaning resumed. The sin took hold of him. Stuart wanted to walk away but instead found himself leaning in for a second look. He peeked through the crack, unable to resist the perversion.

He could see Eleanor's bed, but she wasn't in it. "Where are you?" he mouthed, barely aware that his hand was rubbing the front of his slacks.

He shrieked when Eleanor sprang out of the darkness, her sad face appearing in the opening inches from his. He fell backward onto his buttocks. She stared at him with false eyes before slamming the door shut.

His face burned with humiliation. Stuart gathered himself and wormed his way into his room. He crawled into bed and lay in silence until his heart and breathing slowed. How he hated himself.

He closed his eyes, begging sleep to come. When at last it did, his dreams were filled with her.

§

Stuart lurched up in bed, sweating profusely. His sheets and pillow were damp. His eyes began to focus. Eleanor's happy mask stared him in the face. Her hand was stroking his penis.

"Eleanor, you must return to bed," he squeaked. "This instant!"

Eleanor didn't listen. She pushed his shoulders down against the mattress then returned to his pelvis. Stuart swelled inside her hands—hands that shouldn't have been capable of the sins they were committing, that shouldn't have had the skill they seemed to possess. Hands he lacked the strength to remove. They guided his penis inside her.

"Forgive me," Stuart cried and fell victim to her rapture, submitted to his lust.

He climaxed soon after. Eleanor's head rolled back. Her body glistened with sweat in the starlight pouring in through the window. A strange cooing resonated from the hole in her throat as she swayed in time to music only she could hear.

Stuart's pubis and inner thighs were drenched with what he assumed to have been the results of her orgasm. He had never had sex before, but he didn't think it was supposed to be that wet. Concern stifled the guilt blossoming in his mind. For a moment, his thoughts were only on the wetness. He reached between his legs. The liquid he found there was thick and warm.

It felt like blood.

Stuart scrambled out from beneath Eleanor and kicked the sheets away from him. Huddled against his headboard, he inspected his upper legs and saw that they were stained dark. He checked for wounds but saw none. The blood wasn't his.

Eleanor moved closer. She reached for his flaccid penis, perhaps not understanding why they had stopped. Despite it all, despite the fact that he had just desecrated every vow he held sacred—the vows of his church, the vows of his morality, the vows of a *father*—a part of Stuart craved more. He felt himself becoming aroused again. He pushed Eleanor away.

Perhaps too fiercely.

She fell off the bed, gasping through the hole in her neck. Had he hurt her? No, not even discouraged her. She rose to her knees, a supplicant reaching out her arms, inviting Stuart into them.

"Get away from me, you demon! You... you... *whore!*"

Eleanor cocked her head, and he could see his words were sinking in. She stood, trembling, and reached for the wall, then felt her way back to her room. If she could have cried, Stuart had no doubt she would have.

God knew he wanted to. But at that moment, he was sure God wanted nothing to do with him.

He walked to his door and closed and locked it. *What have I done? God forgive me, what have I done?*

§

The sun arched high in the sky before Stuart got out of bed the next morning. Dry blood caked his pajamas, flaked off his skin. In the daylight, he could see that it was a lot of blood, more than he imagined could come from a broken hymen. He wondered if Eleanor was menstruating. More blood, still wet where it was at its thickest, painted the sheets. No amount of soap and water would ever wash that blood away. How could she have pushed herself on him like she had?

No, what happened could not be pinned on Eleanor. It was *his* fault. He had been weak. He knew the connection he and Eleanor shared, yet he'd failed to protect her from passion's poisonous fruit. He had failed to protect her from him.

And worst of all, Stuart had blamed Eleanor for it.

The first thing he needed to do was clean himself up. The second thing, a close second: apologize to Eleanor. After that, he would have to begin the long, arduous process of making himself right again with the girl and the Lord.

After washing and donning a fresh shirt and trousers—he left his collar atop his dresser—Stuart crossed the hall toward her room. *I'm a fool. She's just a girl. I've abused her, her trust and the sanctity of our relationship.*

"How do I make her understand that this is all my fault?" Stuart asked the question to an empty hallway, hoping God would see fit to place the answer in his mind.

Letting out a deep breath, he raised his hand to knock on Eleanor's door. He stopped when he saw that it was cracked open. This time, he did not peek through the crack.

"Eleanor? It's me. I've come to apologize." When she did not appear, he called again. "Eleanor?" He placed his hand flat against the door. "I'm coming in, Eleanor."

Stuart pushed open the door. The room was in shambles. Eleanor's dresser lay flat across the floor. The contents of her closet were strewn everywhere. She must have made considerable noise causing the disarray. How had he slept through it?

Stuart scanned the room but saw no sign of Eleanor. A soft whimper came from the corner, a spot blockaded on three sides by two walls and Eleanor's bed. That was where he found her.

Her appearance matched that of the room, a disheveled mess. She sat with her back against the wall and her knees tucked against her breasts, her head buried between them. When Stuart approached, she pulled her legs in tighter.

Eleanor appeared to have been in that corner for some time. She still wore her happy face, though it no longer suited her. Blood smeared across its white surface, turning its exuberant grin into something maniacal. Her hands were covered in blood. Her nightgown looked as if it belonged to the victim of a homicide. Blood stained it everywhere, not just between her legs.

Stuart began to weep and rushed to her side. He paused when he saw the knife.

"Where did you get that?"

Eleanor held a long, serrated kitchen knife in her right hand. The blade was red, with little chunks of meat stuck in its grooves. She must have had the knife for several days, weeks even. Stuart could not recall the last time they had red meat.

With her left hand, Eleanor reached behind her back, groping for something hidden there. She pulled out the apple he had given her yesterday and rolled it at his feet. Its carved face stared up at Stuart.

"Here," he said, reaching for her. Eleanor scurried back until she collided with the wall. *He* had made her like this. *He* had to fix it. A smile as phony as the one she wore fought to hold up his cheeks. "Let me help you up. We'll get you and this place cleaned up in no time." Even as he filled her ears with calming words, Stuart knew there were some stains he couldn't wash away.

Eleanor shrank deeper into the corner. She slashed at the air between them with her knife. It was a warning, not meant to cut. Stuart heeded it.

Maintaining a safe distance, he tried to pacify her. Tears fell from his eyes. "I'm sorry, Eleanor. Everything that has happened, all of it... it's my fault. You did nothing wrong. I was..." The words caught in his throat. He pressed on. "I was terrible to you. I have wronged you in so many ways I don't know if I will ever be able to make them right. But I promise you, I'll never stop trying."

Stuart shook and sobbed, fell to his knees. Snot bubbled out of his nose. The backs of his hands rested upon the floor, palms upward, begging forgiveness. From God. From Eleanor. "I am sorry, truly sorry."

Eleanor cocked her head. *She's listening, at least. Oh, thank God. It's a start.* He wiped his nose with his sleeve and stood. "Let's get you cleaned up, dear. Afterward, I will read you *Gulliver's Travels*, and we can eat apples, all the apples you want, with the Lilliputians."

Eleanor sat still for a moment then carefully rose to her feet. Stuart offered his hand. She fumbled in the air until she found it. Her other hand dropped the knife onto her bed.

Stuart pulled her into his arms and held her close. She smelled of old sweat and older blood. He didn't care. Tears filled his eyes. "I'm sorry," he repeated over and over again, smothering the top of her head with kisses. "I never meant to hurt you. I never want to hurt you again."

Eleanor rested her head upon his shoulder. For a while, they stood, holding each other, Stuart never wanting to let her go. He loved her, he knew, in all ways.

But there was only one right way.

Her hand slid down his chest. It slipped down the front of his trousers.

Stuart pushed her gently away, a softer rejection this time. "We can't, Eleanor. It's not right. Do you understand that? It would damn us both."

The whimper Stuart had heard when he had entered her room returned. It came from Eleanor, though he had difficulty believing it. Her purrs, her moans, and now this sound were all new to Stuart. She reached for his crotch again. Stuart stepped back.

He straightened. "Eleanor, we can't. I was wrong to permit it the first time. In my weakness, I failed you. I won't fail you again. I'm sorry."

Eleanor grunted. She pointed to her mask. The hole in her neck opened wide. "Boot."

Stuart's mouth dropped open. He was stunned, speechless. Eleanor had made a sound, and he was certain she was trying to speak. "Boot?" He had no idea what it meant, but the joy he felt at the possibility of Eleanor forming her first word made him weep.

"Did you just speak?" Stuart laughed, overwhelmed by the moment. He grabbed her shoulders and pulled her close. "Maybe God has not yet forgotten us. Praise be to our Lord!"

"Boot," Eleanor repeated, a sense of urgency in the way she said it. She pulled away. "Boot." She stomped her foot. A hiss followed by a gurgle spouted from her neck opening. Was she trying to form more words? How long had she been practicing in secret?

"Fell," she said at last.

"Fell? Boot fell?" Stuart stroked his chin. "Are you asking me if I think you are beautiful?"

She nodded and placed a finger on her mask.

"Of course I think you are beautiful. You know that."

Eleanor stomped her feet. A growl emitted from her throat, and she tossed her head frantically left and right. Her fingers walked up Stuart's neck to his chin. They spread wide, curled and dug into his skin. With his face in her hand, Eleanor shook him. When she let go, she did the same to her linen mask.

"Boot... fell?"

Stuart thought he understood. She showed a lot of courage asking him what she was asking. She must have known the answer. Stuart hadn't the heart to say it. Hers was the one question that made him dishonest.

"I don't know how to answer—"

"Boot... fell!" Eleanor growled. She pounded her fist against his chest and pointed to her mask. "Boot... fell?"

"It's a mask, Eleanor. You are beautiful in here." Stuart touched her above her bosom. "And we are all beautiful in the eyes of our Maker."

A stinging ache ran through his cheek. He yelped more in surprise than in pain. He couldn't believe Eleanor had slapped him.

"Boot... fell? Boot... fell? Boot fell, boot fell." The words were coming easier for her, and she began to chant them, all the while waving her hand at her mask. Spittle splashed from her neck, her voice becoming wet and slithery.

"No," Stuart said. He looked away. "Your mask is not beautiful."

Eleanor clapped. For some odd reason, the answer seemed to please her. She smoothed her dress with her hands and threw her shoulders back, standing tall and proud.

Before Stuart could protest, she tore off her mask. "Boot fell?"

Stuart yelped. He bit down on his knuckle to stifle a scream. His Adam's apple lodged in his throat, and his eyes widened in terror.

"My God, Eleanor. What have you done?"

Eleanor tried to speak. A steady stream of mucus-like plasma oozed from the hole on her neck. It didn't stop until Eleanor said the word she had worked so hard to say. "Fess."

She ran her fingers down her face. Where Stuart remembered a smooth, vacant surface resembling the shell of a brown egg, marked only by two small black circles he had assumed were nostrils, a long gash ran horizontal across a gore-splattered canvas. Pink tendrils of flesh and muscle hung from the carved canyon's ceiling like bats in a cave. Eleanor had removed a section of her face that might have resembled a slice of melon. Stuart couldn't be sure. He didn't know what had happened to that excised flesh, and he didn't want to know.

Above her nostrils were two more incisions, not exactly evenly spaced, but close. *Eyes.* The contents of Stuart's stomach rumbled. *She made eyes.* One was slightly higher than the other, tilted at an entirely wrong angle. Blood streaked down from all three wounds.

"Boot... fell?"

LOST WORLD

Do you remember when I found you? I remember.

The heat melted the air, our breaths thick and cloying yet salty to the tongue, our clothes soaked through, bodies shedding water faster than we could replenish—never drying, freezing us to the bone at night but blissfully soothing the bites. I don't recall it having rained even once—a funny thing for a rainforest—and perhaps that was for the better. The lush, endless foliage offered plenty of shade and shelter, but the sun nearly killed us nonetheless, baking us in chiminea of teak, rubber, and banana; and those damned stranglers, always reaching with clawed fingers to trip, club, or tear: the sum of all flora weaving a canopy dome over a lost world.

And that's what it was, wasn't it? A rich and dangerous Eden, with cathedral figs host to a congregation of species having no claim to this hemisphere or this era except perhaps enslaved in amber, harkening back to a day when all land was one, and water swallowed the rest. If only Conan Doyle could have seen it… his vision a reality, a place like no other on earth, lost to time and wholly uncivilized, at least by sophisticated notions—Western notions, or Northwestern anyway, from which your neighboring peoples ought to borrow a page. Do they even understand the vast wealth of resources growing, thriving, and proliferating just outside their walls and under their feet? They certainly knew not what they had in you.

But those mosquitos… they were dreadful, weren't they? I'd never seen them so big. I thought Jenkins—he was the journalist who accompanied us, not that you would recall or comprehend—I thought for sure he would die from blood loss, the way those parasites coveted his taste. And their constant buzzing about the ears. God! You could even hear their slurping, their suckers as thick as straws.

Honestly, I don't know how you bore it. In that dreadful place, I suppose we might have faced worse terrors than swarming insects, but... your world... such a harsh place. We did you a favor, taking you away from there. I wonder if your trifling mind can fathom it or, at the least, accumulate some modicum of appreciation. There, you were in constant danger: countless hazards stiflingly close, so many horrors lurking just over your shoulder, prowling in the underbrush, or lying in wait at your feet.

Here, you only have me.

I suppose in simple things, a lack of understanding results in a failure to recognize threat or opportunity. You acted as if *I* were that which you should fear, fighting tooth and claw to escape what you no doubt perceived as capture, not knowing I could offer you culture and cultivation, or at least a life with only controlled and predetermined hardship, an existence superior to what you had in every way save, perhaps, the size of its bloodsuckers.

I see you now, watching me from your glass enclosure with your dark-pool eyes. And I talk as if you might answer, knowing full well you cannot. Still, in these late hours and with my increasing visits, I find more and more comfort in your company. For you are special, not just to me, but to mankind—a cottage industry unto yourself. Every part of you has limitless potential, from the strength in your muscles to the virility in your heart, the agelessness of your cells, and the antibodies in your blood. You are an answer to disease, to deterioration... maybe even to death itself! What might we accomplish as we unlock your secrets? As we begin to understand you?

You slide a long nail under your steel collar, wheezing as if it were too tight. And I remember what happened the last time someone fell for that trick; what happened to Sampson. A clever beast you are. But all beasts must be broken if they are to mingle in polite society.

Do you remember *how* I found you? I remember.

Traipsing through that dense brush, hacking a trail until our limbs ached and muscles fought against our wills to persevere, I thought our guide a meandering fool and us fools for following him. The superstitious lout often recounted folklore of no import to a *scientific* expedition, even stopping several times to offer prayers or pleas to you. I'm uncertain which, as his gibberish was hard to understand, but in the end, with enough cajoling, he saw things our way and fulfilled his purpose adequately. The simpleton probably idolized you until his dying breath, when you tore him to shreds, an admittedly unfortunate way to have found that which he sought.

And then, the chase was on, and what a chase it was! It's true, I didn't expect a fraction of the intelligence you showed in eluding us and have since shown. But it's not real intelligence, is it? Baser lifeforms often exhibit survival instincts that almost seem preternatural at times, and even the stupidest dog can learn a whole bag of tricks. Still… you continue to surprise.

But the locals… ha! What they thought of you! They called you a monster and a demon, revered you like a god while simultaneously shunning you for a devil. From the stories they told, passed down no doubt through generations of inbreeding and mutation in both people and lore, we half expected to find something akin to a chupacabra or some other fantastical nightmare. The ignorant fear what they do not understand. Who was it that said that? Tolstoy? Machiavelli? It'll come to me, I'm sure. The point is: those locals, as all yokels will, labeled wrongly that which they feared.

And I see you now, staring at me like you are, unthinking, unintelligent, unblinking eyes boring holes through mine. Your mouth curled in that perpetual scowl, I might be tempted to project the same ignorance upon you, but I am not afraid. Anthropomorphism, I believe it's called. A fang borne, just slipping over your lower lip as you rake your talons—always sharp no matter how many times we hammer them off—down the glass. You assert only an apex predator's posture—innate, not calculated, and wholly uncouth. Savage surely, but monstrous? No, I shouldn't be so daft to think so.

Still, my more fanciful thoughts sometimes turn to pondering how a creature like you, devoid of advanced cognitive processes, might view me. Am I your monster? Perhaps to you, our poking and prodding, the rougher treatment when you misbehave, may seem unkind, maybe even sinister. But that's only because you cannot comprehend the goals we hope to achieve from these slight misgivings at your expense or the benefit you— and more like you, God willing—could have to *our* way of life.

There I go, anthropomorphizing again. Contempt, and even the perception of mistreatment, require an intellect beyond your capacity. Through the carrot-and-stick approach, you've been taught appropriate and inappropriate behavior, and you have taken to it exemplarily. What strides we've made in domestication since your... feeding, for lack of a better word... on Lewis. The rod should not be spared, as it has been unparalleled as a teacher, so if I seem heavy handed, it is only to ameliorate the relationship for master and beast alike. Honestly, I don't know why I fret, as I'm sure any perceived cruelty is soon forgotten.

And yet I hear you now, those sounds you make, sometimes so rhythmic I'm almost fooled into believing them language. Much like a dog barks and a cat meows, it is, no doubt, a manner of communication, but the syntax and variables are so many and complex I sometimes feel as though you might be trying to speak to me. The idea is laughable, of course. What of consequence would an animal have to say to a man?

Still, a monster you most certainly are not. An animal only, though whether feline or primate or something wholly new, defying classification, we've thus far been unable to determine. Perhaps you are a distant cousin, if Darwin is to be believed, or an ancient mammalian ancestor who evolved along a uniquely divergent path. That is beyond my own expertise to decide.

I dare say, though, that not even the Neanderthal seemed quite so barbaric, so... so... primitive. I think back to the manner in which you dispatched Rogers and McHale when, after days of chase, O'Connell— that crack shot—felled you from your distant perch. Struck with enough tranquilizer to sedate an ox, you dropped the forty feet or so onto your hindquarters, the landing silent and graceful. At least two more darts hit you then, and you collapsed. I wonder now if you were only feigning unconsciousness to lure us closer or if your body had expelled the toxins at an extraordinary rate. Perhaps exuded through the pores, similar to how a shark expels urine through its skin? I must make a note to include this hypothesis in our testing...

But I digress. Do you remember how we proved our mastery over you? I remember.

As we moved in with your collar and chains, you were a wonder to behold. And you had us all fooled, didn't you? Your movements, lithe as a ballerina and faster than a cheetah, were nothing short of awe-inspiring. Before anyone could react, Rogers was on his knees, clutching his neck, blood spurting between his fingers. Beside him one second, twenty yards away the next, you moved in a blur, impossible to track. Many men fell, injured and disarmed, before the next round of darts finally hit you. Some men, like McHale, resorted to the use of actual bullets, and if I didn't know better, I might have thought you understood the graver threat they presented from the way you almost seemed to target them. Probably a reaction to the sound of the gunshots, I suppose.

Like an acrobat—and isn't it strange to continuously use such human description for something so clearly inhuman—you injured so many of our kind. And McHale, you had that poor sod disemboweled before the whole expedition opened fire. As you fell, your ebony skin and fur dotted with blood, I cried out, almost shed a tear—for *our* loss, you see, and the chances of advancement lost to the ages. *I* ran to you: *I,* your savior, and when I saw you yet had breath, wasted only a moment before clasping on your collar. The others rushed in with your wrist and ankle shackles as well as the bit, that brave soul Donahue tempting fate as he jammed it unceremoniously into your mouth.

Even then, it took six able-bodied men to drag you into your cage— poor Spriggens, stumbling in the effort, falling in with you. We could do nothing for the man as you decapitated him with a length of your chain, arterial spray coating your fur. Again, if I hadn't known better, I would have thought I saw you smile.

Despite the gore and viscera, the savagery of all that is you, what I saw in that moment—I'm somewhat ashamed to admit—was beauty. Like a panther stalking its prey in the cover of the brush, precise and deadly, there was a sense of artistry in your brutality, a grace in murder. Pure, unadulterated beauty.

I look at you now, and it's still all I see. You are far more enchanting than we might ever have imagined from the locals' tellings. Strange how they couldn't recall a single instance of your having harmed a human or threatened their way of life, wretched as it may be. Yet they spoke of you as if they should have always had their pitchforks at the ready. Unsophisticated brutes, every last one of them. Blind hate: that's all it was, really. That, and an unwillingness to understand promulgated by a history of apprehension.

Place the yoke on lesser folk, I always say. Beat pitchforks into plowshares, and let the enlightened class lead all to greener pastures. May those of indelible worth reap what the plebeians sow.

And what you sow. I wonder: what would you sow if I were to set you free? Would you return to the rainforest, return to squalor and boorishness, feeding only to survive when you might eat of our fruit while we take from yours?

Your calling is here now, to serve. To make the enlightened world whiter, safer from the darkness, from shadows within and without the mind.

I see you. To be sure, I see you now as I saw you then, and since, and always, with a growing tempo in my heart and unbridled yearning spawned in my own dark places. You stand naked and chained, broken yet undeniably magnificent, savage and raw, and it stirs within me my own savagery, a cyclonic force mounting inside me, threatening to render me asunder. Teeth gnashing, throat growling, blood boiling, feral lust. We are not so different in that regard.

Can you see inside me? Smell the pheromones I emit? Taste my flavor in the air?

Yes, I see you, and my desire reverts me to a baser form, spurs me forward even as logic dictates that your touch is damnation. But you are mine by right, as I have vested my claim to you, and you are mine for the taking.

And I see you now as I step closer. Your muscles relax, your expression softens. Have your fangs retracted? Your eyes taking me in—all of me— and I them, lost within those abyssal pools. Does the awareness behind your eyes have the same intrinsic needs? You sashay your hips, flit your tail, bewilder me with feminine guiles. An invitation? Your low purr more than suggests so. I know I shouldn't, but the desire—first a spark, an intrigue, no more—now a conflagration, your body torturing me nearer with its siren's song. I'm feverish, intoxicated, entranced, and powerless to resist.

Enchanted.

Not a very scientific state of mind, I concede, but what does science know of the dryness in my mouth, the clamminess of my palms, and the want that thrums through me? I half-heartedly struggle, make a show of propriety, appeal to my inner self for a return to reason and decency. But who am I to deny what I am at my core? What all men are, I should think.

My hand is over yours now. The sheet of glass between us is not enough to dispel the heat of your form so close to mine. I titter like a schoolboy, wage war in my thoughts, but in truth, I'm merely waiting for my mind to admit what my body knows even now: that I've already lost the fight. Like last night and the night before and all those several nights when my daring first upstaged my façade of incorruptibility.

I wonder if others might call me brave or rather foolish, irreverent and impious. Would they pretend to be my betters? But they cannot know, can never know, for they would covet and scheme for that which does not belong to them. That which is mine alone.

Do you remember the first time you let me approach? Let me pet you, adore you, coddle you like a master does his prized spaniel? Each time since, I've wanted more. I've taken more, and you showed your obedience. You are my prize. If only you could grasp the depth of my sentiment.

Your soft coos are calling me to the door. I unlock it, open it, then step inside, within reach. You wait for me to close the door behind me. Bound to the floor as you are, it is out of your reach, so I needn't lock it. I take another step inward, my hand out before me, and your lips pepper it with kisses. I think at night, in the quiet of the lab while all others are away, we are as we should be.

And tonight, I see you. You rub your cheek against my leg, lap gently at my hand, draw my fingers into your mouth. I remove the key from my pocket—the true key, not the imposter I brought in those first times to test your guile—and undo the shackles that bind your wrists and ankles. Your hands free, they roam over my body, exploring. Your tongue flitters against my neck.

My eyes roll back as the thrill of you consumes me. With a soft whimper, pouty lips, you pull back. The chain affixing your collar to the bolt encased in cement at your feet, having been drawn taut and now slackened, clamors against the concrete floor. The key to the clasp is in my hand, the same key for all your locks. You have not tried to take it from me, never have despite the fact that I am no match for your strength and speed. I'd be easy prey. But you see more in me than that, don't you?

As you have learned, you do as you are told. I tell you to sit. Before removing your collar, I consider the risks, it and myself being the only remaining bastions between you and freedom. I have never gone so far as to take off your collar, but it has become a trivial contrivance. This is the home you know now and the company you both require and, perchance, aspire to keep. You will obey the rules you must follow.

As if reading my thoughts, you nuzzle my thigh, that low hum so much like a purr rising anew from your throat. I am certain you have learned your new place in the world. You exist for me.

I unlock and remove your collar, and you spring upon me so quickly that I cry out, but the lab is otherwise empty, no one left to hear my troubles or provide aid. You mount me, thighs straddling my hips, claws pressing into my chest, not hard enough to break skin. I feel your every flex, the heat of your sex, and the wetness of your breath as your lips close in on mine.

Oh, how I've waited for this, for you to understand! And you do now, don't you, my pet? How you must improve my life if you wish to improve yours. This is it! This is the personal and scientific success I've been striving toward: to have you, to own you in every way.

To keep you.

As your eyes gaze into mine, their dark pools swirl—and behind them, the projected contempt returns. My blood curdles and retracts from my extremities. This is not the animal I have cowed. This is not the tempter to my sins.

This is something far more terrifying. The scowl has returned to your face, that one fang protruding over your lower lip. I tremble beneath you, order your retreat, but when I try to rise, you pin my shoulders to the floor.

Your mouth forms sounds, and I pick up a hint of archaic Portuguese or Spanish or some blended ancestor of them both. They come out with obvious struggle, broken and mumbled, your tongue obviously not accustomed to forming human words. You trip on the syllables, strain for the sound, but I cannot understand them.

Yet your meaning is clear.

All at once, I see you now and your intelligence—*real* intelligence, and more than the smile on a dog—laboring behind your eyes. The contempt you have for me is real, not projected or anthropomorphized. You are not my kind, you know not my ways, but you are worthy of deference, reverence, and compassion… of so much more than I've shown you. I *have* been a fool. A hollow pang stabs my belly. I begin to cry.

Through my sniffling, I try to apologize, try to explain, but even to me, my words sound empty. I can never undo what has been done. Things should have been different, I say. I didn't know, I say. Even if I could make you understand a language foreign to you, from a world forced upon you, how could I convince you that my intent was noble, that in subjugating you—in domesticating you—I did these things out of… what?

I thought you were no better than a beast, I whine. How could I treat as equal something I could not understand? Your glare is scolding, chiding me in a way a mother might on that which should be obvious even to a child's comprehension of right and wrong.

I'm sorry, I wail. I beg for your forgiveness. In your silence, I have brief time to consider what might have been had I only shown you love.

The thought dissipates as your nails dig into my flesh and my mouth opens in a scream.

STARRY NIGHT

Officer Joel Crombie rubbed his temples and studied the bloody trail leading behind the barn. "What's the nature of your complaint, Mr. … Haggard? Is somebody hurt?"

"That's Merle Haggard Forsythe," Merle corrected, throwing a thumb into his chest. "Named after the greatest country-and-western singer this side of the whole damn earth." His too-few-toothed grin faded. "Anyway, ain't nobody hurt. The problem's like this: Lester's dog went missing last night. When it came back, it wasn't his dog no more, if'n you catch my meaning."

"I don't." Joel withdrew a small pencil and notepad from his breast pocket and flipped the pad open. He bit his lower lip, trying to distract himself from his throbbing forehead with new pain elsewhere. "You're saying someone took Lester Houlihan's dog and replaced it with a different dog?"

"No. Why would anyone do that?" Merle frowned. "I'm saying, same dog but, you know, different dog."

Joel lowered his head, took a deep breath, and counted to three. When he raised his eyes and saw Merle's mouth hanging open, a tiny, oval orifice circumscribed by an outgrowth of grizzly graying beard, oddly shaped in the form of a W, he counted to three again. His gaze fell past Merle's sizeable belly, down his mud-caked jeans, to the thick streak of matted grass, the blood spread over it curdling faster than spoiled milk and smelling doubly as sour.

Joel buried his nose in the crook of his arm. "I thought you said this blood came from Mr. Houlihan's dog."

"Some of it."

"And the rest?"

"Well, I suspect some of it used to belong to Lester."

Joel studied the older man's impassive face. He didn't know whether to reach for his gun or his radio, but the sudden movement to his belt failed to raise so much as a flinch out of Merle. He grabbed his portable and called in. "Evelyn, it's Joel. We have a possible homicide down at the Forsythe Farm out on Route 10. Send backup and an ambulance ASAP. Over."

"Homicide?" Merle rubbed his chin. "Homicide, homicide, homicide … you mean like murder? Ain't nobody been murdered here, Officer. Just a little tiff between a dog and her master. Everyone's fine. Dog, too, 'cept I got no idea where that ol' mutt got off to."

Joel raised an eyebrow. "I thought you said this was Lester's blood."

"Some of it."

Joel stared expectantly at Merle, but any further clarification wasn't forthcoming. "And?"

"And some of it's the dog's."

Joel swung his arm over the blood smeared around their feet. The biggest strip was about two feet wide. It ran in a fairly linear track, appearing as if someone had painted a heavy coat with a rake-sized paintbrush. Or a man-sized one. He stamped his foot. "So whose blood is all of this?"

Merle crossed his arms and spat. "Are you daft, son? I done told you like four times now. It's Lester's dog's mostly, and probably some of Lester's too."

Joel tensed then hurriedly followed the still-wet path around to the back of the barn, Merle plodding along behind. There, the trail ended abruptly, no sign indicating why or how it had come to its end except for what appeared to be gopher holes randomly dotting the landscape within a bowling alley-sized lane. The lane led from the barn to a lush forest. The metallic taste of blood hung in the air, combined with something much worse. Joel's eyes watered as he covered his mouth and nose again, wondering if Merle's dairy farm had recently become a tannery. "Right, so … where are the bodies?"

JASON PARENT

"I think I saw Lester playing in the trees over there." Merle pointed to the forest at the edge of the property. Tall firs, dark and uninviting, stood like fence pickets in close rows and delving as far south as Joel could see. To the east and north, the land rolled hill over valley, each crest higher than the one before it; those on the horizon were jagged mountains. Merle's farm was but a mote of dust lost in a vast acreage of largely untouched land, dirt roads the only evidence of human trespass outside of Merle's curtilage and that of his only neighbor, Mr. Lester Houlihan. The closest town, and Joel's base of operations, was nearly forty miles due west, raising serious questions whether his police department, or *any* police department, had jurisdiction over that isolated frontier.

Still, Merle had called for help. Joel would do what he could. But he had never seen so much blood. Not from any two persons, never mind a man and a dog. He shook his head. "You're sure he's alive?"

Merle crossed his arms, staring coolly at Joel.

"All right, all right." Joel radioed dispatch. "Evelyn, go ahead and cancel that backup. Send animal control instead." He lowered his arm, but after another look at the blood, raised it again. "Still send the ambulance. Over."

Merle shook his head. "You ain't gonna need it. Lester, he ain't never been healthier. I ain't seen him run and jump like that in, oh, forty years."

"And the dog?"

"That old bitch is around here somewhere."

Joel fixated again on the blood, still unable to accept it belonged to just a dog and a person. He frowned and squinted at Merle. *An elaborate joke?* "Maybe you should just tell me what happened. From the beginning."

"Well, it's like I said. Bessie—that's the dog—she up and disappeared 'bout dusk yesterday. Now that dog, she ain't left Lester's side in sixteen years. So I'm figuring she went out to the woods, found someplace to curl up and die."

Merle raised his arms in a *whatta-you-gonna-do* sort of way. "Lester, he nearly chewed my head off when I told him just that. Said he went looking for her, heard her howling something awful. Said she fell down some hole." He waved an arm out. "Them holes are all over these parts. Caves as deep as the devil's asshole. If she fell down one of them"—he swished his palms

179

over one another—"good as gone. No one and nothing's gone down below and come back. They say the sound plays tricks on you in subterrestrial caverns like that. Help might sound as if it's right on top of you but could really be miles away."

"Subterranean?"

"Huh?" Merle raised an eyebrow. "Anywho, Lester gets it in his head to go on in after her. I called him a damn fool, but he starts walking. So's I make him a deal: sit down, have a swig of my famous moonshine, then we both go out looking for Bessie. We got drunk instead and passed out. The next day was business as usual, for me anyway … 'til I sees the dog."

Joel leaned closer, then checked himself. He gave a curt nod. "Go on."

"Bessie's face was all scratched up, like she'd got into it with a badger, and she had this giant black lump on her back, fat and swollen like a deer tick a thousand sizes too big. She was all teeth, snarling and snapping and staring at me like I killed her pup. Now, Bessie weren't never fond of me, nor I her—I don't know whose farts are worse, hers or Lester's—but we kept the peace."

"So what did you do?"

"I just backed away slowly, went inside the house, picked up the phone, and told Lester he needed to get his sorry ass over here. When I peeked out the window, that dog was standing in the same spot, still snarling and snapping, and it was *still* like that when Lester come over to the yard. Ain't never been so happy to see him leave, the dog with 'im."

"Back up. Did you find out what was wrong with the dog?"

"Can't says I rightly know. But the dog seems okay now." Merle ran a hand down his face. "But she bit Lester. Damndest thing. Them two were always thicker than thieves."

"Thick as thieves." Joel rolled his eyes. "So does Mr. Houlihan require medical attention?"

"Nope, we wrapped that sucker up. But that's when things got really strange."

"Where were you when the dog bit Mr. Houlihan?"

"I was here."

"And where was Mr. Houlihan?"

"He was there." Merle pointed to a structure dark as a shadow on the next lot. "His place."

"You didn't see him get bit?"

"No. Lester, he came running over here like a rabid wombat, bleeding all over my doorknob. So I let him in and fixed him up. Ol' Lester, he said that dog weren't right. Said it must'a run afoul of something. Me, I don't know what a dog might *run afoul* of that'll give the sonna-bitch tentacles growing out its freakin' back."

Joel's eyes felt as if they might shoot from their sockets. "Tentacles?"

Merle chuckled. "Yeah. Darn thing looked like an octopus, except the dog's extra legs were trailing ooze."

Something scurried over the grass behind Joel—something small, probably just a chipmunk or a squirrel, but big enough to make Joel's breathing hitch.

"Dog doesn't seem to mind the extra limbs, though," Merle continued. "Just sorta meanders around, half hobbling, half … I don't know … squirming, sniffing the grass, the barn, my truck … and baring its teeth at anyone or anything that moves."

Merle squinted. "Oh, and licking them tentacles. Just licking and licking, and chewing real quick, like you know how they do sometimes when they have ticks buried in their paws. I swear, when that dog gnawed off one of them sucker-things, well, that tentacle gushed like Old Faithful. Blood as black as oil coated that poor mutt's face, got into her mouth and ears. Poor thing didn't know what to do. Just ran in circles, yapping and snapping, like she was trying to eat off her own tail."

Joel grimaced. He didn't know what to make of Merle's story. If the call had been a hoax, Merle was totally invested in it.

"But I'll tell you one thing: that weren't no oil. Sure, it *looked* like crude—bubbled like it too—but it stank worse than that coon that done crawled up under my porch to die last spring, even after the two weeks it took to find the bugger."

Despite the whole tentacled-dog story being a bit hard to swallow, Joel couldn't help but glance about nervously. He didn't necessarily think Merle was lying … not exactly … but a sick or rabid dog was all it was.

Had to be.

His collar felt a little tighter. He shook off a sudden chill. "Uh, maybe we shouldn't discuss this out in the open."

"I follow you, Officer." Merle drew a massive handgun that had been tucked into the back of his pants.

Joel went for his sidearm, shaking hands fumbling with the holster. He'd been too slow to pick up on the crazy, and now he was going to be gunned down by an honest-to-god, aliens-probed-my-dog-and-the-government-controls-our-minds-through-the-water-supply kind of lunatic. His eyes widened, mouth dry as a cracker.

Merle pointed the gun up to the sky. "Just in case. But they don't seem to want no trouble now. They're just sorta, you know, frog licking." He tucked his gun back under his belt.

Joel let out his breath. "Frolicking? And who are *they*?"

A sharp, shrill whine came from the tree line. Joel pointed his gun. Silence followed.

"That doesn't sound like frolicking."

Merle chuckled. "Ol' Bessie worked up an appetite in them there caves. That's the fourth animal she's gotten yet."

"And that doesn't alarm you?"

"Everything's gotta eat."

"I thought you said you didn't believe Bessie had fallen into one of those holes you mentioned."

Merle puckered his lips. "Well … maybe I do and maybe I don't."

"Has Bessie attacked other animals before?"

"Nah. She was too old to even be chasing squirrels."

Joel opened his mouth to speak but sighed and shut it as animal control pulled up the dirt drive. The SUV stopped about twelve feet from where he and Merle stood, its halogen headlights blinding.

Joel shielded his eyes, but the animal control team killed the engine a moment later. From the passenger side stepped a tall man with stovepipe arms, rail-thin legs, and a cocksure grin. The driver, a tiny mousy woman with spectacles and a meticulously cleaned and tucked uniform, stepped out and walked to the front of the truck, where she met her partner. They stood there for a moment, whispering to one another as an ambulance pulled in beside them.

The two paramedics, also a male and female, got out and headed toward Joel. Animal control followed.

"Where's the injured party?" the female paramedic asked, all business. Joel had seen her once or twice, had an eye for the athletic blonde, but he had never mustered the courage to ask her name. But he could read, and her nametag read *Briggs*. He'd never seen her baby-faced partner before and saw no nametag.

"Somewhere over there." Joel pointed at the woods.

Briggs didn't so much as raise an eyebrow. "Extent of injuries?"

"He was bitten by a dog—"

"On the hand, and I dressed it," Merle said.

"—at least once," Joel finished.

The male animal control officer stepped in front of Briggs. "Where's the dog? Officer …"

"Crombie. Joel Crombie."

"The name's Lou." The big man extended a hand. Joel shook it.

Lou threw a thumb over his shoulder. "That there's Gina."

Gina mouthed a *Hi* then stared back down at the ground, possibly looking for animal tracks.

Joel pointed again at the forest. "The dog's also over there."

"So we got an aggressive dog and an injured man, both somewhere over there," Lou said, puffing out his chest. "Anything else we should know?"

Merle and Joel exchanged a look. After a moment, Joel said no, but his voice went so high, it sounded like a question.

The party broke up, the paramedics returning to the ambulance for some first-aid basics, the animal control officers grabbing their leashes—four-foot-long poles with cinch cords at one end. All four power walked past Joel and straight toward the woods.

"Uh," Joel said, then raising his voice, "I haven't cleared the scene yet."

"We got this," Lou said without bothering to turn around.

Joel shook his head and hurried to follow but stopped when he realized he was alone. He turned to face Merle. "You coming?"

Merle stood still, arms crossed. "Nah. I do believe I've had enough excitement for one day."

Joel hesitated then turned and ran after the others, his reholstered gun at his side.

When he reached the property line, he nearly plowed into Gina. She, like her partner and the two paramedics, had stopped short at an opening in the forest. Though the night sky was clear and full of stars bright enough to see well on Merle's open lawn, it was another story under the thick canopy of leaves, branches, and pine needles. Joel clicked on his flashlight and peered into the dense undergrowth.

Through the brush, a three-foot-wide trail had been blazed. Ferns lay pressed flat against the ground, pinned there by a thick layer of ooze. Something about it reminded Joel of marmalade spread over toast.

"Just how sick is this guy?" Briggs asked. She peered into the opening.

Joel grabbed her arm. "Maybe I should go first." Hearing no objections, he was about to step into the forest when the rookie male paramedic, ignoring protocol and swelling with the machismo Joel had expected from Lou, beat him to the punch.

As the young man stepped onto the flattened flora, he slipped. He landed facedown on a Slip 'N Slide of the snot-like substance.

No one helped him up. He crawled, hands and knees, off the newly blazed path. The others watched dumbstruck as he stood, his skin glimmering a fine sheen in the moonlight.

"I think I swallowed some," he said, tearing off his shirt. He turned it inside out and used it to wipe his face. "God, it reeks!"

Briggs put her hands on her hips. "We're gonna have to hose you down. You aren't getting in the van like that."

Her partner grimaced. His shoulders drooped, all machismo drained out of him.

Briggs allowed Joel to pass her on the side of the trail. "I can't tell what all this says about his condition, but it's obvious he can move."

The trail ran deep and straight. After several minutes of stomping through ferns and roots, they stopped. The trail had come to an abrupt end.

"Well?" Lou grumbled, somewhere behind Joel. "Where is he?"

A scream, loud and close, chilled Joel's blood. It cut off like someone had cupped a hand over the screamer's mouth. He turned and saw confusion on the others' faces—three of them.

Lou was missing.

Rustling came from above. Looking up, Joel instantly wished he hadn't. Tentacles, slick and scaly like black mambas with rows of yellow suckers on their undersides, coiled around both of Lou's arms, drawing him up, higher and higher. The body of the tentacles' owner, whatever it was, remained out of sight, hidden within leaves and darkness.

But the head ...

Joel drew his gun.

"Shoot it!" Briggs yelled.

"I-I-I ... I can't!" Joel squinted down the barrel of his service pistol, mind racing as he stared at what looked like a giant, stemless rose, pulsing and enveloping Lou's entire head. The bulbous thing—*a mouth?*—had grown out of the top of what once could've been a man's head. Not understanding how it could be, Joel nevertheless concluded he had found Lester Houlihan. He shone his light up and shuffled from side to side. "I can't get a clear shot!"

Lou's headless body crashed down beside them. For a moment, the others stood stupefied. First to react, the male paramedic ran. The others quickly followed. The trees rustled above Joel, and he ducked. Swinging like a monkey from branch to branch, the Lester-thing passed over Joel and the two women as it closed on the lead runner.

"Look out!" Joel shouted, running no longer *away* from the creature but *toward* it, with little time to question the soundness of that decision. The Lester-thing reached for the male paramedic. Joel fired, again and again.

The thing squealed so loudly Joel had to cover his ears. It fled to the treetops, dripping black oil all over the foliage. Joel keeled over, hands gripping his knees. His side felt as if someone had given it a good poke with a carving fork.

He caught his breath even as Briggs passed him, Gina on her heels, both gaining on Briggs's partner. The monster had retreated. For the moment, they were safe—

A spiraling whirl of tentacles rolled out of the brush, tackling the young paramedic like a safety spearing a receiver leaping for a pass up the middle. It and the paramedic went airborne and smacked down, unseen, in tall grass.

Two tentacles capped with pointed bones resembling scorpions' stingers rose above the grass. They struck their unseen target like snakes, whiplashing back and forth, over and over again. Joel could do nothing for the paramedic, whose crippling wails had stopped Briggs and Gina in their tracks. They turned and raced back to Joel, huddling behind him for cover.

The tips of the grass blades were stained like sacrificial daggers. The sounds of agony ended, snarling and thrashing all that remained. Joel held his breath. The creature—a *second* creature—stepped out of the grass.

In the center of the squirming appendages, two bloodshot eyes glared at Joel from behind a snout. A low growl emitted from between curled-up lips.

The dog? It can't be. But he knew it to be true. He was just beginning to wonder how many other mutated critters were in the forest when Ol' Bessie charged.

Briggs and Gina turned and raced toward Joel. He planted his feet, stood his ground, and raised his gun.

The first shot went wide, but the second hit home: dead center in the mass growing out of the dog's back. The beast didn't even slow, seemingly unfazed by its wound. Joel fired a third shot, a fourth, a fifth, each hitting its mark.

Still, the creature came. It leapt. Joel fired, but the gun only clicked. He dove to his right, the landing jarring his flashlight from his hand. He gripped the gun tightly in his other.

The dog fell next to him, panting heavily, a forked tongue lolling from its mouth. A six-inch stinger stabbed the dirt inches from Joel's face. He rolled out of reach.

By the time he stood, the dog wasn't moving. Cautiously, he took a step toward it. Then another. He jolted upright when something seized his arm.

"Don't touch it," Briggs said. "In fact, don't even go near it. We don't know what's going on here, but clearly, humans can catch it."

"Oh my god, oh my god, oh my god," Gina chanted as she paced. She clung to her pole leash as if it might protect her against—

Against what? Joel ran a hand through his hair. "Should we burn it?"

"Let the CDC or whoever decide that. Brow furrowed, Briggs studied the treetops. "We should get the hell out of here."

His eyes followed her gaze, but he saw nothing in those trees, the only movement being their gentle sway in the breeze. "Agreed."

"Oh my god, oh my god, oh my god—"

"Gina!" Joel barked. She froze and stared at him with wide, tear-filled eyes. "You good?"

She gulped and nodded.

Joel popped in a fresh clip, the only one he had with him. "Stay close." He looked from Briggs to Gina. "Let's move."

Bellowing came from the trees. Joel couldn't pinpoint its source. It seemed to come from everywhere, and for all Joel knew, it did. Too painful to bear, he fell to his knees, clasping his hands over his ears, Gina sobbing and doing the same beside him.

Then silence.

"Fuck this," Briggs said. She took off running.

"We have to stay together!" Joel shouted.

"Why?" Briggs called back through heavy breaths. "The way I see it, there's three of us and one of it. If we split up, two of us have a chance!"

Rustling came from over her head, and Briggs slowed, giving Joel and Gina time to catch up. "On second thought, let's stick together." She glanced at the gun in Joel's hand and fell in behind him. "How many bullets you got left?"

Joel shook his head. "Not enough."

"But you hit it," Gina whined. "It's wounded."

"Maybe." Joel was still considering this when a whoosh of air prickled the hair on the back of his neck. He slowed and looked over his shoulders.

Briggs let out a low grunt as if all the wind had been knocked out of her. A long, spear-tipped tentacle protruded from her chest. She started to rise.

Joel dove for her feet, hugging around her ankles. Briggs coughed above him, wet barks laced with blood. He planted his feet, halting the creature's efforts only briefly before he, too, left the ground.

Reluctantly, Joel let go. But he didn't give up on Briggs. Swirling his gun in the air above him, searching for a clear shot, he fired twice into the branches, hoping to get lucky.

Gina grabbed his sleeve and tugged. "It's too late for her. We have to go!"

Joel let Gina take him by the hand and lead him out of the forest. They were only a hundred yards or so from spilling out into the moonlight when Joel's legs were knocked out from under him. He didn't know whether he'd been struck or had merely tripped over a log, but he assumed the worst as his body jettisoned into the air, arms Superman-like out in front of him. He crashed with a grunt onto the trail of slime then pressed his lips together as he began to slide.

Momentum carried him onward. Flailing and sliding faster and faster, he shot across the trail like a puck over ice until he burst out of the forest and tumbled onto Merle's lawn. Scrambling to his feet, he spat the gunk off his lips then froze and listened for the sounds of pursuit.

Twigs cracked and brush shook. Joel raised his gun.

Gina barreled out of the woods, still carrying her pole. "It's coming! It's coming!"

A wall of branches exploded into splinters behind her. Joel turned to run then stopped. Gina needed cover.

She raced by Joel before the Lester-thing emerged from the woods. As it squirmed into the field, it paused to sniff the air. Joel got a better look at it then. Merle hadn't been too far off with his octopus comparison, except the thing had likely sprouted more tentacles since Merle had seen it—so many of them, coiling like a nest of snakes or tree roots twisting over and around each other.

And in its center, the outline of a man.

A man suffering from what could only be described as severe leprosy, Ebola, and a boatload of gangrene. Skin hung loose, tinted green-purple like deli roast beef when it started to turn. The tentacles themselves seemed bigger, no longer mambas but anacondas, wiry and boneless save for their pointed protrusions. Their suckers secreted the viscous substance that coated the front of Joel's uniform.

Joel swallowed, his phlegm thick with revulsion and pity. The creature's bloodshot eyes locked on his. It lurched forward.

Joel fired four times before the creature closed the distance, each bullet seemingly wasted. The abomination wasn't stopping, wouldn't *be* stopping. The world blurred, went preternaturally silent as he saw his death unfolding. In that final moment, he only hoped Gina had managed to escape.

A roar came from behind him, followed by a trumpeting horn and blinding lights. A half second more passed before Joel registered their meaning. He gasped and rolled to his left even as a slick, pulsating tentacle curled around his waist—but before it could clamp tight, it went limp and retreated, driven backward by the animal control truck as it plowed through the creature.

The crack of bones snapping almost made Joel hurl. He burped and covered his mouth, managing to keep in his lunch. The truck bounced on its axles as its front wheels went over Mutant Lester then again as the back wheels followed suit. As Gina hit the brakes, the truck fishtailed on the slime, righted, then came to rest, its front end curled around a tree, horn blaring unceasingly.

Joel stood, one eye on the creature and the other on the truck. The thing wasn't moving. Neither was Gina.

He holstered his gun, ran to her aid, and found her slumped over the steering wheel. Her head was cut open and already bruising as he pulled her from the wreck. Sitting her on the ground, her neck resting in the crook of his elbow, he saw the steady rise and fall of her chest and knew she was only unconscious. He lightly tapped her face. Slowly, she came back to the waking world.

Her eyes looked past him. "Where ... where is it?"

Joel turned then reached for his pistol. The creature was gone.

"It—it—it can't be alive!" Joel's gaze darted in every direction, searching for the beast. "You smashed the hell out of it!"

A formless mass Joel had at first mistaken for a boulder began to swell, larger and larger, only forty yards away. A single red eye—embedded in a now-jawless face, swiveling from a craggy neck, jutting from a contorted frame—stared at him with a sort of contempt Joel had only seen in the worst criminals his department had taken into custody: the sadists, psychopaths, and supremacists, those whose very nature was violence and hate.

He lifted Gina to her feet then caught her when she staggered. She was probably concussed and wasn't fit for moving quickly. But if a goddamn two-ton truck couldn't take out that thing, running was the only option left.

He held her by her cheeks, looked deep into her eyes. "We have to go. Can you run?"

Her cloudiness lifted. She sucked in her drool and nodded then started to lope unsteadily, only to stop, turn, and reach into the open door of the truck. She pulled out the tool of her trade and awaited instructions.

Joel couldn't suppress a pained smile; the absurdity of four-foot Gina thinking her four-foot pole might save her was almost too sad to bear. He grabbed her under the arm and shuffled her forward.

She shook him off. "Go. I'm right behind you."

The strength in her voice reassured him, and even if it hadn't, the swelling mass of tentacles was plenty to spur him onward. "To my cruiser!" he shouted, never looking back.

He sprinted across the lawn, past the barn, and around the front of Merle's house. His car sat right where he had left it. "No-no-no-*no!*" The two tires he could make out were flat. They looked as if they had been slashed, and he slowed to inspect them.

Gina breathed heavily behind him. "Don't stop! Keep running!"

He headed toward the foothills, their much bigger siblings looming over the horizon, miles away. His only thought was that somehow, he might gain the advantage if he could just make it to higher ground. A tiny voice at the back of his mind told him he was being stupid, but it was the only plan he had.

Sooner or later, he would again have to make a stand.

As he crested the first hill, a howl whipped through the air like a hurricane. His heart jumped, and his body locked up midstride, and he fell down the opposite side of the hill. At the bottom, Gina helped him to his feet, and the pair raced across the valley to another steep rise. As they began to climb, a grotesquery bounded down the hill at their backs.

The Lester-thing was halfway up the hill when Joel made it to the top and realized he had nowhere left to go. After a plateau no more than ten feet wide, the land dropped off sharply into a stadium-sized crater. In its center was another hole, a tiny pupil in a great eye, plummeting into darkness. Joel wondered what had formed the depression—a meteorite, he guessed—and how long it had been there. It reminded Joel of a funnel, from which the chances of escaping were next to none should that goddamn monster chase them into it.

No. Joel set his jaw and drew his gun. He guessed he had eight bullets left at most. They would have to do. "Get behind me."

Gina circled, stopping at his back, standing so close her metal pole pressed against him. Knowing she was there, feeling her presence, was somehow comforting. He wouldn't have to die alone.

The sharp point of a tentacle speared the ground of the hilltop. Joel aimed but waited, wanting to hit the thing center mass, for each of his bullets to count. Another tentacle planted into dirt then another, a monster crawling spiderlike up to its prey. The bulbous head emerged.

Joel fired. He wasn't sure just how many shots he'd gotten off before he was slapped aside like a mosquito under the hand of a giant. When he tried to sit up, his back and hip squealed in protest. He squinted and bit his lip, forcing himself through the pain.

When he opened his eyes, he saw the unbelievable. Gina had the noose end of her pole around the creature's broken, human neck. She dodged strike after strike from the hydra she had ensnared, all while trying to drag it toward the cliff's edge.

The beast was too strong for her, and Joel could see Gina tiring. He ran to her side and grabbed the pole. Adding his strength to Gina's, Joel heaved the creature over the lip. Screeching and snarling, it fell into the crater.

A tentacle whipped around Gina's ankle, jerking her to the ground. Before it could snatch her into the hole, Joel slammed his gun into its holster, dove to the ground, and wrapped his fingers around her wrists. Together, they were dragged over the edge.

The crater was steep but not a straight drop, slanted enough to keep ground under him. Jagged stones scraped Joel's chest as he skidded down and down, vision obscured by a cloud of dust and dirt. His knuckles collided with something hard, and Gina slipped from his grasp, disappearing in a mini sandstorm.

After that, Joel concentrated on slowing down. He figured he was nearing the bottom of the crater—and a second drop-off—because the decline grew slighter. Clawing the earth, he managed to spin himself around and eventually stopped sliding altogether as his hand caught onto a tree root. He coughed through the dirt ensconcing him, blinding him as he stopped short. He called out to Gina but received no answer. Wiping his eyes and blinking furiously, tears helping to wash them clean, he scanned his surroundings.

The creature was gone. Gina hung from the edge of the fourteen-foot-wide hole at the center of the crater. Her grip was slipping.

Between Joel and Gina, her animal control leash lay discarded. Joel raced toward her, scooping up the pole as he ran.

"Grab onto it!" he yelled, baseball-sliding toward her retreating hands. As her fingers tightened around the loop at its end, Gina dropped into the darkness.

The pole jerked out from under Joel, but he clung to its base even as it pulled him closer to the edge. Crawling up its length, he tucked it under his body, pinning it to the ground. "I've got you! Hold on!" Though he couldn't see her, he knew Gina still had the other end because of the force of the pole pushing against his chest.

Too much force. *That thing still has her leg!*

Keeping atop the pole, Joel edged closer to the hole. He drew his gun and peered into the abyss. The glint of Gina's glasses, like a lone star in empty space, sparkled with hope.

"Help … me …" she groaned.

Joel couldn't see anything to shoot at. His finger flexed over the trigger, but before he could take a shot, blood sprayed up onto his hands. It came from Gina's mouth. Her eyes rolled back. She let go of the noose.

"Gina!" Joel shot to his feet, hands clawing at his hair. He dropped back down to his knees, defeated. There he stayed, catching his breath and trying to make sense of all that had passed that evening. He heard nothing more from Gina. She was dead. And if that monster wasn't, at least it was down in hell where it belonged.

"Heck of a thing, that was."

Joel's heart slammed against its cage at the sound of a voice behind him. He yelped and jumped to his feet, spinning around with gun raised to face a man who was delightfully free of tentacles.

Merle chuckled. "Easy there, Officer. You're too young to be giving yourself a heart attack."

"Jesus Christ, Merle!" Joel took long, deep breaths. "You scared the living shit out of me." He lowered his gun.

Merle stepped closer. He had a strange twinkle in his eye. "My family, we've been on this land a long time, long before this here hole was here and whatever those things are began their ... co-habituation."

"Cohabitation?" Joel frowned. "What are you talking about?"

"Well, you see, most of my kin, they're down there now. Ol' Lester too. They're hungry, and like I said, everything's gotta eat." He lunged forward. "I'm sorry, Officer."

Joel's eyes widened as he realized Merle's intent. He tried to catch Merle's arm as he plummeted back into the hole, but he was too late. He dropped several feet, rolled down a short hill, then dropped again, finally landing on cold, wet stone. He ached everywhere, but nothing seemed broken.

Groaning, he staggered to his feet, his eyes trying to adjust to the pitch black, but not even the moonlight shone through at the entrance somewhere above him.

"I can't let my family, my friends starve," Merle called down, his voice echoing through a cavernous space, the acoustics so unnatural it was impossible to locate its source. "You understand."

"Merle?" Joel's lips quivered, but he snarled in anger. "Merle! You get back here! You—"

Pebbles skittered off to his left. A thump came to his right. Sounds emerged from everywhere around him. A guttural purr, a low growl, bodies dragging through dirt.

Sliding and slithering closer.

Joel fired into the dark, the spark of the blast illuminating his immediate surroundings for half an instant. Still, he saw nothing. He fired again.

A scream caught in Joel's throat. In that flash of light, he swore he'd seen faces, some old, some young, all of them drawing nearer, all of them hideously mutated. His whole body trembled. He wanted to run, but fear kept his feet planted, knees shaking, weakening beneath his weight.

He raised his gun again to fire, hearing those monsters closer now, smelling their putridness, feeling the heat of their breath, the warmth of their flesh.

He pulled the trigger. The gun clicked. And the darkness swallowed him whole.

MORE?

Poverty drove us below ground. Who knew it would be our salvation? I've been down here so long I've forgotten the sight of the sun, the feel of its warmth on my skin; all that remains is a vague memory of a day at the beach, parasols and sand castles, before the oceans were too toxic to swim.

A lifetime ago, or so it seems. Time is relative in endless dark.

Still, it's been at least a couple decades since the world above annihilated itself, and the walls around me continue to tremble. I suppose now there is no sun to see, blotted out by corrosive clouds. Perhaps that's for the best, for I fear what its light might reveal. What might seep down here, where it's safe.

Relatively speaking.

Another quake sends me stumbling, arms out from my sides. It comes and goes swiftly, just a little one this time, but always without warning. I live in fear of the next tunnel collapse, though we've become adept at digging each other out when bones aren't too badly misshapen. We need each other, and even the dead have value.

I shudder, remembering all my lost brethren, my *kin*, for we are family, united by our resolve, our shared, almost symbiotic coexistence. We have become what is needed to survive, if not as individuals, than as a species. And it makes us stronger than those topsiders, those Have-a-Lots, ever were.

I inhale the musty, dank air and run my fingers along the dirt-encrusted walls. Roots tickle my fingertips, daring me to pluck them, to ingest them, but to do so would be folly. How they yet grow when their crowns must surely have been obliterated is a mystery. We learned of their poison as we learned of all things down here: the hard way.

Yet what once felt claustrophobic, an earthen tomb, suffocating and swallowing, has become a womb ripe with life. The tunnels we burrow expand our world, while Mother Earth wraps us in her coddling embrace, shrouding us in warmth and permanency, nurturing us, her heart our home.

That's how it's always been for those who were down here long before the privileged broke our bodies, ground and discarded us, so that they might have their trinkets and gadgets—fancy toys for fancy people, technology to laze away their days while we labored to keep their Towers of Babylon climbing higher. Endless hours we toiled, fracturing dirt and rock for the precious metals they desired so that they might glitter and glow. A vanity and selfishness worthy of destruction.

Our reward for our efforts? Scraps they would otherwise have thrown in the garbage.

Look at them now. A laugh escapes me, and I am startled by the sound of it. I clamp a hand over my mouth as pebbles cascade down the earthen walls. The soil above is wet, and I wonder if we've burrowed too close to an underground river or lake bottom, a necessary evil, for water is the source of all life.

Especially when it can be purified.

When all settles, I continue forward. We should shore up more of this path, but our eagerness makes us reckless. We are so very close now. A strange chittering comes from my companion. He thrums with excitement. The fruits of his labors, his burrowing, so very close indeed.

Burrowing. I scoff. *Like moles.* That's what the Have-a-Lots used to call the subway folk: Mole Men. My friend studies me with his gray-red eyes, and I must look away, for I was once guilty of the same ignorance. Before I came to understand them. What a strange thing, to name an entire class of people after what they eat.

They were unknown to us, these Mole Men—no, these *human beings*— just folklore and rumors before the bombs fell and we became trapped.

Like fallen angels ascending from the depths to reclaim their wings, they revealed themselves to us as we scrabbled helpless in the dark, became our guiding light in a place that saw none. With stilted words and gestures, they taught us how to survive, to find food—moles, worms, insects, and other burrowing things—and to make do with what the encompassing earth offered. And we taught them how to reinforce tunnels, to excavate with machinery, to rapidly expand their domain. When our supplies ran out, we had thought we had outlived our usefulness. Until we figured out how to use bone.

I smile at my friend, the under dweller, and he smiles toothily back. We are one in purpose. It never mattered to me that his skin was paler, grayish even, like meat starting to turn. His eyes, with a sheen that repels light, never saw in me anything less than a brother nor I less than one in them. As he stands beside me now, I see my reflection in those hopeful eyes. Am I paler?

I still cling to the miner's helmet and its rechargeable light as if it were a life preserver. But it shines a little too brightly for my taste of late. My friend gets by just fine without one. I will need to learn to let it go sooner or later, for the gas fueling our generators is in short supply.

And so it is with all our rations. We eat what we can catch, but lately, it seems the insects have truly inherited the earth. Do you know how many ants one must eat to keep his belly full? Of course, we've taken to eating our dead as well. Such a bountiful source of sustenance cannot be left to waste. And when food is at its scarcest, we all understand that the herd must be culled.

The under dweller by my side—I know not his name—urges me forward. But we have reached the tunnel's end. I run my fingers down the cool metal surface blocking our passage.

My friend understands my intention. He claws at the metal, works himself into such a frenzy my hand on his shoulder cannot steady him. Sharpened teeth scratch and scrape but are no match for the barrier before us. At last, he tires, his huge doleful eyes seeing so little yet expressing so much. He sniffs the air. Though I do not doubt his superior senses of hearing and smell, it's hard to believe he can detect what lies beyond a blockade of steel. But I must believe, for he has led us to this place.

To our salvation.

I inhale deeply through my nose. The air is stale, the odor of my friend staler still. Once I found his unique fragrance a thick odor, like black mud at low tide, but like anything, I suppose, I grew accustomed to it, grew to like it even, basing myself in a new normalcy. His smell means he is near, watching over me. Something natural, something primal lies within his scent. Or perhaps I am just smelling me.

But I cannot smell *them*. Perhaps, in time…

The under dweller bares his teeth and nudges me, shaking me from my reverie. He is losing patience. Down here, we must all do our part. Friends quickly become enemies when one stands between the other and his innate entitlements. I whistle, and a few of my crew—their names… why can't I remember their names?—wheel a massive contraption past us as we hug the wall. Ironic that such a fancy, expensive gift from the Have-a-Lots should be used in such a manner.

I forget the name of the tool and even the name of the gigantic, subterranean capsules where so many of the Have-a-Lots had fled, trying to escape the reaping owed. These memory lapses are occurring more frequently, but I suppose they're the least of my worries. Even after they reduced the world to less, less, less, the Lots found a way to still have more, more, more. Lots more.

Though I don't recall the machine's name, I do remember how to use it. I yank a lever, and it lurches forward, large conical gears rotating and screeching, grinding and twisting metal into jagged ruin. Sparks fly, their brightness forcing my eyes shut.

And I start to salivate. This isn't our first… *bunker!* That's what the Lots call them. And there'll be a lot of them inside. I shuffle on my feet, my friend shuffling beside me. Is there anything harder than waiting?

With a pop, a cacophony of creaks, and finally, the high-pitched whine of an unencumbered drill, the machine breaches the wall. The hole is not big enough to pass through, though my under dweller friend cannot stop himself from trying. I yank him back, though I wish someone would do the same for me, my restraint teetering on a crumbling precipice.

A child is wailing, and I bite into my lip, the sound of such a morsel so near filling me with desire, threatening to overwhelm reason. They will have weapons, but we have the numbers, and we alone have earned the right to live down here. We could take them in, I suppose, but where would we keep them in a herd already in need of culling?

I run my tongue over my canines. I'd be lying if I said I don't take pleasure in this. The child's screams, the panic and the chaos, the reduction of those who always felt they were so much more to something so much less: a comeuppance many lifetimes in the making. For certain, the Lots have brought this upon themselves. They had to take and take from us, from their fellow man, from the world we shared, until there was nothing left to take. And in their bunkers, they toil away safely, still having so much more than us. Lots and lots more!

I sneer then snigger, for tonight, I will feast. I will have more and more Lots.

My under dweller friend points to himself then to me. "More... Lots?" he says as if reading my mind. Except, in his garbled, clicking voice, it sounds a little more like *locks*.

I laugh again. A strange thing, to be named after what you eat.

THE ONLY GOOD LAWYER

Innocent until proven guilty: that was his mantra. No matter how guilty Bradley Walsh knew his client to be, he'd make sure justice remained blind. He'd bury the truth in a murky sea of "facts" and misdirection, obscured by a school of red herrings. Reasonable doubt was his ally, a vixen who seduced jurors with an alluring cloud of deceit.

The trial was his to control. The participants—the witnesses, the victims, the prosecutor, and even the judge—were his unsuspecting pawns. The courtroom his playing board, Bradley ruled the game. And that day, just like all the days before it, he had performed masterfully.

Bradley dismantled the prosecution's case with carefully crafted cross-examination. His questions could only be answered one way, limited so much in their scope that witnesses answering them had no room to wiggle. He'd never ask them the material questions, those that would damn his client—not unless the state wanted to pay him the exorbitant amounts his clients were willing to shell out. No, private practice had swelled his bank accounts and his ego well beyond those of the inferior masses.

Victory was so close he could smell her perfume. Only one witness remained. After that, Bradley would move to dismiss the case, and he would succeed, the state having failed to put forth any credible case against his client. The jury would not have the chance to convict on gut feeling alone. His client would never have to set foot in the witness box.

Bradley glanced at his client, his eyes smiling upon a guiltless canvas. Clint Billings, a convicted drug dealer with a rap sheet that read like a Manson confession, stared back at him, a smug grin marking an otherwise hardened face.

The face of a killer. Bradley was sure everyone present thought it. But who could prove it?

Billings was evil, pure and simple. A six-foot-six, three-hundred-pound weapon of mass destruction without compassion or conscience, Billings ran a crew of thieves, rapists, drug dealers, and murderers, the sort who took what they wanted no matter the consequences. He was a monster inside and out. Monsters like him didn't think twice about suffering and torment unless someone intended to inflict either upon them.

That was what the state had in mind for him. But Billings had learned long ago the cardinal truth behind the criminal justice system: threats, bribes, and unscrupulous representation were far better than innocence, particularly since innocence was supposed to be presumed.

Bradley was happy to accommodate so long as his pockets were stuffed. He cared little for innocence. For the right price, he could serve innocence up on the proverbial platter. He'd even steal it from the scales of justice.

"No more questions, Your Honor." Bradley backed away from a rattled college student, the prosecution's star witness to the brutal murder of Jeanette LeFevre. Once a beautiful teenager filled with dreams of a bright future, Jeanette now lay naked and mutilated on a cold metal slab as lifeless as she was. She had been abducted from outside her dormitory, bludgeoned repeatedly and defiled—postmortem—in the woods nearby.

The young man on the stand, a fellow university goer with no apparent reason to lie, testified on direct examination that he'd seen Billings force Jeanette into his black BMW at gunpoint. By the time Bradley had finished with him, the student could no longer say with certainty the color of the car Jeanette had entered, the time or day of the alleged abduction, the circumstances under which she'd entered the vehicle, or the identity of the man with whom she'd left.

The student's testimony had unraveled against questioning designed to discredit, confuse, and confound. The case was all but over. The victim's father, a witness of no factual consequence, was the sole barrier between Bradley and yet another win.

"The state calls Pepe LeFevre to the stand," the prosecutor announced, projecting confidence Bradley found as phony as unicorns in space.

A dark-skinned man rose from his seat in the back of the courtroom where he had sat alone, unnoticed. Small in stature but large in presence, he stepped out from behind the crowd and walked toward the gate separating the officers of the law from the rest of the rabble. All eyes were on him, including Bradley's. He walked through the swinging half door and paused until a court officer directed him to the witness box. His part in what masqueraded as the administration of justice was about to begin.

As LeFevre passed, Bradley watched him with the shrewd confidence of a falcon stalking a field mouse. *Easy prey.* But on closer inspection, the little mouse didn't seem so meek. LeFevre was clad in a royal-blue blazer thrown over a black tee shirt and black dress pants. The afterthoughts of a fire scarred one side of his face. His mouth was hideously deformed, the corner of his lips missing where the scar tissue began, his teeth partially exposed. It made him look as though he might be smiling sinisterly, mouth curled like something between a dog's snarl and the smirk of a psycho clown in a horror film. His teeth were stained yellow and unnaturally spaced. A few were black and rotted.

But it was his eyes that bitch slapped Bradley's composure—completely colorless, cataract plagued, and milky. LeFevre must have been as blind as a mole. But he wore no sunglasses, and he was sure-footed. There was conviction in those eyes, a strength unbefitting the man's four-foot-nothing frame.

And Bradley saw it well. LeFevre's gaze never left him. Bradley wanted to retreat from that stare. That ghost of a man, that nobody among giants, made him feel small. He swallowed hard. Something in LeFevre's eyes caused the attorney's hands to shake. His tie tightened around his neck. He tugged at his collar. Sweat pooled in his armpits.

What's wrong with me? Bradley couldn't make sense of his fear. He had shaken hands with the Devil, represented beings far worse than LeFevre. Yet this mongrel, straight off some ill-begotten raft, likely without a dollar in his pocket or a friend with any clout, had unnerved him with nothing more than a stare?

He's nothing, Bradley tried to rationalize. But his uneasiness wasn't so easily staved. The upper hand was his to lose. He needed to pull himself together. He needed to stall. So he stood.

"Your Honor, before swearing in this witness, perhaps now would be a good time for a break?"

Judge Mia Nevarro peered over the thick bifocals propped on the end of her nose. Bradley knew she despised him. He had played fast and loose with the rules of procedure in her courtroom many times too many. She looked at the clock hanging high on the back wall. "Mr. Walsh, it's only twelve fifteen. As you are well aware, lunch break isn't until one. This case seems to be nearing conclusion, so I thought we'd press on through lunch. I see no reason—"

"Fifteen-minute bathroom break, Your Honor?"

Judge Nevarro let out a long, heavy sigh. "Very well."

She stood and turned toward fourteen blank faces aligned in two rows: the esteemed members of the jury and the alternate jurors. Bradley saw them as fourteen people too dumb to know how to get out of jury duty, fourteen people who would eat up his bullshit all day long.

"Jurors," Judge Nevarro said. "Same instructions as I gave you before the last break. No discussing the case with anyone, including each other. We'll take a short break and be ready to resume in fifteen minutes. I trust that everyone who needs to use the facilities will have done so by then." She cast a sideways glance at Bradley.

"Thank you, Your Honor."

"All rise," a court officer hollered. Like sheep, all in the courtroom complied.

While waiting for the judge and jury to exit, Bradley shuffled absentmindedly through papers on the table before him, keeping his eyes downcast, away from LeFevre's stare. But his brain eventually betrayed him; he looked up just as LeFevre stepped from the witness stand. Again, their eyes locked.

Bradley watched as thin lips pulled back, revealing diseased gums. Now he was sure of it: LeFevre was smiling.

A court officer, who Bradley thought was named Len, escorted LeFevre between the lawyers' tables to the gate. As they passed him, LeFevre opened his jacket. A patchwork doll with green button eyes and a stitched-on smile was affixed to the inner lining. Its hair looked real; it was light brown and parted to the side. The doll wore a stylish blue pinstriped suit, white button-down, and canary-yellow tie. It matched Bradley perfectly.

"He... he..." Bradley pointed at the doll, but he couldn't get the words out. Words were his weapons, yet the doll's appearance made him forget how to wield them. He'd heard of dolls like that. He understood their significance. Though he didn't believe they held any supernatural power, he sure as hell didn't like the threat. Bradley didn't just feel threatened; he was downright terrified.

LeFevre jabbed the doll with a sharpened fingernail. Pain burst through Bradley's side as though a spear had pierced it in exactly the same spot. He keeled over, bracing himself with a palm against the table. LeFevre winked and exited the courtroom. The court officer returned to his post.

"What's the matter with you?" Billings asked from his seat beside him. Bradley's lawyering had secured his client that seat, as well as the absence of an orange jumpsuit and shackled, cuffed wrists so that he'd look less guilty. But the ankle shackles remained. His client had to stay put. That was the deal.

"I gotta take a shit," Bradley answered, not wanting to alarm his very big and very violent client. He waved the court officer over and headed out of the courtroom.

Outside, the court officer, who matched Billings pound for pound, glared at Bradley with questioning eyes. *This had better be good,* the eyes said.

"Thanks for coming out here with me, Len. You're not going to be—"

"The name's Lou."

"Right. Lou. Sorry." Bradley pointed to LeFevre, who was standing twenty feet down the hall. "I know this is going to sound strange, but that man has a voodoo doll of me attached to the inside of his jacket."

Lou frowned. "You serious?"

"Could you just ask him to open his jacket, please?"

Lou huffed, but he did as asked. Bradley watched as he walked over to

LeFevre. The two talked. Then they laughed. LeFevre opened his jacket. He took it off and handed it to Lou, who shook it and sifted through its pockets.

Bradley heard Lou say, "Sorry for the inconvenience." The court officer walked toward him with palms held upward, a satisfied look on his face. He shrugged and returned to the courtroom.

"But…" Bradley tried to protest, his lower lip quivering. His best bet for a comrade-in-arms had wiped his hands clean of the situation, leaving Bradley alone and defenseless in that hallway. Now he really did need to use the restroom. He hustled toward it and away from LeFevre.

The courthouse was decades old, and its restrooms were no better than outhouses with running water. Bradley pushed open the wooden door to the men's room, staring blankly through a bubbly opaque-glass window that framed everything on the opposite side in shadow. The door creaked. Bradley scanned the bathroom for life, but it was empty. He walked over to the sink and splashed cold water on his face, happy to be alone.

He's fucking with me. Bradley stared through his reflection in the mirror, his mind replaying the events in the courtroom. *Stupid mind trick—that's all it was.*

He hit his palms against the sink, angrier at himself for being duped than at LeFevre for duping him. *He thinks he can shake me off my game?* Bradley scoffed at the notion. The knots in his shoulders, wound tightly by LeFevre and his little toy, began to unravel. He would not be bested by some manipulative freak.

He unzipped his fly and strutted toward the middle of three adjacent urinals, all unoccupied. As his stream released, his stress released with it. He stared at the wall in front of him. "Justice is blind" was scribbled on the tile.

Bradley laughed. *Yeah, but it sure is lucrative.*

The restroom door creaked. The sound of footsteps did not follow. Bradley thought nothing of it until he felt a presence to his left, then another to his right. He cleared his throat, shook himself, and tucked his manhood back into his pants. As he zipped up, a chill ran down his spine. Without rhyme or reason, nausea hit him like a punch to the gut. His mind screamed for him to look left, simultaneously warning him against such action. He stole a glance to his left.

Bradley screeched as his eyes met the cold, dead stare of Pepe LeFevre. He stumbled back, bumping into the man to his right.

He released his breath. *Thank God I'm not alone with LeFevre,* he thought, feeling the warmth of the stranger's shoulder against his back. It gave him confidence, emotional support. He would not be terrorized—not by LeFevre, not by anybody.

"Mr. LeFevre," he said, trying to sound coolheaded. "I can't even begin to imagine what you are going through. Your daughter deserves justice. But respectfully, sir, I think you'd be better served if you pushed the police to find her real killer. I'm sure they will help you in every way they can."

LeFevre didn't move. He didn't speak. He didn't so much as blink. He just kept on staring that thousand-yard stare. Bradley imagined gruesome cinematic depictions of his own death playing upon the backs of the man's eyes. All the while, LeFevre's eerie-ugly smile never vanished.

"In the meantime," Bradley continued, again needing to clear his throat. "Your threats against me have got to stop, or I'll have no choice but to report you to the authorities. Am I clear?"

Though LeFevre made no hint of aggression, Bradley saw something malevolent beneath his smile, darker than anything in the faces of the hundreds of criminals he'd plucked from judgment—a glimpse at the essences of hatred, rage, and murder. Real evil. It chilled him to the bone.

But what could LeFevre do with a witness standing right next to him? Bradley turned to apologize to the man he'd bumped, his rope out of this pit of fear.

Pepe LeFevre stared back at him.

"What the fuck?" Bradley's jaw dropped open. His heart tried to leap out of it. His thoughts raced out of control. And into the abyss he plummeted, the darkness dragging him down.

Instinct preserved Bradley. He spun to his left. No one was there. He spun right. LeFevre number two had also vanished. Bradley could hear his pulse pounding in his temples. He scanned the bathroom. LeFevre was gone.

But something remained. When Bradley saw it, he raced to the sink where it had been perched. He reached with both hands, wanting to throttle

LeFevre but willing to settle for this little doll. But silly superstition halted him in his tracks. *What if…?*

Blood rushed into Bradley's head. His face turned apple red. "That's it!" he shouted, the words coming out with a growl. He kicked the wall, putting a hole through the plaster. He picked up the doll.

Someone had drawn Xs over the eyes with a Sharpie. The mouth was no longer smiling—the stitches ran flat, expressionless. The hair was styled the same way he had styled his hair for the last twenty years, parted left to right. Most strands were light brown, and some were gray—the same as his hair looked in the mirror before him. He felt it. The hair felt like his, too. Just like his.

He flipped. "Motherfucker!" Bradley kicked the wall until the small hole he had made grew to the size of a manhole cover. Clutching the doll, he stormed out of the men's room.

He stormed into the courtroom, where he placed the doll in his briefcase and slammed it shut. Billings jumped. Bradley found it nice to know he wasn't the only one on edge.

He waved Lou over.

"What is it now?" Lou huffed. "More doll issues?"

"You'll see," Bradley said. "Please inform the judge that counsel would like to speak with her before the jury returns."

Lou shrugged. "All right, but it's your funeral. You know she's not going to like another delay."

"I think she'll understand. *This* warrants her attention."

Grumbling, Lou disappeared through a doorway behind the bench. Moments later, he returned with Judge Nevarro in tow. She did not look happy.

She sat down in her chair. Leaning over the bench, all the while glaring at Bradley, she crooked her index finger. "Counsel, you may approach."

Bradley grabbed his briefcase and hustled to the bench. The prosecutor was slow to follow, his face reflecting his confusion.

"This had better be good," the judge warned.

"Your Honor," Bradley began, his voice like silk. "The victim's father has been threatening me. Since his testimony has no relevance to this case, I ask that he be stricken as a witness and removed from the courtroom."

The prosecutor leaned forward. "Mr. LeFevre's testimony will place his daughter's whereabouts at the time of her abduction—"

"Which is undisputed—"

"*And* will detail the numerous occasions upon which he'd seen the defendant's automobile outside his home. As to any threats made against Attorney Walsh, this is the first I'm hearing of them."

"Mr. LeFevre's testimony is relevant. He will be allowed to testify." Judge Nevarro stroked her chin. "But Mr. Walsh's claims are troublesome, to say the least. I am extremely hesitant to remove Mr. LeFevre, given his obvious interest in the outcome of this trial and the public nature of this courtroom. Still, I take threats very seriously. Do you have proof to support your allegations?"

"I most certainly do, Your Honor." Bradley felt smug. The judge grimaced but said nothing.

"He created a voodoo doll with my likeness. It's here in my briefcase." He lifted his leather case and placed it upon the bench. Lou stepped forward, but Judge Nevarro waved him off.

"Let me just…" Bradley unclipped the latches. He never finished the sentence, for when he opened the briefcase, the voodoo doll was gone.

He shuffled around his folders. He reached beneath his documents and deep into the inner sleeve. Bradley could feel Nevarro's eyes upon him, judging him—as judges did.

Come on. It has to be in here somewhere. Bradley panicked. He dumped the contents of his briefcase onto the floor.

"Mr. Walsh…"

If the judge said more, Bradley didn't hear her. He crouched and sifted through pens and papers scattered about the courtroom floor, looking for something that clearly wasn't there, unwilling to concede the obvious truth.

"I don't understand," he murmured. "I never took my eyes off it. He must have…" Bradley gathered his things into his arms and stood. "I don't know how he did it, but it was here; I swear it."

"Swear all you like, Mr. Walsh," the judge replied. "You've never had much credibility with me. If I find out you're playing some kind of charade to keep Mr. LeFevre from testifying, I'll have you jailed for contempt."

Peering over the rims of her glasses, her unblinking eyes narrowed on Bradley. Judge Nevarro meant it. Bradley was stunned. He had many tricks and employed them freely, but this was not one of them.

"Now pick up the rest of your things. Lou, have Mr. LeFevre approach."

Bradley dumped the contents of his armload in a heap upon his table. He collected the few sticky notes and pens that remained on the floor and added them to the pile. Billings watched him with a raised eyebrow.

"Everything's under control," Bradley whispered. He hurried back to the bench just as Lou was returning with the demon who called himself Pepe LeFevre. Bradley scowled at him, but LeFevre nodded respectfully to the judge.

"Mr. LeFevre," Judge Nevarro began, "I'll get right to it. Have you been threatening this man?" She jabbed at finger at Bradley.

"I'm sorry, *jenn fanm*," LeFevre answered, a heavy Haitian accent lacing his words. "By chance, we had a rather uncomfortable meeting in the restroom, but I made sure not to say anything at all because I didn't think he and I were supposed to talk to one another. Mr. Walsh appeared angry with me, though I am not sure why. I'm afraid my appearance does seem to alarm people at times. Perhaps this was one of them. I left the restroom as quickly as I could."

"He's lying!" Bradley blurted.

"Settle down, Mr. Walsh." Judge Nevarro sounded like a mother scolding her child. Bradley kept his mouth shut, not wanting to press his luck.

"I can't believe I'm asking this, but have you created a voodoo doll or any other type of doll or figurine that looks like Mr. Walsh?"

"No," LeFevre responded, smirking. "Of course not."

"Did you bring any dolls or figurines with you to this courthouse today?"

"None whatsoever."

"Will you agree to stay away from Mr. Walsh, to not approach him or speak with him except to answer the questions he asks you while you are giving sworn testimony in the course of this trial?"

"Certainly," he said, his smile disappearing. He nodded at Bradley. "I have nothing to say to Mr. Walsh."

"Good enough for me. Counselors, take your seats. Lou, have Mr. LeFevre return to the stand then bring in the jury. Let's get this trial done, gentlemen."

"But—" Bradley tried to protest.

"I've made my decision."

Defeated, Bradley sulked back at his table. A moment later, the jurors filed in, and the prosecutor began his direct examination of Pepe LeFevre.

Bradley glanced at his Rolex. Fifteen minutes had passed. In that time, LeFevre had failed to advance the state's case against his client in any meaningful way.

He's just whining about the loss of his daughter. Boo-dee-fucking-hoo. Cry me a river. He cracked his knuckles then went back to doodling on his legal pad. LeFevre was no threat to his defense. He began to wonder why he had ever been worried about him in the first place.

He panned the jury box. *Sure, they feel sorry for him. They're eating up his sob story like a bunch of old ladies watching soap operas. But he hasn't even pointed a finger at Billings, and it doesn't sound like he's going to, either. I won't even have to cross-examine the bastard.*

Bradley folded his fingers behind his head and leaned back in his seat, smiling inwardly. The case was coming to an end. He winked at Billings. *A most favorable end, indeed.*

When the prosecutor rested, Bradley flashed him an arrogant grin. He had never been above gloating, and with another victory just moments away, he swaggered out from behind his table.

Two words would end it all. He opened his mouth. Words formed upon his lips. "No questions" was all he had to say. If he didn't want to show off so badly, he wouldn't even have to show the court proper deference by standing to utter those words.

He did stand. He did strut. And he did speak. But the words that came out of his mouth were not the words he intended.

"Mr. LeFevre," he heard himself say. "Who is Clint Billings?"

The question had flowed from his mouth though his mind had never formed it. The judge eyed him queerly. The prosecutor looked downright flabbergasted. Everyone in that courtroom knew he had won. Yet for some reason, Bradley pressed forward.

Was it black magic? Did LeFevre have an accomplice, someone manipulating the voodoo doll while he testified? What kind of sinister incantation had programmed it—and, through it, him—to speak? Bradley tried to scan the courtroom, but his head wouldn't turn. At that moment, he knew he was in real trouble.

His eyes were forcibly locked on LeFevre's. He peered deep into those milky-white globes. They seemed viscous. The more Bradley stared, the more the lines of LeFevre's sockets blurred until his eyes were like egg whites spreading in a frying pan.

He wanted to scream, to run from that courtroom. But his body was no longer his to control. If only his outside reflected what he felt on the inside. Couldn't Judge Nevarro see his panic?

Help me! he shouted, the words imprisoned within his mind. *For God's sake, won't somebody help me?*

LeFevre gritted his teeth. Their yellows blended with the whites of his eyes, his face a featureless monstrosity. The courtroom around him glazed over. The flesh of the judge and the jurors melted like cheese. Their hair ran down their faces like mascara in the rain. Their mouths were cast in horrific poses, silent screams, and unnatural shapes impossible for the human form. *Is this what Hell looks like?*

Still, he couldn't close his eyes. He couldn't even blink. Terror seized him. The fear made him howling mad, particularly because he could do nothing about it.

Though he could no longer recognize LeFevre, Bradley knew he still faced the man. Somehow, he knew the son of a bitch was enjoying this. He hadn't answered the question, instead savoring the moment, letting Bradley squirm inside while an unseen puppeteer acted out a script the lawyer hadn't written.

"Clint Billings is the man who…" LeFevre choked up. His gaze fell away.

Bradley's breath returned. So did his movements. He blinked away the blurred world. He was free.

Now's my chance! Thinking fast, he spoke. "No more—"

LeFevre's head shot back. "Clint Billings is the man who brutalized and murdered my beautiful daughter," he said at last, his tone righteous. A fire burned behind LeFevre's eyes, and Bradley knew he saw Hell. Somehow, Hell had regained its hold upon him.

"And how do you know that?" his voice asked. "Because he gave you the metal pipe he used to beat her with. You put it in a safe at your office. My daughter's blood was still on it."

More than one juror gasped. Another ran his hands down his face. Most stared on with their mouths hanging open. For a moment, silence pervaded the courtroom. Then the murmuring started, the peanut gallery's hushed voices collecting into a low rumble. The prosecutor stared at Bradley, accusations dancing in his eyes.

Judge Nevarro pounded her gavel repeatedly. "Order! I will have silence in my courtroom."

And Bradley's pride fell. His shoulders slumped. His heart sank. He had been tried and convicted in the minds of those who'd heard LeFevre's claim, reduced to the lowest form of criminal, revealed as the lowest form of man. He was guilty until proven innocent.

It wasn't the first time Bradley had helped conceal a crime, but it was the first time someone had found out about it. All his other indiscretions—the hookers, the gambling, the drugs—could be covered up by greasing the right palms. But this allegation had been presented to a courtroom full of palms, some of which would not take kindly to greasing.

Judge Nevarro shook her head. "The jury will disregard that last remark. No evidence or testimony has been presented that would substantiate or corroborate Mr. LeFevre's statement, nor is the witness speaking from personal knowledge. Further, I'm ruling that the answer given was nonresponsive. It shall be stricken from the record."

Bradley sighed. The judge had actually cut him some slack. But though the testimony had not come into evidence correctly and was properly stricken, Judge Nevarro had no love for him, and the prosecutor wasn't going to object to a gem like that.

Suddenly, he lurched forward, nearly stumbling into the witness box and the vile man who sat within it. The strings controlling him had been severed. His body was once again his, though he didn't know how or why. He'd waste no time minimizing the damage done.

"No more questions," he blurted, expecting some force to cut him off again.

The prosecutor stood. "The state rests."

"Your Honor, at this time, the defense would like to…" Bradley started. *Move to dismiss* is how his mind envisioned ending the sentence. A cold tingling surged throughout his body like thousands of thin tendrils penetrating through his pores. There was nothing he could do. His body submitted once again to another's control.

His words that followed were, "Call myself as a witness."

Clint Billings shot up from his chair. He looked as though he wanted to rip Bradley's head off. Lou must have gotten the same impression; his hand rested upon the grip of his gun.

Bradley hoped he would come for him, maybe break the invisible bonds with his pummeling fists. Unwillingly, his arm rose, a flat hand held out to pacify his client.

"This is rather unorthodox," Judge Nevarro said. "Are you sure you know what you're doing?"

"Your Honor, Mr. LeFevre has brought my name into this case. I feel it will do the jury a great service to hear the truth."

"What is the state's position?"

The prosecutor stood, his face revealing his amusement. "No objection, Your Honor."

"Very well. I'll allow it, but only to the extent of addressing the comment that was made. I'll remind you, Mr. Walsh, that the statement is not in the record, and the jury cannot use it for any purpose whatsoever. But if you insist on clearing the air, by all means do it quickly. I'm giving you a little rope here, counsel. See that you don't hang yourself with it."

Bradley already felt as though he were dangling from the rope. The noose around his neck squeezed tighter and tighter. Hope left him. He was at the mercy of a vengeful father. He was a prisoner unable to act, forced to watch from the confines of his mind.

His legs were set in motion. They carried him to the stand. Lou followed closely. Was he laughing?

At the stand, Lou administered the oath. Bradley raised his hand and swore to tell the truth, the whole truth, and nothing but the truth, so help him God. His mouth kept that vow.

"What Mr. LeFevre claimed I did is true. I accepted the weapon my client, Clint Billings, used to slaughter Jeanette LeFevre. I kept it in a safe at my office for a time until I found an opportunity to dispose of it. I dropped it off the East Bridge."

The words sounded so calm and collected. Bradley could not believe they were his, their tone a stark contrast to the turmoil within him. With more dignity and poise than he could have mustered on his own, under the circumstances, he stood.

"I now rest my case. I hope the jury will see that justice is served."

From that point on, the remaining semblance of law and order was shattered. The spectators burst from their seats. Cries of anger and outrage filled the air. The judge banged her gavel as if she were driving in a railroad spike. The prosecutor slunk low in his chair, perhaps fearing that bullets would fly. The jurors froze with anxiety as if they were on a roller coaster heading toward the big drop. Court officers tried to order chaos. Clint Billings charged at his attorney.

"I am going to beat you far worse than that bitch ever got!" he shouted, his massive frame barreling forward like a charging rhino. Even with his ankles chained together, he made it to Bradley before anyone could stop him, if anyone had tried.

"You're dead, Walsh," Billings said between clenched teeth. Spit flew from his mouth. His hands wrapped around Bradley's throat. "So fucking dead."

Chaos became a cluster fuck. Court officers and attendees swarmed Billings, taking shots at him freely. Some went for Bradley. He was kicked, punched, and beaten, all while an angry behemoth throttled his neck.

A jolt of electricity shot through him. Then another. And another. With each jolt came mind-blanking pain. The courtroom flashed white. For a moment, he was blind.

When his sight returned, Bradley saw Billings pinned to the ground with Lou clenching his legs between his arms. Another officer drove his knee into the back of Billings's neck. A third cuffed him. Still others were holstering their Tasers. Bradley had no idea where they all had come from, but he now had a good idea what had caused his teeth to chatter.

It took many officers to hoist Billings from the floor. His face bled from multiple locations. One of his eyes was swollen shut. A deep gash ran across his lips. His mouth poured blood, and several teeth were cracked or missing altogether.

Yet even as he was being dragged away, Billings laughed the laugh of the defiant. He swore revenge against everyone in the courtroom. He had some particularly choice words for Bradley.

Most of the crowd had hit and run. The judge and jury had disappeared, likely hiding out in the judge's mysterious inner sanctum.

Bradley rubbed his temple. It ached something awful and was trickling blood. Soreness ran throughout his body, but with the pain came the realization that his body was his again—a not-so-small consolation.

He walked sheepishly back to his seat, where he nearly fainted into his chair. He stared blankly at his table, unaware of the passage of time and the goings-on around him. He still sat speechless when the judge returned and notified the attorneys of her decision to give their predetermined jury instructions behind closed doors and send them off to deliberate. Slowly, some of the crowd crept back in. Billings did not return.

The jury came back with a verdict in less than ten minutes. Billings was found guilty on all counts, including murder in the first degree. A sentencing hearing would determine whether that finding included a death penalty, if the beating Billings had just taken didn't kill him first.

With the verdict read and the jury dismissed, the courtroom emptied. Judge Nevarro ordered the attorneys and Lou to remain. She stared at Bradley with a disgust he'd normally let slide over him. But in his pitiful state, her revulsion sharpened the sting.

"In all my years on the bench, I've never seen anything quite like that. What you did took guts, Mr. Walsh—a heck of a lot more guts than brains, that's for sure. But it doesn't even come close to excusing your revolting conduct. I'm recommending immediate disbarment. I'll leave it to the state to decide whether it wants to press criminal charges."

The prosecutor leaned toward Bradley. "Don't plan on taking a vacation anytime soon," he whispered.

"Yes, Your Honor," Bradley stammered, his voice no longer boastful. He shoveled his papers into his briefcase and hurried from the courtroom.

Confused, terrified, with his career on its last legs, Bradley yet found himself grateful. He was alive and free of alien control. He ran into the parking garage, threw his belongings into the back seat, and jumped behind the wheel of his brand-new Mercedes CL-Class, paid for with monies illicitly begotten.

Inside his car, he felt safer. He let out a breath, ready to forget the day by any means possible, glad it was over. He'd return to his home, drink as much bourbon as it took to obliterate his fear, and pass out with his collie, Jenkins, resting over his feet. Tomorrow, he'd begin his slow crawl back to the top.

It'll be okay, he told himself. Always the stellar lawyer, he was even able to convince himself it was the truth.

He turned the key in the ignition. His Mercedes sprang to life. After fastening his seat belt, Bradley turned to back out of his parking space. As he did, his eyes caught a glimpse of something black and white sitting on the passenger seat. His heart lunged into his throat. Slowly, he turned his head for a better look.

It can't be! How the fuck did that son of a bitch get it in here?

A familiar smiling replica of a man, decked out in a fancy suit and polished leather shoes, lay across the seat. The corner of a small piece of paper jutted from the miniature briefcase the doll held in its hand.

Bradley checked his anger. He swallowed his fear. *You've won,* he thought, the dams behind his eyes threatening to burst. *What more do you want of me?*

His hand trembled as he reached for the briefcase. Its detail was amazingly accurate. Bradley might have been impressed had it not been so terrifying. He clicked open two tiny gold clasps with the edge of his fingernail. The paper fell out of the briefcase and onto his lap. It was folded several times until it formed a neat square. He opened it and read.

My friend belongs to you now.
Keep him safe.

Bradley picked up the doll. Its stitched-on mouth had changed, now curled into a big smile. Its green-button eyes shined as if they had been buffed, round and open, no trace of the black Xs that had marked them earlier.

"It doesn't even look like me," Bradley scoffed. He wanted to rip it apart, to make sure he'd never see the damnable thing again, but the thought caused his pulse to quicken. He placed the doll delicately back on the seat. Then he backed out and drove toward the parking garage's exit. He swiped his pass, and the gate opened. He pulled forward into the bright afternoon sun.

Blamm! Shots thundered through the air. His back passenger-side window disintegrated into crystallized fragments. They speckled his back seat and his sleeve. Several loud thuds followed in rapid succession.

"Billings!" Bradley said. It wasn't the man himself, of course, but his enforcers had wasted no time avenging their boss. They weren't just trying to scare him; they meant to kill him. He pressed his foot to the floor.

A moment later, he heard a loud crash behind him. In his rearview mirror, Bradley saw that a police car had T-boned a Chevelle Supersport with windows tinted so dark they were black. More blasts filled the air. The officers scurried out of their cruiser, one behind the other out of the driver's-side door, and returned fire at three or four gunmen blazing from the Chevelle. Bradley's foot eased off the gas only slightly. He kept on driving.

He didn't get far. His Mercedes began to sputter. "Come on!" he yelled, striking his palms against the steering wheel. "Not now!"

He glanced at his fuel gauge. "What do you mean, empty? How can you be empty? I filled you this morning!"

When he looked up, Bradley saw a man standing in the middle of the road not more than twenty feet in front of him. His car would surely run the man down unless he acted fast. He swerved and veered into the breakdown lane. With a grinding sound, his hubcap skidded along the curb before his wheel rode up on the sidewalk. He hit the brakes. Finally, he stopped.

That was Pepe LeFevre. Had the realization come sooner, Bradley would have floored it.

"What the fuck?" he screamed. His head felt as though someone had jabbed a bicycle pump into it and kept on pumping. Soon, it would burst. Now was the time to confront LeFevre, the moment when rage expelled all caution. Bradley had had enough. LeFevre was going down. Bradley had no doubts that he would have coldcocked LeFevre if only he could have found him. He looked left. He looked right. He even checked under the car. LeFevre was nowhere to be seen. Yet his presence lingered, fouling the air. The odor was familiar, one Bradley detested. What was it?

Gas!

Bradley ran to the back of his Mercedes. A trail of cola-colored fluid led from up the street to beneath his car, where it trickled from a couple of deep holes.

He slapped his palm against his forehead. "Can this day get any fucking worse?"

The sensation that shot through him at that moment told him it could. The hair on his neck stood erect. His stomach went sour. Someone was behind him. Someone now stood where no one had been standing just a second before.

In the reflection of what remained of his window, Pepe LeFevre's dead white eyes seemed to stare right through him. The man puckered his lips as if he were whistling.

An icy breeze ran up the back of Bradley's neck. He coughed. Smoke engulfed his head. Heat swelled beneath his reddening cheeks. His temples throbbed. His jaw clenched. He swung around without thought, acting in tune with his most animalistic instinct. His arm swung with him, a powerful backhand meant to rend LeFevre's head from his shoulders.

But Bradley hit only air. The cloud of smoke dispersed. In it, he saw a single lit cigarette, suspended at chest level, held up by nothing but sorcery or imagination. The power, whatever it was, released its grip. The cigarette fell, spiraling downward, onto the—

Oh, fuck me! Bradley turned to run. Sure enough, the gasoline that had been at his feet ignited.

Dodging traffic, he sprinted across the street. A car horn honked, but he made it to the other side intact. He panted like a fat dog after a run as he checked himself for flames. He was fire free. He was safe.

From the opposite sidewalk, Bradley watched the blaze grow. Soon, it swallowed his Mercedes whole. The fire burned bright and clean, a beautiful sight on an otherwise dreadful day.

Then Bradley remembered the doll, still sitting where he had left it on the seat. He ran to his car. The gas tank imploded. Flames lashed their hot tongues into the car's interior. Bradley began to sweat. The skin on his arm sizzled, then ignited. The pain drove Bradley to his knees.

The car combusted. So did Bradley.

A PROVIDENCE THING

"What's with the pineapple?"

Josh squinted at the strange statue overhanging Atwells Avenue as the car crawled toward it. His gaze fell, and he glowered at the bumper-to-bumper traffic in front of them. "And why do they call it the Hill? Seems pretty flat to me."

Lauren snorted. "One, it's not a pineapple. It's a pinecone. And two..." She stared blankly over the steering wheel. "Well, I don't really know why it's called the Hill. It kinda goes downhill at one point."

Josh examined the statue, his face nearly pressed against the windshield, the car's front fender idling under the archway over the Providence district. "I *guess* it could be a pinecone." He huffed and sat back in his seat. "Still looks like a pineapple to me."

"It's a pinecone!"

"Like that makes any more sense?" He took in the restaurants and businesses along each side of the road. They looked as though they'd been there for centuries, drab and unwelcoming, gray as the sky and filthy as the air, as if they'd never once been renovated. Everything about Providence had thus far seemed old and antiquated, dead. Nothing new, nothing fresh, nothing living. "There sure as hell aren't any pineapples around here, but I bet there aren't a lot of pinecones sprouting from these dingy old buildings, either."

"Will you stop already?" Lauren glowered at him. "You've been dogging this place since you got here. Maybe if you give it a chance—"

"What's to like? It's dark and grimy and cold, and so far, the best thing I've seen has been a freakin' pineapple."

"It's not a..." Lauren let out a long breath. "It's an Italian thing. Supposed to represent... I don't know, prosperity or something. Anyway, who are you to insult another's culture?"

"I'm not trying to insult anyone's culture. If anything, I'm insulting the skill of the sculptor."

Lauren groaned and slapped her palms against the steering wheel. She dropped her right hand into her lap. She slumped. "Look. This is my home. This is where my family is. If that isn't enough, we've got a ton of good things here you haven't even seen yet, like..." Her brow furrowed. "Like coffee milk and-and-and Thayer Street... and Olneyville!"

"That hot dog place you told me about?"

"Hot *wieners*. They're not the same thing."

"So hot wieners, coffee milk, and pineapp... pinecones. Got it."

"It's obviously way too much to ask that you actually *want* to do this for me, but could you at least *pretend* as if you want to do it for me?"

Josh glanced up one more time. *It's a stupid pineapple.*

He closed his eyes and massaged his forehead. Lauren was right. She was going through something hard, and she didn't need him making it worse. The trip was not intended to be a vacation, and he had no right to think of it as such.

A loud pop came from the bus in front of them, followed by a plume of smoke that billowed over the car, turning the air fouler and the gray sky grayer. He crossed his arms.

Why anyone would choose to live here, I'll never know.

He sighed and took her free hand in his. "You're right. I'm sorry. I just... I haven't been to a funeral since my dad's, and you know what a shitshow that was."

"I know, babe. I get that. But think about how hard that was for you." She squeezed his hand. "That's how this is going to be for me."

Josh frowned. "You were close with your uncle?"

"Yes and no. He's family, and we Wests never die easy."

He squeezed her hand. "Well, I'm here for you. Whatever you need."

She smiled warmly as he released his grip so she could turn the wheel. They traveled in silence down one short street then another and another, before pulling up to a late-nineteenth-century home, the kind usually converted into three-family tenement housing. As she put the car in park, her expression brightened. "I thought of one thing here that you might think is cool, you being a horror buff an' all: H. P. Lovecraft."

"The tentacle guy? He's all right. I think I've seen a few Nicholas Cage movies based on his stuff." He laughed. "Nic Cage… that guy will take any role, but you know what? A lot of his movies are actually pretty—"

"That *tentacle* guy?" Lauren said through clenched teeth. "Really? *Tentacle* guy?" She poked him in the sternum. "More like a leading voice in weird fiction and a master craftsman who had and continues to have a profound influence on modern horror. And yes, inspired at least one Nicholas Cage movie." She poked him again. "And, I'll have you know, one of my ancestors."

Josh snickered, but he saw no humor in Lauren's expression. "You're serious? But… how can that be? You're Black."

"And?"

"Wasn't he, uh, well…"

"Hypocrisy abounds. Maybe that's why he kept his affair with my grandmother secret."

"Grandmother? Just how young was she when—"

"That, or he didn't want anyone to know where he got all his wild ideas." Lauren softened. She stroked his arm. "Anyway, are you ready to meet my family?"

Josh nodded. "As ready as I'm going to be. You're sure they know I'm coming? And that I'm white?"

"Yes, for the hundredth time. And what about you? You haven't told anyone about us or where you were going, right? You know I wanted to ease them into it first before it's posted all over Facebook."

Josh mimed locking his mouth shut. "Not a soul."

She kissed his cheek. "I promise, after this trip, we can announce it to the world." She unclasped her seatbelt. "Let's go. Leave your things in the car. We can get them later."

He looked down at his T-shirt and jeans. "Won't I need to change into—"

"You're fine. This won't be your usual wake."

Before Josh could open his mouth to protest, Lauren had opened the door and was stepping out of the car. He blew out a breath and followed.

As he climbed the wooden steps to a small porch, he detected the antiseptic smell of cleaning products and, underneath it, the fouler scent of what those cleaning products were meant to mask. A fly buzzed near his ear. He wondered if something had died under the porch.

Lauren opened the door, and both odors grew stronger, clearly coming from inside. A gray-haired gentleman in a fine black suit bearhugged Lauren as soon as she entered. Through the finely tailored fabric, Josh could see well-developed muscles. He didn't relish the possibility of crossing the man.

After he put Lauren down, the man turned to Josh and extended his hand. "You must be Josh. Welcome. Curtis West."

Lauren smiled. "Josh, this is my father."

"Nice to meet you." Josh hated the meekness he heard in his voice but quickly added, "So sorry it has to be under these circumstances."

"Yes, yes. My brother Steven lived a full life and is ready for his next one. Funerals are not only a time for honoring the dead but for celebrating life." He waved an arm out, directing Josh's attention to a casket not much longer than any Josh had seen but easily twice as wide.

Surprise must have shown on his face because Lauren was at his side in an instant, hooking an arm around his and whispering, "It's not what you think."

"That he was grotesquely overweight?"

"Not at all, actually. It's the bloat," she said, matter-of-fact, as if that explained everything.

Josh did not want to imagine just what this *bloat* might be doing to a decaying body that it would require a double-wide coffin, so he took in the rest of the room instead. Though the coffin, the hardwood floor, the podium, the flower arrangements, and the rows of aluminum chairs resembled setups he'd seen at funeral parlors, the similarities ended there. A sofa and matching chairs had been pushed against the wall, and a flat-screen television hung on the opposite wall. A coffee table rested on its end in one of the corners, likely to make room for the expected guests. A woman in a black dress perched on one of the chairs, a black veil hiding her face. She did not rise to introduce herself, nor did anyone introduce Josh to her.

Josh did not let his gaze linger on the woman. Instead, he searched for a bathroom, hoping to be prepared should the need arise. The adjacent room appeared to be a kitchen and dining area, and he assumed the stairs to his right led up to bedrooms. This was someone's home.

"Are we staying here, or is this just where the wake is gonna be?" he asked in a whisper.

Lauren playfully bumped him with her shoulder. "Both."

Does that mean I'll be sleeping over the body?

A gurgling sound interrupted the uneasiness growing inside him then jump-started it anew when he thought it had come from the coffin.

"Sorry," Curtis said. "My stomach won't stop rumbling." He chuckled. "I haven't eaten a thing today. Come, let me introduce you to my wife."

Josh assumed that Curtis would lead him over to the woman seated on the chair. She appeared to be watching him through her veil, but Josh couldn't make out her eyes. Instead, Lauren's father led him into the dining room, where another woman in a black dress sat at a notched and worn table.

"Josh, this is my wife, Christa," Curtis said.

Josh straightened his spine. "Please to meet you, Mrs. West."

She nodded politely but frowned. "Slight fellow, isn't he? Not much to him."

Lauren gasped. "Mother! Be polite!" She stroked Josh's arm. "She's become blunter and *ruder*"—she glared at her mother—"in her old age."

"You don't look a day over forty," Josh said, trying to win over his girlfriend's mother. In truth, she had very few wrinkles and, if not for her graying hair and Lauren's age, he wouldn't have guessed her much older than that.

She snorted. "When I was forty, young man, I was—"

"Mother!" Lauren's eyes shot open. She rolled them toward Josh. "Be. Polite."

"Why? It's not like he's the one, is he?"

Lauren blushed. "Too soon to tell."

Josh thought he saw Lauren's head shake slightly, but that could have been for any number of reasons, not the least of which was her mother's crassness. Given what she'd told him about her family, he'd expected some opposition and had been prepared to take it in stride.

A sudden electrical current pulsed through the floor and walls, through Josh himself. It came with a hum and chill that sent his skin crawling. He blinked, and an infinite cosmos flashed behind his eyes, a deep, dark, empty void. As soon as his eyes opened again, it was gone, along with the vibration and its nauseating touch.

"We should begin the ceremony," Christa said, rising. "Everyone should be here now."

"I thought you said you had a large family," Josh said to Lauren under his breath. A dull murmur came from the living room. They followed Christa toward the sound.

Josh stared wild-eyed at the mourners that had gathered in a matter of moments. All the seats had been filled except for the front row, where the black-veiled woman sat beside four empty chairs. Several more attendees stood along the wall in the back. It was as if the crowd had materialized there, Josh not having heard anyone enter. He assumed they must have all been awaiting Lauren's arrival and been summoned by the veiled woman in the minute or so in which he'd been in the dining room.

As he followed the Wests to the empty chairs, he took in the crowd. All eyes were on them. No, they were watching Josh specifically, and he didn't see another white face in the brief moment he had to observe them. He also hadn't seen anyone dressed as casually as he was either. Perhaps they thought him disrespectful for being clothed as he was. He had a pressed suit in the car and had had every intention of wearing it. *Maybe I could sneak out and change before—*

"Thank you all for coming." The veiled woman stood in front of the casket beside a portrait of a young Black man wearing what appeared to be the blue uniform of a Union soldier. The large oil canvas was a work of art commissioned from a master, no doubt, exquisite in every detail, except for the eyes. The artist had, in some strange fit of creativity, dilated the pupils to an unnatural degree, such that they resembled black holes into which all the color and life of the piece seemed to be drawn. Peering into those eyes, a great unease washed over Josh, reminding him of a trip to the beach that'd been soured by red tide. The slick fronds of kelp—and the itchy, creeping, slimy creatures with which it was infested—still showed up in his nightmares several years later. As silly as it was, he couldn't shake the feeling that something watched from the other side of those eyes and dared not imagine what kind of entity could hide in the miniscule space between canvas and frame—a sensation of wrongness accompanying his awe so strong that it tangled up his insides.

It must be a great piece if it can affect the viewer so much, he thought, trying to shed his discomfort. Surely, the rendition of the deceased, for who else could the portrait depict, must have been a joke, like those old-timey photos where people dress up like flappers or pirates, everything filtered through dull sepia.

The woman lifted her veil to reveal a beautiful face so much like Lauren's they could be sisters. Josh assumed she must be Steven's daughter. The woman stepped behind the podium.

"As you know, my beloved Steven has returned to the Deep Dark. The Cold One has called him home, but he is not forsaken. For he is again one with our Lord as we carry our Lord within us, his lightless chambers beyond time and space sheltering us before rebirth."

Josh leaned forward in his chair, offering a sideways glance to Lauren, who either ignored him or didn't notice. Her religion caused him to raise an eyebrow, and he realized their conversations had never turned toward it. He'd always assumed she was Christian. If that's what he was hearing, it wasn't like any denomination's sermons he'd ever heard before.

"Steven is with Him now," the woman continued. "Our Lord, the Lord of All, King of All. Shapeless, amorphous, a snail cast from its shell, floundering in primordial ooze, our Steven lingers at the base of His dark throne, at the center of all things and no things, where chaos undying reaches with infinite tendrils to bleed into our world, and in turn, bleed our world so that we might know His touch and strive to know Him."

Josh glanced at the door, unblocked and no more than seven feet away. He squirmed in his seat, not understanding the words he was hearing but drawing a serious cult vibe from them nonetheless. His skin prickled, and his heart beat a bit faster, sensing danger from a group that had shown him none. The silence that pervaded the crowd amassed behind him heightened his anxiety without reason, some base instinct screaming at him to flee.

"... to share infinity. But to obtain infinity, there must be sacrifice. Rejoice in the Sleeping Chaos! Rejoice in Azathoth! Rejoice, for in his darkness, Steven will rise again!"

Josh shivered as any remaining warmth was vacuumed from the air. The silence became unnatural, the room—and the entire world around it—as lifeless as oblivion. Neither a breath nor the creak of a chair could be heard. His breathing hitched as the unnaturalness shrouded him in a cloak of putridity and pulsed through him like electric eels slithering along his skin. He couldn't shake it, wanted nothing more than to break for the door despite how foolish he knew he would look. He wasn't safe. Of that, he was certain. And yet not one in attendance had shown him the slightest harm.

Whatever his wants, he remained seated. His eyes were drawn toward the casket. Discordant tones, monotonous and shrill, broke the silence like woodwinds resonating through water. This time, Josh was certain they came from the closed box.

Wait... not closed. The coffin lid was ajar, raised a crack, though not enough to reveal the decaying thing within—only darkness, infinite and obsolete as death itself.

Wisps of black smoke filtered from the cracks as if a fire had somehow started in the dead man's gullet. They rose like charmed snakes, swaying to the cacophony. Josh turned in his seat to see a gathering of toothy smiles and black-hole pupils gazing upon him. He dared not peer too long into those eyes for fear of what he might see beyond them, his mind hanging on the fringe at the glimpse of something immense, unclean, darker than the night. Lauren, too, had those eyes, and her smile was bigger than all the rest.

He rose on shaky legs, and the crowd rose with him. He backpedaled toward the door, and no one followed. The casket exploded open. An amorphous blob swelled from the dead man's engorged stomach, burst open like an over-inflated basketball. The tendrils—*no, tentacles*—were not gaseous at all but solid. They shot toward him even as he turned to run.

"Lauren! Help me!" Slimy cords curled around his limbs and dragged him toward the glistening, gelatinous mass in the corpse's hollowed-out stomach. He reached for Lauren, but she slapped his hand away. As he fell into the casket, into the awaiting void, he screamed. The darkness closed around him, flowed into him, devoured him. It seeped into his head, permeated his thoughts with visions of a great nothingness and in it, a writhing mass, monstrous and ever-changing, the end and the beginning of all things driving his sanity to the brink. Anguish sent it over the edge.

As he cackled and clawed at his own skin, unable to rid himself of the Deep Dark's vile touch, he heard Lauren say, "Welcome back, Uncle."

SCAN FOR LIFE

Eight minutes and forty-two seconds.

That's how much time I have left before my air runs out. The digital number on my visor's display continuously counts down to zero. No one can stop time.

Not that I'd want to. In the seven hours, fifty-one minutes, and… now, thirty-eight seconds, that I have been drifting, I've gone through the five stages of grief. The first four were ugly. A lot of denial, hysterics, anger, weeping, and pleading to a god I'm not sure I believe in.

And finally, acceptance. Or at least resignation.

I am going to die, and there's nothing I can do about it.

As I look at the life support and operational functions flashing in red over my visor, I'm unsure if anything I have to say will be recorded, though I have the com open. The visor itself responds to my verbal command prompts, and all its display options appear to be working fine, though nearly all my suit's critical systems are offline. Thrusters worked for half a second, just long enough to stop my spinning. Not that I have anywhere to go.

Oxygen's working, but that's running out faster than I can make this entry. Anticipating further technological advancement, I optimistically estimate I'm twenty-plus years away from rescue… er, retrieval, rather. On the off-chance someone, somehow, some way, someday hears these, my final words and last moments not on Earth, I will attempt to relay what happened to me and the crew of the *U.N.C. Erebus*, a ship that was, thirty years ago when we left Earth, a state-of-the-art Epsilon Class interplanetary vessel.

And I've only got about seven minutes, so the short version will have to suffice.

My name is Sasha Kozlov, First Lieutenant aboard the *Erebus*. The date is March 5, 2176. My crewmates are dead. Our ship, for lack of a better word, exploded.

We were tasked with assessing Chernobog Minor, a diminutive, Earth-like planet in the shadow of Alnitak in the Horsehead Nebula, for resource and colonization purposes. The journey went without issue, but as soon as we dropped out of warp, we nearly collided with the planet's sole satellite—a bleak, gray, desolate thing not unlike Earth's only moon. All our navigational charts and calculations put us exactly where we landed, but with Chernobog Minor's moon on the far side of the planet. It was almost as if the damn thing had reversed its orbit while we slept.

Our ship's thrusters ripped us free of the moon's gravitational pull, and we made haste along Chernobog's equator until we had circumvented half the planet. We had barely begun atmospheric sampling when we experienced a second proximity alert.

This time, we saw no moon. All *Erebus*'s sensors indicated an anomaly still many klicks beyond the bow but closing rapidly. Over the next few minutes, Captain Barlow ordered a multitude of evasive maneuvers, but nothing could shake whatever it was that had homed in on us. It moved as we moved, as if it could sense our actions before we could even enact them. Nothing on Earth could maneuver so fluidly. Nothing technological, anyway. It glided like a shark through water.

But, of course, we weren't on Earth.

Captain Barlow eventually gave up on trying to outmaneuver the incoming projectile. Instead, he raised the shields, deployed antitorpedo missiles and barrier mines, and braced for impact.

It never came. We all stared at our viewscreen, watching half our ship's artillery float away uselessly. Aside from the planet thirty thousand klicks off our starboard side, only space—black, empty, and endless—lay between us and more space.

Then... something.

I couldn't be certain whether it was truly there or just a mere trick of the eye. It looked as if a segment of black nothingness was moving, swirling in the airless expanse, darker than space itself except where it glittered like the stars. Some sort of translucent miasma approached. Tendrils wisped over the viewscreen.

The *Erebus's* sensors blared. Jervis tried to scan it, but the readings that appeared on his dashboard might as well have been in Mandarin. No, even that would have been better because Zhao might have understood them. Whatever was out there, it was made up of no known elements. Nothing natural. Nothing… earthly.

As if that should have surprised us. We do not belong out here. There are places humans were never meant to go, things we were never supposed to comprehend. Space is infinite. Our minds… not so much.

We stared in awe and dread as darkness engulfed the ship. The brume wisped like wind through spiderwebs, delicate fingers probing over our hull. We felt nothing in a physical sense—no collision, no movement, no nothing. We killed the alarms, yet heard no sounds. But the look on the others' faces—pale, wide-eyed expressions, gazes darting about—told me they felt what I felt: something wrong. Something terribly wrong.

An eerie howl, like a whale song underwater with all the lamentation of a dirge, pierced the silence. A rank odor—rot to a level I've never smelled before—seeped in through a supposedly seamless hull. The ship began to rattle.

Beep. "You have three minutes of oxygen remaining."

Twelve people… twelve brave men and women crewed that damn vessel, and I was the only one to move. Being first to react saved my life. Well… prolonged it, anyway. I'm not sure why I ran for my suit, abandoned my post. Something about the very air in that ship felt unclean, curdled my skin down to the bone. It was suffocating, maddening even. They say all ships are like that on long journeys—suffocating, closed as tightly as a coffin.

Enough to drive anyone mad…

But this was not mere claustrophobia but rather a presence that has to be felt before it can be understood. Just thinking about it comes with nausea and the bitter taste of revulsion. Something was in that ship with us. I couldn't see it or touch it, but it touched me, reached inside my skull and explored my contours. It *invaded* me, seeking I know not what but defiling every part of me it explored, souring it. Souring me. And upon feeling it, I had to be free of it.

You will either believe me or you won't. I can only hope that some other evidence will corroborate what I'm telling you, proof falling short of you experiencing that festering cloud for yourself. I wouldn't wish that upon any person.

Thankfully, as quickly as it had come upon us, it had gone. But it had changed everything.

I had just managed to clasp on my helmet when the ship fell apart around me. Panels separated from their niches on the walls. The floor dropped away. All the synthetic polymers and all the screws and bolts beneath them just undid themselves as if they couldn't stomach each other's company any longer. Pieces shot randomly in all directions. Tubing impaled Mikhailov before my very eyes. Zhao went insane, tried to tear off my helmet and take my suit, an act that, had he succeeded even partly, would have left us both dead. I… I had to dispatch him myself.

My suit sustained damages in the struggle. Moments later, I floated within an asteroid belt of shiny, expensive debris, the now-scrap metal that had previously been the *Erebus*. As the ship finished… not exploding, as I said earlier, but *dismantling* itself, I took even greater damage, fortunately mostly to the suit's outer lining and digital components.

Or unfortunately, given my current circumstances.

And just before the ship drifted apart, I could hear Com.R.A.D., *Erebus*'s AI, scrambling captain's log entries to repeat a message I couldn't make sense of: "In its shadow, a dead god dreams." It played through the intercom patched into my helmet.

Then, the silence of space, all around me. Someone—Villanova, I think—floated by me, his skin shining like purplish-silver armor. His death was immediate. I assume the rest of the crew met similar fates.

I envy them now.

Beep. "You have two minutes of oxygen remaining."

There you have it. Two minutes before I start dying.

Some part of the ship—it looked like the toilet—knocked me askew, and I used the three seconds of functioning thrusters I had to right myself. For nearly eight hours, I've been orbiting the planet, its gravity drawing me closer. I suspect my body and this suit will burn up entirely as I enter Chernobog Minor's atmosphere, and this entire record will have been a complete waste of time. But fret not. At least I will have suffocated long before I'll feel even a modicum of heat.

Warmth. Where life belongs. Humans cling too fiercely to their one-sided notion of reality to walk in the wide, empty spaces between known quantities, where only cold, incalculable privations await.

I should not be here. You don't volunteer for a mission like this if you've got someone or something back home worth staying for. But you don't realize what's worth staying for—the little things, like... I don't know... bike rides and ice cream, fine wine and finer music—until you can't experience them any longer. I was homesick for a home I thought I wouldn't miss before I had even left its atmosphere.

The quest for knowledge is a fundamental flaw in the human condition. We can never leave well enough alone. We live on a speck of dust in a great, dark sea, and in our arrogance, we think we should venture far. The cosmos does not tolerate carbon-based life.

I've thought about removing my helmet...

But the planet below me—it's so beautiful, so much like Earth. Its vitality brings me some comfort, to know I am not all that is alive out here. Alone out here. With my visor's magnification on high, I can see so much of it now. Oceans and forests and mountains and so much of all the stuff that made our planet wonderful.

Home. Even after mistreating it so badly, we should never have left. This new world doesn't deserve us. Part of me hopes neither I nor it are ever found.

I've given up trying to decipher what caused our undoing, either the *Erebus*'s or our planet's. Life's too short. Ha! I'll chalk it up to bad gas and try to appreciate the view while I can. There is still too much out here we can never understand.

Wait... What is... "Command: magnify one hundred percent."

It... it can't be... a... a civilization? "Command: increase magnification another forty percent. My God... If you are listening to this, Chernobog Minor shows signs of habitation. Intelligent life!"

Beep. "You have one minute of oxygen remaining."

"I-I-I can't believe it! Those structures... so many of them, tall as skyscrapers, shimmering like glass castles. Something lives here. But where? Command: scan Chernobog Minor for life."

Beep. "No lifeforms detected on the planet."

But those structures... they have to be artificial. No manner of natural phenomena, not even out here, could have constructed those formations. So many straight edges and right angles. So many repeated geometric shapes, interconnecting rails, but... broken now, like shattered teeth. A crater at its center. It's massive, odd-shaped, elliptical, infinity, infinite.

"Command: scan for life." Surely, there must be life.

But I see none. Where have they gone?

Beep. "One lifeform detected."

"Where? Show me!"

A flash comes from my peripheral. My helmet's computer is directing my gaze toward the planet's moon. Could life from the planet have relocated there?

But how is the moon... It can't be here. It should be somewhere on the other side of the planet by now, orbiting as I am orbiting. Surely, I couldn't have circled the entire sphere?

Beep. "You have ten seconds of oxygen remaining. Ten."

The moon—it's huge! As big as the planet. "Command: scan out."

"Nine."

Still so big. Its gravitational pull has somehow ripped me from orbit.

"Eight."

Impossible. It's moving. Unfolding. No moon...

"Seven."

An eye? Hideous, as wide as an ocean. Watching me.

"Six."

Full of contempt, and... beneath it... "Command: magnify four hundred percent."

"Five."

A thousand faces! Millions! Humanoid, but not quite...

"Four."

Eyes wide, screaming, clawing. Trapped. A transparent membrane. Trying to get out.

"Three."

A tentacle, large as a freight train, whipping toward me, emanating that hideous mist.

"Two."

I can hear it in my head! Unintelligible, yet its meaning is clear. Calling for me. Sucking me in!

"One."

My heart pounds in my chest. My body—so cold, trembling. You can't have me! Mind unraveling, my fragile sanity holding only because death will embrace me before that-that... Oh God, what have we found out here? What now sees us?

The appendage draws nearer. A chorus of howls carries across the void from the civilization trapped beneath the titan's skin.

Beep. "Oxygen offline. Seek alternative source immediately."

I laugh, choke, then wheeze. Death must come before that thing can touch me. I can feel its presence, so much stronger now than I did back in the ship. Tears stream down my face. My arms flail to no effect as I try to swim away. I must escape. Death is the only escape.

The being, so close now. In a moment, it will have me. I laugh madly between gasps. I suck at air, my body craving to go on where my mind can no longer.

My eyes roll back in my head as the miasma radiates over me, creeping in like swamp mud into a boot. My skin revolts against its touch.

It has me, I know, but it is too late. Everything has gone black.

Its presence, louder now in my mind, its voice razor sharp, tearing at the fabric of my soul!

And with its touch, my breath returns, if only to fuel my screams.

ACKNOWLEDGMENTS

The author would like to thank Sebastian McCalister, Evans Light, Carrie Abatiello, Kenneth Cain, Kevin Rego, Frank Spinney, Erin Al-Mehairi, and all the friends and family who have supported me through this last decade-plus of publications. I would not be here without you. The author also would like to thank the great team at Red Adept Editing as well as Curtis Lawson, Joe Morey, and Weird House for their hard work and partnership in making this collection come true.

ABOUT THE AUTHOR

Jason Parent is an author of horror, thrillers, mysteries, science fiction and dark humor, though his many novels, novellas, and short stories tend to blur the boundaries between genres. From his EPIC and eFestival Independent Book Award finalist first novel, *What Hides Within*, to his widely applauded police procedural/supernatural thriller, *Seeing Evil*, to his fast and furious sci-fi horror, *The Apocalypse Strain*, Jason's work has won him praise from both critics and fans of diverse genres alike. He currently lives in Rhode Island, surrounded by chewed furniture thanks to his corgi and mini Aussie pups.

ABOUT THE ARTIST

NICK GREENWOOD graduated from East Carolina University with a BFA in illustration. He has worked as an illustrator/concept artist/designer in the advertising, gaming, and publishing industries for over twenty years.

A brief list of clients include AT&T, Modiphius, Rubbermaid, Dias Ex Machina, Hardee's, IBM, Goodman Games, Green Ronin Publishing, Wyvern Gaming, and Poisoned Pen Press.

Nick lives in Jamestown, NC, with his wife of 30 years and is the father of four daughters, two dogs and a cat.

GALLOWS WHISPER

Made in the USA
Middletown, DE
22 July 2023

35362311R00151